Reflection

A WHITE COUNCIL NOVEL

Brandon Hargraves

Brandon Hargraves

Copyright

Copyright © 2021 Brandon Hargraves All rights reserved
The characters and events portrayed in this book are fictitious. Any similarity to real persons, living or dead, is coincidental and not intended by the author.
No part of this book may be reproduced, or stored in a retrieval system, or transmitted in any form or by any means, electronic, mechanical, photocopying, recording, or otherwise, without express written permission of the publisher.
Cover design by: Neiris
Printed in the United States of America

For Zealand Hargraves

Your mother and I may not have met you yet, but we love you unconditionally

Preface

Being a Christian for much of my life, I grew up with all sorts of self-help books. Books for all sorts of people to improve their lives through practical means. The problem I noticed early on, is only so many people will read a personal development book. It reaches a very specific grouping of people, and often times the people who really need the help are ignored, because they will never pick up one of these books. That is where the idea of this book came. There are so many people who struggle with issues of identity, depression, or trauma, who need a outlet that can give them practical ways to grow and begin their healing journey. Hopefully this book can help people who would never pick up a personal development book begin to experience their own personal healing

Contents

Preface		vii
Prologue		xi
1	Break Of Dawn	1
2	Alone	15
3	Reavers	25
4	The Guild	38
5	Wastes	61
6	The Great Canyon Pass	79
7	Danger on Every Side	96
8	Imprisoned	107
9	Civil War	123
10	Through the Dark	139
11	Kytas	154
12	Exodus	165
13	At the Gates	175

14	Seabound	194
15	The White Council	209
16	The Citadel	221
17	Hilios	232
18	Ulumbra	242
19	A New Dawn	259

End of Part 1	267
About The Author	269

Prologue

Stef never thought he would kill a person. Yet here he was, preparing for an assassination. He stepped onto the cold stone stairs, his mind snapping between his accomplices striding next to him and the surrounding streets. He watched, gazing into the shadows of nearby alleyways.

"Focus, Stef," his brother, Ambrose, commanded as they ascended the stairs connecting the Lower Barlo District to the Upper District Bridge. "Your nerves won't do you good anymore. We are already in this. There is no turning back."

None? Stef thought. He wouldn't dare speak it. Ambrose had been planning this for months now, and would never allow Stef to back out.

"Nerves are good," the third man, Gus, stated. "Nerves will keep you alive. Keep you aware. As long as they don't paralyze you."

"I'm not paralyzed," Stef demanded. "But now that we are here... I just... I don't know."

"You had better figure it out pretty quick, little brother," Ambrose stated. "We are here."

They ascended to the top of the stairs where a large bridge led toward the Upper District of Barlo. Centered on the bridge stood a behemoth of a man, taller than any of the three. He stood atop the bridge wall and spoke out over a crowd that had gathered on the overpass. His words were eloquent, though Stef hardly understood them. *All their religious jargon,* he thought. *If they don't make any sense, then their lies seem more believable.*

The three approached the crowd, quickly splitting into separate sections. Ambrose waded through the throng of peasants to the center, while Gus and Stef positioned themselves on the outsides of the gathering. They watched the priest intently, feigning to listen to his words.

"Your lives have been purchased by Fos himself!" He stated. "He wants us to have true life, yet we live as though we are dead!"

Stef scoffed under his breath. *The arrogance of these people,* he shook his head in disbelief. *If he wanted us to have life, then we would not be suffering like we are.*

"Excuse me, sir," a small feminine voice whispered from behind him. He flipped to see a young girl, maybe twenty years old, with red hair gazing at him. "You are a little bit tall. Could I ask that you move aside a little bit?"

Stef exhaled a relief and side stepped so the girl could see the priest. She stepped up to fill the gap, and turned toward him again. "You don't usually attend street sermons, do you?" The girl asked.

Stef glanced at her, but quickly shifted his attention forward again.

"I can tell by the scowl on your face," the girl continued.

"This doesn't seem much like your domain. What brings you here today?"

Stef tried to ignore the girl, but she stared at him, unblinking. Finally, he turned to her. "My sister died recently. I want to know what to do next."

It wasn't a complete lie. Him and Ambrose's sister had died years ago when the great plague infested the city. All of Cirrane had been on lockdown attempting to fight the deadly disease. While Stef and his brother never experienced the hell of contracting the virus, they both had to watch as their entire family fell to it one at a time, beginning with their father and ending with their sister.

"I'm sorry to hear," the girl apologized. "Hopefully you can find comfort in Fos' hands."

Stef scoffed again, louder than he had anticipated. The crowd turned to him, watching his movements. Stef stood silently. Immobile. As if staying still would make him invisible.

Just then, Gus drew a blade, cursing as he charged the priest standing on the bridge. Stef watched with wide eyes as his ally rushed forward, unhindered by the inhabitants of the congregation. Too simple…

As he reached the front of the crowd, the priest quickly drew a blade hidden in his tunic and sliced through the air, ending the encroaching madman's life. The throng screamed and scattered, terror rushing into all different directions. Stef too, overwhelmed by the sheer enormity of the situation, rushed away, but Ambrose had found him and gripped him by the arm. "Our mission is not completed! This is just a minor bump in the road!"

The red-haired girl lingered nearby, now drawing a blade from a sheath on her back. She made eye contact with Stef, and his gut lurched.

"They knew," he whispered to his brother. "This is no priest!" He brandished his own blade as the girl and the faux-priest closed in on them.

"This is it, Stef," Ambrose shouted. "Are you ready?"

Stef glanced at his brother, who had a calm smile on his face. He hadn't even drawn his sword. "What are you thinking?" Stef shouted.

Before there was time to respond, Ambrose grasped Stef's arm and chanted something under his breath. His foul words were soft, yet menacing. Suddenly, Stef felt a surge through his body, followed by instant pain from his head to his toe. He screamed at the sensation, unsure what was happening. He gasped for air, but his lungs betrayed him. Strength in his arms and legs gave way and soon he collapsed on the floor, still grasped by Ambrose's cold grip. He gazed up at his brother. Unable to vocalize any words, he just looked into his eyes. Hurting. Afraid.

Ambrose looked at Stef. "This was the only way, brother."

***

Kaela watched as Ambrose drained the life out of his partner on the bridge. She looked up to her brother, Ephras, who had dressed himself in a preacher's rags for the day's mission. He solemnly watched the scene unfold. Wind blew all around them, heavy and unforgiving. The sun darkened in the sky, casting a large shadow over the city of Barlo.

"Your plan has failed, sorcerer!" Ephras shouted. "Give up and let us take you in to face the Council!"

Ambrose laughed. "I would rather die here on the street like a rat than face the Council's judgement, peacekeeper!" He spat onto the stone bridge.

Ephras sighed. "If death is what you wish, then we shall gladly oblige."

Quickly, Ephras rushed forward with his sword, slashing at the sorcerer's feet. Kaela charged behind him. She hacked her sword toward the assassin, but it felt awkward in her hands. All her life she had trained with a spear, but the stealthy nature of the mission didn't allow her most valued weapon.

As they unleashed an endless barrage against Ambrose, he ducked and twisted himself unnaturally out of the way. Kaela cut toward his head, but he spoke a soft word and was suddenly nothing but a puff of smoke in the air.

Ephras spun around, looking out over the bridge. He grabbed Kaela by the arm and pointed to the stairs that overlooked the Lower Barlo District. As she turned, she saw the man leaping down the stairs, out of sight.

Quickly, the fighters rushed after him, stamping the stone city streets beneath their feet. Ephras led the way, leaping out over the stairs and falling nearly 4 stories. Before he hit the ground, a blast of wind exploded from his feet, halting him in the air and slowing his descent enough to land safely.

Kaela attempted the same, but expelled the wind too late. As she landed, she rolled into a wall and smacked her shoulder against the rock. With no time to grovel, she leapt back to her feet and limped quickly toward Ephras who had continued his chase.

She could hardly see the man they pursued, except for moments when he would jump up over walls, or climb up onto the roofs of the city's buildings. If it weren't for her brother's quick pursuit, she would have lost him long ago.

She followed closely behind as the chasers raced through the city. Behind buildings and through alleyways. Ambrose impressively avoided all streets stationed with Sacred Order guards. He knew exactly where he was going.

She watched as the man jumped up a wall and climbed swiftly to the roof. *I can cut him off!* She thought, turning down an alley and rushing toward the assassin. She pierced through the shadows, bouncing between buildings until finally she was underneath the pursuit.

The sorcerer leapt back down to the street. Kaela extended out her hand, yanking backwards to pull a strong gust of wind towards her. Ambrose jerked through the air, crashing into a pile of stacked crates.

Kaela charged forward, but Ambrose quickly shifted and shot a blast of fire from his hands. She ducked out of the way, dancing to stay on her feet. When she finally reclaimed her balance, the sorcerer had jumped back to his feet and squared off with the young peacekeeper.

Kaela watched his hands, but suddenly he clapped. She was immobilized; she couldn't even lift her arms. As if she were encased in ice, she stood still. Held under the power of Ambrose's magic.

An evil laugh resounded past the sorcerer's disgusting orange teeth. He pointed a finger at his prisoner; an orange glimmer expanding from the tip. A final blast of deadly fire. But Ephras emerged from an alleyway behind them, shooting his own fire at the mage. The charging blast evaporated as Ambrose jumped out of the way, releasing Kaela from his spell. He flipped back around and ran away from the pursuers yet again.

Kaela stepped to give chase, but Ephras grasped her by her arm. "Don't be too eager," he said. "Slow down and pace yourself. Otherwise, you will fall into his despair. A clear head is your best weapon." Kaela took a deep breath, forcing out her adrenaline in a single exhale. "Tell me," Ephras continued. "Where did he go?"

Kaela scanned the street where the man had raced off, but he was nowhere to be found. She glanced from alleyway to alleyway, watching for signs of their target.

"Not like that, Kae," Ephras encouraged. "You can still see him."

Kaela sighed, pressing her eyes shut. The world around her suddenly lit up in vibrant colors in her mind. She could see the glowing city street and the aura of the city dwellers. Each person glowed a different color, revealing their true selves. Kaela glanced from street to street until she noticed the yellow aura of fear racing away from them.

Her eyes ripped open, pointing down the road. "That way."

The siblings stepped forward in unison, following the steps of the assassin they chased. Ephras peered through alleyways until he saw the man duck into a large stone building shaped like a dome. The Observatory. He tugged at Kaela's shoulder and led her toward the large structure.

Inside the massive stone doorway there were large plants hanging on the walls, unlike anything that grew natively in the White Islands. Giant plantations of blood red flowers expanded throughout the cavernous room with bright orange vines smothering the plants nearby. Dark blue trees speckled with white hanging fruit on its branches. Kaela admired the beauty of the foliage that grew within the Observatory.

"This place always gave me the creeps," Ephras said. "Unnatural things here."

They traversed the other-wordly terrain, stepping through pools of thick glowing water as well as more species of plants and foliage. Kaela peered through the manufactured wilderness, watching for signs of life that didn't belong. To her dismay, she didn't see anything. Not even people who were to be working in the gardens and assisting in the growth of the wildlife. Was it abandoned? She hadn't heard of anything happening at the Observatory, but she knew this wasn't how it was supposed to be.

He knew exactly where he was going, she thought, heart pounding in her chest.

They entered a grotto of wild red and orange flowers, where Ambrose sat in the center of the room on a giant brown mushroom cap. A red light illuminated the room from within the bioluminescent wildlife. He watched them with unwavering eyes. "You shouldn't have followed me here, peacekeeper."

"No more games, assassin," Ephras stated, grasping tight to his sword. "And no more magic."

"No more magic?" Ambrose scoffed. "Do you know where you are?" Suddenly the earth shook and the red light dimmed in the heart of the Observatory. Ambrose stared at the peacekeepers with evil in his eyes, raising his arms above his head. "You have come to the heart of Seor himself!"

As Ambrose moved, a portal opened behind him. Darkness breathed out of the mouth of the threshold, ready to expel the disease that lingered within. The dark sorcerer laughed as little demonic monsters rushed into the grotto with small blades in their hands. They were nearly reptilian in appearance, but with an eerily childlike stature. Two by two they exited the portal, charging the peacekeepers.

Ephras and Kaela swung their swords violently, maneuvering between the horde of little monsters that flooded the room. For every demon they slay, four more emerged from the mouth of the portal. The beasts snarled and bit at each other as they fought amongst themselves over who would draw the life from their prey.

The demons flooded the room until the peacekeepers could hardly see any of the foliage left. Bereft of his remaining patience, Ephras finally plunged his sword into the floor and shouted loudly, sending a shockwave throughout the grotto. Suddenly each of the demons had evaporated into the air. The portal had closed, leaving behind a dark, sticky residue.

Ephras gasped for breath, reaching for any energy left within him. He glared toward Ambrose, who had also been blasted back by the magical attack. Kaela rushed over to the sorcerer, and before he could find any footing, she knocked him back to the ground and pressed her sword against his neck.

"Who hired you?" Ephras shouted, hobbling to his sister.

Silence.

Kaela pressed her blade farther into Ambrose's skin until blood dripped onto the steel. Ephras asked again. "Who hired you? Where did you learn this magic?" His voice echoed loudly throughout the grotto.

Ambrose swallowed nervously, but as he opened his mouth to talk, a dark, shadowy flash burst in the room, and suddenly he was writhing on the ground. Grasping at his throat, but unable to scream. He squirmed in pain until he finally lay still, gazing up at the ceiling with lifeless eyes.

Ephras turned in just enough time to see a flash of purple and black, removing whatever figure had been standing in the same room, watching the events unfold.

"Two dark sorcerers in one day," Ephras exhaled. "Something isn't right, Kae."

The peacekeepers examined the room, watching to see if the person who was watching them would return. As they walked through the grotto, Ephras discovered the mushroom Ambrose had been sitting on had shifted under the magnitude of his shockwave, and revealed a staircase leading down beneath the Observatory. He motioned to Kaela, and they made their descent beneath the floor.

At the bottom of the stairs, the luminescent flowers had disappeared. Ephras snapped his fingers to summon a small ball of light at his fingertips. The room was cramped, but purposeful. Symbols from an ancient language that Ephras didn't recognize decorated the room. Cloaks hung on the walls, as well as blades that were designed for skinning and gutting hunted animals.

A round table stood in the center of the room. Ephras and Kaela approached cautiously to find a map laid out over the top. It was a map of Quarrine, the western island of the White Islands. Placed on the map were different small figurines; one was shaped into the head of a lion, and the other was a teardrop set atop a cross.

"What does that mean?" Kaela asked out loud to herself, not intending for Ephras to answer.

Ephras investigated where each of the figures had been placed. The lion head had been set upon the Quarrine capital city of Oasis, along with several other cities. The teardrop symbol had pierced into Port Aurora, as well as an unnamed town on the far west of the island.

"I don't know what it means," Ephras muttered. "But I think we need to go to Quarrine."

REFLECTION

1

Break Of Dawn

Change is painful. Sometimes, before the sun can return to light the morning sky, life as we have always known it can go up in flames.

Dawn was ignorant of this reality. She woke up that warm fall morning the same way she always had: preparing herself for a morning hunt. She had followed this routine for many of the nineteen years of her life. Her father had taught her everything she needed to know about surviving in a small village in the middle of the Quarrine Wasteland, and hunting for food was of prime importance. She tip-toed between the expertly made huts of her family and friends with her bow in her hands, and entered the bleak wilderness.

Miles away from her village, the air was still. Not even the leaves were rustling. Dawn snuck over the sand and silently through the brush. Nocking an arrow, she readied herself for her shot. The antlers of her prey protruded out of the bush in front of her. Her target was clear.

"Dawn!"

Like lightning, she released her arrow into the trees, branches snapping under the force of the bolt. As the shards of trees fell to the ground, Dawn's target scurried off into the woods. A young dark-skinned man cleared a way through the brush with his own bow in hand, revealing himself to the hunter.

"Dang it Maron!" Dawn shouted. "Waste of a perfectly good kline. You had to have seen it! I was readying a shot!"

"Sorry, I didn't!" Maron responded, holding back a smirk. "Though, it's what you deserve! Cheating like that."

"Cheating?" Dawn snarled back.

"Yeah! Getting a head start and then rubbing it in my face how much faster you are once you get back!"

Dawn rubbed her forehead in frustration. "I have told you a hundred times, it isn't a contest! You aren't even in my league!" A smirk flashed across her face.

"That's why you need a head start?" Maron frowned.

"Oh, you boys," Dawn laughed. "Just sooo competitive." She motioned Maron to follow her deeper into the wilderness. "That is a part of hunting, Maron. You get an early start, and then you can get food back before nightfall. If you sleep until midday like a bum, you're not going to like your results."

"Hey! My strategy is just as good as yours!"

"If that were the case," Dawn turned toward the boy with a coy smile, "then you would have beaten me by now."

"You admit it!" Maron started, but Dawn silenced him

with a hand signal. Just ahead, there was another rustle in the bushes. Dawn nocked an arrow, aiming into the thicket, and quickly released it. With a *THUD* they heard it hit. The kline cried out, and took off into the woods. The hunters followed quickly behind, watching for drops of crimson and waiting for the hybrid beast to finally fall to Dawn's well-placed shot. As they passed through thickets, Dawn was thankful for the leather she wore to protect her pale skin from the thorns. She unsheathed a short blade to clear some of the path.

The sun peeked over the desert trees and reflected off Dawn's deep maroon necklace. It was a stone, oval in shape, with an engraving carved into the face; a teardrop sitting atop a cross. Normally when she hunted, she would replace all loose articles, necklaces, or baggy clothing, with something tighter to ensure nothing got snagged by branches when she was rushing through the thicket. Today was different though. She felt an urge when she woke to wear the necklace her father had gifted her when she was born.

Hours passed and the hunters chatted small talk until they finally came across the animal lying in the dirt; a long body of scales and rough skin, antlers crowned its head. Its long, snake-like tongue rested on the dusty ground. Dawn began to make the cuts necessary to lighten the load while Maron watched in horror from a tree nearby. "Gross!" He shouted as she sliced the beast open.

"You know, most of the time a man would be a gentleman and help the lady who seems to be doing all the work?"

Maron laughed. "Lady? You're funny! You make it sound like you're a princess in need of her brave knight." He swooned, teasingly. "You should try to be more like your mom. Or your Aunt Eva!"

"Our village has enough cooks as it is, Maron," Dawn grunted, working her knife into the slain beast. "I don't need to take after my mother. And Aunt Eva is a tentmaker in the Citadel. What am I supposed to learn from her?"

"It isn't their trade you need to learn," Maron sighed. "You just need to learn how to be a lady!"

Dawn rolled her eyes, tying the kline to her back. The two made their way back to their village sooner than she expected. Maybe Maron was right and she had started a little earlier than she needed to, but her family would be happy to see her return so early.

As they approached the village, little Cammie ran after them and met them in the open field, tugging on Dawn's arm. "You are back so soon! Can you show me some tricks today?" His young, high pitched voice pierced their ears like a knife.

"I'll drop this off at Merlyn's shop and then I will come find you, OK?" Dawn replied with a smile.

Cammie left in high spirits, getting ready for a session of training with Dawn. "I guess that's my cue," Maron laughed, raising his hand to his head in a salute. "Kid's got nothing to learn from me."

"Don't be like that," Dawn smiled back.

"Like what?"

"Acting like you have nothing to offer!" Dawn responded.

"I didn't say that!" Maron laughed. "When Cammie is older and needs help courting his lady friends, I will be there for him."

"Glad I never fell into that trap," Dawn laughed.

"But when it comes to manly things, like fighting and stuff, he doesn't need me," Maron placed his hand on Dawn's shoulder. "Same time tomorrow? Maybe I can beat you this time."

Dawn smiled back. "It's a date."

Maron made his way to the opposite end of the village as Dawn walked into Merlyn's hut to drop the kline onto his cutting table. "Not the biggest catch, but it should last for a couple days." She said with an exhale of exhaustion.

Merlyn smiled back at her, "You know, not all the responsibility of the village falls to you. There are other people here that can lighten your load." He glanced at Cammie through the door. "You are allowed to relax every once in a while."

"Who else does he have?" Dawn replied, glancing back to her protégé. "His grandma? Maron? They're not going to show him how to defend himself. They won't show him how to wield a bow, or a sword. Somebody has to."

"I agree." Merlyn said, untying the kline and hanging it in the back of his shop to finish draining. "Somebody *does* have to. But you don't always have to be that someone. You can only pour out as much as you get filled up."

Dawn shrugged coyly and left the shop, not entirely agreeing with the butcher's words, but knowing in her heart that he was looking out for her. She spotted Cammie at the training grounds, beating a wooden sword against the straw training dummy. Dawn noticed the opportunity in front of her. She grabbed her bow, and a training arrow with no head. While he was pounding away, she released the arrow into his back. Cammie flipped around, stomping his feet into the dirt. "Hey! That's not fair!"

"That is your first lesson today," Dawn replied with a smirk. "No matter how dangerous you think the enemy in front of you is, you have to stay aware of the things around you. You won't face off one on one in a battlefield. You'll never see the arrow that takes you down."

The two started sparring with their wooden swords. Dawn reminded Cammie of how to stand when wielding a weapon, and how to react to an opponent's strikes. While she taught him, a tall figure approached behind her. "Care to show him what a real fight might look like?"

Dawn spun around and saw her father standing with a wooden sword in his hand. Cammie shouted, "Yeah! That would be so much fun!"

Dawn sighed as she turned her sights toward her father. "I have grown a lot since last time," she said with a whimper.

Dawn's father stepped forward eagerly, ready to test his daughter's confidence. Without any warning, he swung his sword. Dawn raised her's just in time to stop it from contacting her head, but that was just the beginning. Her father rained an endless barrage of strikes coming from all different directions, and Dawn only had time to react by blocking the attacks. She knew if she could just dodge one without having to use her blade, she could counter swiftly and end the fight, but her attacker was merciless. One swing after another he whittled down her strength until blocking these swings became a task all by itself. Her arms grew tired, and her father seemed to have a never-ending supply of energy.

Dawn knew she would lose if she didn't change up this fight. She had to find a way to move to the offensive. If she could rush forward, it could throw her father off balance and give her the upper hand. She waited for an outside strike, and then made her move, throwing her shoulder into her father's gut.

He stumbled backward, sword steady in his hand. Dawn attacked, but her father was prepared. As she swung her sword, he used his strength to his advantage and swung back at her, knocking her blade loose and throwing her off balance. As soon as she regained her footing, her father's sword was at her neck, a defeat.

Cammie screamed in satisfaction, "That was so great! I want to fight like that someday!"

Dawn's father replied, "If you go seeking trouble, you will find it." He slid his blade into the sheath on his hip. "Don't go looking for a fight, or the fight will find you."

"Drake! You are scaring the poor boy," Dawn's mother, Mia, said in response from her viewpoint on the side of the training ground.

"Yes, Hon," Drake picked up his daughter's sword. "Hopefully Cammie never needs to see what a real fight looks like. But we will teach him how to handle himself if one ever arises." He turned to Dawn, "You did well. That was a good move to gain the upper hand. If you had thought of it before I had tired you out, it might have even worked." He slowed down and locked eyes with his daughter, "Know your own body. Know your weaknesses. Just as well as you know your strengths. The better you know your weaknesses, the better you can cover them."

"What is your weakness?" Dawn asked, wondering what she could have done better to win the fight.

Drake paused, "You are."

As the family discussed the fight, the sound of horses drew near. Drake quickly moved Dawn and Cammie over to Mia and approached the two strange horsemen trotting through the village. Merlyn the butcher also found his way to the commotion.

"They are reavers," Mia said quietly to Cammie and Dawn. "Monster hunters."

"Why are they here?" Dawn asked with a glare in her eye.

Mia shook her head, not knowing the answer. A shiver shot through Dawn's spine. Her mind immediately thought of Cammie's safety. If there is a monster nearby, how safe could they be? And how dangerous are these men?

Dawn slowly crept toward the weapon rack and grabbed her bow, nocking an arrow to be ready. She noticed the men glancing over at her. Drake turned toward her and shouted, "Dawn! Come here for a second."

Surprised, Dawn dropped the bow and walked over to her father and the strangers. As she approached, she examined the characters. One was a katze, a tiger-like being of great stature. It stood on two legs and towered over the humans. Very intimidating. The other was a man, middle aged, with long hair and a gruff face. He seemed weathered by life, as if his posture and demeanor were scarred by his experiences.

"Dawn, this is Cain, and the katze is named Ragnar. They are reavers," Drake gestured towards the men as she stepped up. Dawn made uncomfortable eye contact with the man, whose gaze was captured by her necklace. "This is my daughter Dawn. She can show you to the edge of the village and towards the ruins. They are a few days' walk northeast. You may not be able to get there on your horses. The trails have overgrown heading in that direction."

"Could we leave our mounts with you here?" Cain asked, almost as if it weren't a question. "When we come back this direction, we will take our horses with us."

Drake nodded, and the men dismounted from their horses. With a glance from her father, Dawn led the reavers toward the northeast edge of the village. Walking next to the giant cat made her uneasy, but she still strolled with her head up, and her shoulders back.

As they reached the edge of the village, Dawn turned to find Cain staring at her, as if he was peering into her soul. She averted her eyes to Ragnar, pointing to the wilderness. "The ruins are straight that way. The greenery will start to become less lush and you will see the mountain in the distance."

There was an awkward silence. Dawn glanced back and forth between the two men's eyes. "Thank you, Dawn," Ragnar said, finally breaking the silence before the reavers set out.

That night, Dawn locked herself in her room with the lute her aunt had gifted her as her mind dwelled on the reavers. What was that guy's issue? He couldn't take his eyes away. And why did he keep glancing at her necklace? Her fingers danced around the fretboard as a melody slipped past her lips.

I am fall leaves under the frost.
The chill is in my blood.
I'm unsure if what I feel is pain.
I'm unsure if it is not.
Can I endure this hopeless winter?
Will I be sleeping through the night?
Or will my heart stay cold and bitter?
Even as darkness turns to light.
For now, I wait for spring.
Where the sun will return and glow ever brighter.

As she sang, her mother called out from the main room. Dawn set down her lute and moved to sit with her family around a fire for dinner.

"The Wastes are dangerously cold at night," Mia spoke. Something Dawn had heard her say hundreds of times. She poured a bowl of kline stew for her family. "I hope those reavers know how to keep themselves warm."

"It isn't that bad," Drake stated. "You remember when Maron the moron fell asleep on a hay bale and stayed outside through the night? He survived until the morning."

"Don't call him that!" Dawn defended her friend. "You know he hates it!"

"All I'm saying," Drake continued, "is if the kid can survive, then reavers should have no problem. Especially a katze like that."

Dawn turned to her mother. "You said they were monster

hunters," she stated quizzically. Drake scoffed from his seat nearby, but she continued. "What kinds of monsters?"

"They are said to hunt demons from the Other," Mia responded with wonder in her voice. "The Fallen they call them."

"The Fallen?" Drake responded mockingly. "There aren't any Fallen left in the world. Not even the great Moldolor himself, the greatest dark sorcerer ever to live, could bring the Fallen back."

Dawn shivered at the name. Moldolor. She didn't know much about him, except that he started the revolution against the White Council nineteen years ago, just before she was born. Her stomach dropped as if she was eating stones.

"No," Drake continued. "The worst things that reavers hunt are dragons. And the orcs have done most of that work for them!" He spooned some more stew into his mouth.

"You can't deny that the Fallen are real though!" Mia rebutted Drake's statement. "Even if they are ancient. They did, at one point, exis…"

"Quiet!" Drake whispered, bringing their attention to the noises outside. Dawn heard the sounds of footsteps and whispering right outside their home. Not voices Dawn had ever heard before. Drake quietly walked toward his sword, and strapped it to his hip. "Dawn, take your mother; go out the back of the hut, and run. Go quietly to the Wastes. Wait for me at the entrance of Boar's Head Cave. If I am not there in two nights, move on."

"Drake, you're scaring me," Mia trembled. Shouts and screams arose just outside the front door.

"Just go!" Drake barreled out of the warm hut into the

dark cold of the night, swinging his sword into a bandit standing near the door. Dawn rushed to grab her bow, a few arrows, and a sword for her waist. She was now her mother's protector.

Dawn and Mia retreated out the back door. The flickering flames of what was now a burning village brought dim light to the suffocating darkness. The sound of steel clanging against steel rang through the air. Dawn nocked an arrow and led her mother silently out of the village. One step after another they made their way toward the wilderness. As they looked around at the carnage left by the raiders, Dawn saw the body of Merlyn slumped over a bale of hay, three arrows protruding from his back.

The two kept moving toward the wastes, avoiding everyone in the village, friend or foe. Nothing could compromise their stealth. They scurried like thieves from one shadow to the next, each movement an attempt at stealing their freedom, until they finally saw the desert's edge. Dawn looked back to reassure her mother who was walking right behind and caught Cammie in her vision, drawing a sword to fight off the invaders. She glanced back toward her mother, "Wait here, I will be right back."

Mia protested, but Dawn was already out of earshot. She needed to protect Cammie. A party of raiders approached him, and Dawn released her first arrow into one of them, trying to ready her next shot as fast as she possibly could. Cammie swung his sword at the bandit in front of him, but he was clearly outmatched. Dawn released another arrow, taking out the nearest bandit, but she wasn't fast enough to nock another arrow. A third raider knocked Cammie's sword out of his hands, and plunged his own blade into the young boy's stomach.

Dawn screamed, clenching her fist around her sword to blitz the remaining bandits. She was a much better fighter than they were, but the emotion that filled her body blinded her. She swung her blade once. Twice. Thrice. But the bandit parried each blow. Through her rage she finally overpowered the first enemy before the other two approaching could arrive on the scene.

She knew she couldn't take on two at once, so she dropped her sword and started to ready another arrow as she backed away from the bandits. They realized her plan and rushed toward her, but it was too late. Dawn fired into the first bandit. The second was approaching fast, but Dawn was faster. She ran the opposite direction until she had her arrow ready, and when she turned around she released the arrow into the man's gut, and he fell. Dawn knew that her shot wasn't fatal, so she marched over to the final bandit, removed the arrow sticking out of his gut, and prepared a final strike to finish the job. She jerked back the bowstring, aiming directly into her enemy's foul grimace, but the bandit grabbed her leg and knocked her to the ground, sending the arrow flying into the night.

The man turned over, clenching his gut and drawing a knife from an ankle sheath. As he attempted to crawl on top of Dawn, she kicked as hard as she could into the man's face, sending him flying backwards into the earth. She jumped back to her feet, and grabbing the last arrow from her quiver, she rammed it into the man's heart.

Securing her bow, two arrows that she could find

around, and sheathing her sword, a symbol on the bandit's cloak caught Dawn's attention; a teardrop atop a cross. Confused, Dawn started back up toward where she left her mother, but she was nowhere in sight. She called out, "Mom?" as she ran towards the wilderness. When she finally approached the edge of the wilds, she found her mother lying in the sand, with an arrow protruding from her chest.

Devastated, Dawn knelt down to assist her mother, who was quickly bleeding out into the soft, dark earth. "No. Mom. No. We have to keep going. You have to make it. Mom. No."

Unable to find the breath to speak, Mia quieted Dawn with her hands, placing one finger on Dawn's lips, and with the other hand she grabbed hold of Dawn's pendant. As quickly as the arrow was shot, her breathing stopped.

2

Alone

Shadows suffocated the cold desert air. Dawn sprinted through the thorny brush; tears rolling down her face. Faces of her family and friends went flying through her mind. Cammie, Merlyn, her mother. Why was she even running? Her whole life was behind her in flames. What was the point of fighting for her life if she had no life left to fight for?

As she lingered on these thoughts, noises echoed across the desert wasteland; shouts rising from the direction of her burning home. Her attackers were drawing closer. Quickly, Dawn jumped into a creosote thicket. Under the daytime sun, anyone with eyes would have been able to see through her new camouflage, but the dark cover of night had now become her greatest ally.

Footsteps drew closer. The hoarse voices of her pursuers grew louder each and every second. Finally, Dawn tuned out the noises of the wind and brush to listen in on what the raiders were saying:

"I thought it was supposed to be here?" One particularly rough voice shouted back at some followers, who seemed like his subordinates.

"There may have been one or two that escaped, sir," his lackey's voice trembled.

The raiders were now within several feet of Dawn's hiding place, torches in hand. "If you even try to tell me that some person wandered off, and this was all for nothing... So help me, you will all meet the wrath of Seor! Find the ones who escaped! Bring them to me!"

Dawn shivered as she crouched in the bush. Though the desert wind felt like ice on her skin, cold sweat still dripped from her brow. Her long brown hair clung to her face. She sat, pursing her lips and rolling her fists into balls, listening to the murderers as they passed by her position.

There Dawn waited, tears welling up in her eyes. Each crack of a branch, or strong breeze through the leaves sent her heart jumping into her throat. After minutes of deafening silence, Dawn slowly peeked out of the bush. Her clammy hand gripped her bow with white knuckles as she started toward the cave.

She took one step. Then another. And another. Until finally she found herself sprinting through the wasteland toward Boar's Head Cave. Her head was on a swivel, eyes never closing, barely blinking. She noticed countless orange glimmers on the horizon, and quickly she shifted her direction to favor the shadows. Each time her leather boots pounded into the sand beneath her, she could hear the sound of her heavy footsteps echoing through the night.

Sweat poured down her back. A shiver ran through her spine as if her pursuer was right behind her, ready to reach out and take her. She thrust her body forward, trying her hardest to out speed those giving her chase. Sounds of the wilderness around her were muffled, until all she could hear was her heart thudding in her ears. *Thump! Thump! Thump!* With each step, she attempted to break her cadence and pick up her pace. Faster. FASTER. *FASTER!*

Until finally, hurling herself into the mouth of Boar's head cave, Dawn exhaled a sigh of relief. Turning, she saw no signs of pursuers and, if only for the moment, she felt safe.

The night pressed on, and the adrenaline rushing through Dawn's veins slowed. The cold air began to bite her skin. She repeated her mother's words to herself again and again, "*The Wastes are dangerously cold at night.*" A cloud puffed from her lips as she exhaled. She gathered some kindling, then moved deeper into the cave so the bright flame wouldn't reveal her location. Banging two stones against each other, she created sparks until one caught. After a few seconds of care, warmth filled the cavern that could last until her father arrived.

"If he is even coming," Dawn muttered to herself.

Nightmarish images of raider's cut down by her own blade appeared like an illusion in Dawn's eyes. Nausea clawed at her throat as she tried to force down the bile, but it was too late. Rushing around a corner, she released the contents of her stomach. She had killed living things before, but never a person. She had been hunting her entire life, but she had been taught to revere the lives of people. They had trained in combat for the eventual possibility of violence, but she had never experienced anything like this.

"Poor Cammie."

Dawn's eyes grew heavy, weighted with tears as the night progressed. Thoughts flooded her mind of raiders outside searching for her and other survivors from her village, if there were any. "I have to keep my head up," she whispered to herself. "I have to be ready. Ready for anything. For whatever might stumble in here. That means no sleeping. Keep your eyes open Dawn..."

Thinking through how to keep her mind busy, her stomach rumbled in a low gurgle. She counted the arrows recovered from her struggle with the bandits; she had only redeemed three. She gazed up at the ceiling, eyeing the shadows in the corners of the cave, but couldn't spot anything out of place.

Without another thought Dawn sat, bow in one hand and an arrow in the other. She watched the entrance of the cave, waiting for her prey to return from their nightly hunt.

Time passed, hours of agonizing silence, and finally Dawn heard wings flapping throughout the cave. High pitched screeches escaping the hot desert sun rising outside. She created a torch out of one of the pieces of wood and snuck through the cave with her eyes fixed to the ceiling and the corners. Once she spotted a small shadow, she set the torch on the ground, drew back on her bow, and fired. The first bolt missed its target, continuing on to smash into the rocks behind the creature, shattering the arrow and startling her victim enough to escape.

She clenched her jaw, growling in frustration. Storming

over to the splintered arrow, she pocketed the arrowhead, seized her torch, and continued her hunt. "Slow down Dawn," she muttered under her breath. "Take your time. Breathe."

Soon she came across another beast hanging from the ceiling of the cave. She readied her shot. She inhaled and pulled back on the bowstring. With a fierce exhale, she released the arrow again. The shot found its mark, and the bolt pierced the bat's abdomen.

She brought the creature back to her fire and prepared it for cooking. Her muscles ached from the physical exertion of the day before. As her breakfast roasted over the fire and the smell of cooked meat lingered in the air, she tried to stretch out and help bring relief to the pain. Each movement exhausted her more than the last.

After the nourishment, Dawn sank against the rocky walls, gazing toward the mouth of the cave. Her mind drifted again, thinking about the next steps in her life. Tears streamed down her face as she thought about moving forward without her family. Without her friends. A yawn escaped her mouth. Though her stomach was full, her soul was starved for companionship. She curled her knees to her chest and wrapped her arms around her legs. Her head weighed heavy on her shoulders. Each time she blinked, it took longer and longer to force her eyes open again, until finally she dozed off into a dreamless sleep.

With a jerk, Dawn's head shot up. Voices coming from the entrance of the cave shocked her heart into a frenzy. How could she have fallen asleep? How long was she out for? Did she miss her father's rendezvous time? She grabbed her bow and nocked an arrow, racing into the shadows of the cavern behind her. She glared at the well-lit campfire, waiting for bodies to enter her sight.

The voices grew closer and Dawn focused. She heard them mention a fire ahead. Two men entered her field of vision, wearing the same cloaks as the raiders. The flames glimmered on the steel blades they brandished. "Keep your eyes up," one man whispered. "Someone must be nearby."

Without hesitation, Dawn unleashed her first arrow into the bandit's chest. His friend stood stunned, eyes wide and mouth locked open. Dawn nocked her final arrow, pulled back the bowstring, and shot the bolt through the darkness of the cave. Both raiders lay lifeless on the ground next to the fire.

Dawn's heart pounded in her chest. *If these men didn't report back to their teams, others would come looking,* she thought. *But I am supposed to meet my father here. If I leave, I may never see him again, if he is even still alive. But if I stay, it could mean death.*

Without her father, or her family, the idea of a permanent sleep didn't sound so bad. "What's even left?" The question slipped through her lips. She touched the amulet at her throat, glancing down at those dead at her feet. Suddenly, dread filled her mind at the thought of life after death, and the uncertainty of it all. "I have fought this hard so far," her shoulders relaxed and her head lifted high. "This won't be the end!" Extracting her two arrows and gathering her weapons, she started for the mouth of the cave.

Dawn reached the front of the cave. The orange glow of the setting sun felt warm on her skin. She travelled back toward her village, keeping her eyes peeled for any unfriendly visitors.

Her pace slowed. As she gazed around the arid landscape, Dawn noticed small creatures in the distance beginning their nightly ritual. The weight of her remarkably light quiver weighed heavy in her mind.

With the sun retracting its light from the world around her, Dawn noticed small orange glimmers emerge from the direction of what was once her home. *They are still there?*

Dawn turned south, where she could lay low until the bandits had moved on and she could investigate to see if her father had made it away. *I can't wait in the cave anymore*, she thought. *It isn't safe.*

Moving on silent feet, she slipped between the rough trunks of the low hanging trees. The setting sun cut through the canopy of flat oval leaves in intermittent bursts, dazing her for seconds at a time, and then disappearing. Cold air blew through the wasteland. Running her hand through her long brown hair, she brushed it back from her face.

Soon the trees began to thin, and Dawn came to a cliff, bare and bleak, overlooking arid forests, with the Sea of Respite in the distance. The water, which would gleam during the days with the sun shining off the surface, was now hidden in shadow. Jagged pinnacles of weathered rocks jutted out in every direction beneath her. This cliff could give her some protection from any roaming packs of raiders, so she began to lower herself down, carefully setting her feet on the grey stones. On the way down, she spotted a few gnarled trees protruding out of the scarred cliffside, twisted and dead, bitten to the core by the freezing eastern wind.

As she placed her foot in the closest hold she could find, the rock split open, and Dawn slithered downwards with a wailing cry. She thrust her arm upward, reaching for anything that could halt her fall. Her hand gripped a pointed stone, but it slipped along the sharp surface, cutting deep into her palm. Shrieking, she tumbled down the ravine, slamming to her back at the bottom of the cliff.

The wind escaped her lungs as she gasped for air. Her hand throbbed as the blood dripped, her ears ringing from the long fall. She lay still, aching from head to toe. Every ounce of energy had been extracted from her body.

Dawn feebly tried to raise herself off the ground, but her arms betrayed her. She slumped back, cheek in the dirt. For a long minute she sat, nothing on her conscience except the ache of her bones and the sting of her hand. She finally found a way to her feet.

Lightheaded and bleeding she collected some kindling and stones, and attempted a fire, wincing from the pain as her blood-soaked hand slipped along the rocks. Minutes turned to hours, and she was no closer to a fire, and the chilling eastern wind burned her sensitive skin.

Tears filled her eyes. She hammered the rocks together over and over and over, screaming into the silent night as she unleashed her anger into the stones. Images of her mother and father rushed to her mind. Finally, she dropped the stones and she curled into a ball on the ground, grasping her necklace. She recalled what her father had told her about this gift, *"After you were born, I wanted to make you something that you could always hold onto. To remember your family, even if we are gone."*

As she gripped her amulet, it began to burn hot and kindled a white light, a small heart of dazzling fire. The darkness that had covered the land receded from it until it seemed to shine like a radiant flame. Dawn gazed in wonder at this incredible sight hanging from her neck. The heat from the necklace closed her wound and stopped the blood flow. She marveled at the token she had so long carried, never guessing its full potency. Did her father know the power of his gift?

The wonder stopped short as noises rustled all around her. Horror stricken, Dawn jumped to her feet and slowly started to back away. Her heart flamed and without thinking, whether it was folly, courage, or despair, she drew her sword. With her blade sparkling in the silver light, she advanced steadily into the arid forest.

Silhouettes appeared from the forest, shadows approaching from each direction. The coming enemies had finally been unmasked, and as reality returned to her, Dawn fled through the darkness of the night.

As figures entered her path, Dawn swung her sword wildly in front of her, hoping to make contact with whatever stood in her way. She sped through the wilderness, every now and again looking back to check for pursuers. Distracted, a tree root grabbed her foot and she tripped, landing with her face in the dirt. She jumped back to her feet, but by that time she was surrounded.

The bandits circled her, waving their swords ahead of

them. One by one, Dawn fended off the attackers. Two of the hooded assailants leaped at her ankles, knocking her to the desert floor. Kicking and squirming she screamed, helpless amidst the suffocating pressure of the men surrounding her.

Then, with a glorious flash, the jewel around her neck burned brighter than the midday sun. Heat radiated from within Dawn, yet she felt cool. Just as fast as the light came, it dimmed, and Dawn's attackers were gone. Relief and exhaustion overcame her, and she passed into unconsciousness.

3

Reavers

Flames erupted from cracks in the city streets. The earth shook and stone homes crumbled and collapsed. The creatures ravaging the streets bore no sense of repentance as they cut down terrified bystanders. Dawn watched her father facing down the dark monsters, but she was paralyzed, glued to the ground where she stood. She attempted to call out, but the words choked in her mouth. With each stroke of his sword, the beasts evaporated into the air. He fought until he was surrounded and Dawn's vision was flooded with shadow.

Suddenly she was falling endlessly into a dark abyss. When she finally discovered the landscape below, her body slowed to a stop, and she stood gazing at two magnificent towers. One climbed beautifully into the sky, decorated with brilliant crystals and ancient elven architecture. The light blues and silvers spoke a majestic radiance throughout the court where she stood. The other tower seemed to hardly stand at all. Grey stone shattered along the sides as rocks tumbled down its broken face. A maroon glow emanated from the center of the dark tower, a flare that began to overcome the luminous shine of the light tower. Dawn shuddered, darkness violently conquering the light.

Just then, a shadowy figure sluggishly approached her. The silhouette stood tall and menacing, looking down at Dawn as it approached. Dawn hardly dared to breathe. A meek question was liberated from the prison of her mind, "Who are you? What is your name?"

The shadow drew closer, "My name?" Its voice was shrouded and distorted, both a high squeal and a low grumble. Dawn shuddered at the sound, a strange cold chill. "You know who I am. You know my name."

Suddenly the figure turned. As if a spell had been removed, Dawn relaxed and stirred. She drew her sword, ready to charge forward. With a roar, the shadow twisted and contorted, limbs and joints cracking and breaking as the body grew massive. Grotesque wings sprouted from its back, and the head spun around. A huge demonic dragon now stood, towering over Dawn's petite body. She stumbled backward in terror at the colossal creature in front of her.

Dawn's eyes inched open. Warmth enveloped her aching body. Every muscle and bone inside her felt tattered and torn. She heard soft voices behind the crackle of the fire.

"I just can't understand your interest in this one," a man spoke in a familiar tone.

"I don't expect you to," another man responded. "You've

never had a family. It's only ever been about the work for you. And it's made you a rich man." There was a pause and a cheerful grunt. "I don't think it's made you happy."

"I don't know what else you think I need! I'm happier wallowing in my riches than you are. The vagabond ranger. Who are you to speak to me of *HAPPY*? You are the most miserable mutt I ever met."

The men laughed. Dawn couldn't decipher it in her mind, but these voices appeased her. Her breathing softened and her heartbeat seemed to slow. Cautiously, she turned around to face the party. Behind the flames sat a large, cat-like creature, and a weathered man laughing together. Dawn swiftly sat up and retreated, pressing her back against the rock wall behind her. She grasped a loose stone and readied herself for attack.

"Hey! The girl is awake!" The katze excitedly shouted.

"Don't be afraid," the man waved his hand and nodded. "We aren't going to hurt you."

"Why should I trust you?" Dawn stared at the shaggy head of dark hair flecked with grey covering the man's head. "You... You're the reavers! You were in my village. Maybe two days ago? Cain and Ragnar, if I remember right."

A solemn look descended upon Cain's face. "I'm sorry for what happened to your home."

Dawn fought back tears, not willing to show weakness to the reavers. Though her breath grew heavy, and quickly her face fell, painted with heartbreak. Quickly, she changed the subject, wiping the pain from her eyes. She drew her arm back again, readying her stone for defense. "Where are we? How did we get here?"

"We are atop Barkut Point," Ragnar interjected. "Old lookout from the great war. It's seen better days, but it still works like it's supposed to."

"We brought you here for protection, hon," Cain spoke with a soft voice. "After what we saw happened to your village, we didn't want to risk an open camp."

Looking around nervously, Dawn rose to her feet. She glanced in every direction, gazing into the shadows of night that pooled in the valleys below.

"Don't worry. Nobody knows we are here," Cain attempted to reassure her. "Whoever may have been following you is nowhere near. You are safe. I promise."

"How can you be sure?" Dawn asked, slowly lowering her arm.

"Been doing this for a while," Cain smiled with an infectious confidence. "Reavers are always aware of their surroundings. We travelled a few miles after finding you before coming here."

The chill of the desert night bit at Dawn's skin. She put the stone down and attempted to move to the fire, but she toppled to the cold stony landing. Cain leapt to her aid, but Dawn stubbornly shooed him away.

"She's got spunk," Ragnar laughed. "I like it!"

"You must be hungry," Cain stated. "Would you like dinner?"

Dawn nodded and the three returned to their seats around the fire. Cain prepared kline meat on a stone and seasoned it expertly for Dawn, which she scarfed down in minutes. The reavers watched amused by her tenacity as she ate. As if there was no other food left in the world. Remnants of the feast flew around her; she was like a beast devouring her prey.

"I know the man can cook," Ragnar laughed. "But wow!" Dawn blushed, wiping her mouth of the juices and crumbs from her meal.

"Food is a brilliant way to help others find healing," Cain stated, returning spices to a nearby satchel. "A way to show how the sublime is just a mixture of many ordinary things."

"Food is food," Ragnar scoffed with a grin.

Cain shot a glare toward his friend. "Ignorant. And all paintings are ordinary to you as well?" Ragnar rolled his eyes. "I guess real art is in the eye of the beholder." Cain tossed a raw piece of meat at Ragnar, laughing under his breath. "You won't mind just having that then?"

After the banquet, intrigued, Dawn looked to her rescuers. "How *did* you find me?" The question had been lingering in her mind. "The last thing I remember, I was surrounded by those hooded bandits. It seemed like the end... But then I woke up and I was here."

Cain and Ragnar glanced at each other quizzically. "We had returned to your village after our hunt in the ruins to the west. But, well..." Cain recounted the last few days with remorse in his voice. "We searched for any signs of life... But we didn't find any. Whoever it was that invaded even slaughtered the beasts. Dogs, horses. All of it. So, we decided to start the journey to Oasis on foot, and while we travelled, there was a flash of light coming from the south. It took us a while to get there, but when we did, it was just you." Cain's eyes glimmered in the light of the fire. "The trees surrounding you had been blown back, and there were ashes coating the ground around you."

"And Mister Sensitive here," Ragnar interrupted. "He just had to make sure you were safe. Carried you on his shoulder all the way out here to keep you nice and warm around our fire."

"What's the problem with that?" Cain retorted. "Life is precious, even if it's not your own."

"Don't get me wrong hon, I am glad you're alive," Ragnar smiled at Dawn. "And I don't think you would be if it weren't for Cain. I just didn't believe you actually *were* alive when we found you. I thought Cain was wasting his time and energy. But here you are! Up and moving. Even eating the food we worked so hard to catch."

A short-lived grin shot across Dawn's face. "Thank you." Even with the plunky attitude of Ragnar, memories of her past life still invaded her mind. "You said you already went to my village?" The reavers both nodded in agreement. "Did you see my father?"

A moment passed as the reavers looked back and forth at each other. The silence was deafening in Dawn's head, the crackle of the flames echoing through the night. Cain broke the quiet, "Well... we weren't looking for anyone in specific. But after seeing what was left behind, I..." He paused, searching for the words. "I wouldn't trust to hope."

Tears welled up in Dawn's eyes. The last ember of faith flickering in her heart, extinguished in seconds. Just a couple of simple words, able to cut so deep. Cain started to approach

Dawn to comfort her, but Ragnar grabbed him, "Give her a moment. Let her grieve."

Cain brushed Ragnar's hand away, and knelt next to the sobbing villager. "Grief is something that you need to go through personally, but it isn't something you need to go through alone. I can't grieve for you, but I can be here with you while you process things."

Dawn dropped her head into Cain's shoulder, moaning in pain. After some time, as the weeping slowed, Cain asked, "Do you have any other family? Grandparents? Aunts? Uncles? Anyone who would want to see you?"

Dawn pondered for a second, wiping the tears from her face, "I have an aunt who lives at the Citadel. Aunt Eva. Though...we haven't seen her in a while."

Cain and Ragnar locked eyes communicating a silent conversation. Finally, Cain spoke up, "I am actually headed back to the Citadel. I have business with the White Council. I can take you with me." Dawn exclaimed, jumping up to hug Cain, thanking him excessively. "We have to stop in Oasis first. Get the supplies for the trip. Without our horses, it isn't the easiest road."

"That is where I will be leaving you," Ragnar stated sadly. "While I wish I could accompany you to the Citadel, child, but my home is in Oasis." Ragnar continued, "We should get some rest. We'll be setting out at first light. We should make it to the city in just a few days if there are no obstacles to hinder us."

As Dawn lay down against the cold stone, her mind wandered, but it didn't last as she was slowly overtaken by slumber.

An orange glow peeked over the walls of the lookout. Dawn's eyes cracked open to the smell of seared meat. "Well good morning!" Cain said with a grin on his face. "I hope you still like kline. They seem to be abundant in this area."

"One of my favorites!" Dawn said, stretching her arms. The desert animals chirped and cooed in the valley below. Flocks of birds flew overhead and sunlight gleamed off the quartz in the broken rock of the watchtower.

The three ate the well-prepared breakfast and readied themselves for the journey ahead. Cain extended his hand toward the fire and a blast of frost exploded from his palm, extinguishing the flames. Dawn stared in amazement, "You're a mage!"

Cain laughed. "We are servants of the White Council! It sort of comes with the territory."

Wonder filled Dawn's eyes. "I always wished I could have been a mage."

"That is a common misunderstanding that people have," Cain explained. "You *can* be a mage. Anyone can use magic. Are you a believer?"

Dawn's eyebrows furrowed together. "What does that have to do with anything?"

Energy flashed through Cain's eyes. "That is all magic is. It isn't something that certain people are born with, and others aren't. It's a gift from the creator Fos. He gives blessings to those with the faith to ask, and some people have learned to harness the power of these gifts in what you call magic. It's accessible to everyone."

The three started down the shattered stone staircase of the watchtower and exited into the wilderness. The red orb of the sun now rose bright in the sky, sending long shadows knifing across the panorama spread ahead of them. As they walked from one shaded spot to the other, their feet scuffed up clouds of dust from the scorched earth. The air hummed with the sound of birds and scampering desert creatures.

They walked for the day until the sun set. Cain showed off his magical abilities again by lighting the fire to keep them warm in the cold desert night. Dawn relaxed more every minute she spent with the reavers.

The next day, the travellers approached a stream, and stopped for refreshment. Taking her shoes off, Dawn dipped her feet in the cool flowing water. "Ahh. I love the waters in Quarrine. I haven't been to the other islands, but there is no way that they have streams and rivers quite like Quarrine does."

"You've never been to the other islands?" Ragnar asked in amazement.

"I've never needed to go anywhere," Dawn replied with a sigh. "My home... My village... It always had everything for me. We have plenty of food in Quarrine. We have beautiful landscapes; all the seasons hit us here. We get the sun, and we get the snow. You can't say that about those northerners in Ardglas right? Nothing but ice and snow up there. If we need city life, we visit Oasis. It's not too far away." Dawn stared into the water rushing around her feet.

Cain stood, drying his feet to get his shoes back on. "But just like this water, we need change," he stated. "The water continues to flow, and because of that, it is clean. It can help us clean ourselves, and it is a pure, cool, refreshing stream. The same can't be said for water that lies stagnant." He gestured toward a small reservoir of the creek isolated from the water's flow. The water was green, with algae floating on the surface. "This water is poisonous. It's dirty. No one wants to dip into this part of the river."

Cain walked over to the dirty cistern and dug a path for it to flow into the rest of the stream. The waters rushed through the murky track and quickly became clear as crystal. "Sometimes all it takes is a little shift to wash someone's life clean."

Dawn dried her feet. "I get what you are trying to say, and I thank you for your sentiment. But everything that happened in the last few days..." Dawn paused to hold back tears. "I'm not going to suddenly thank your god for giving me a 'needed change'. Taking my family? My friends? I understand that there may be a silver lining in every cloud, but I am still right in the middle of the storm."

"Just because you can't see the silver lining, doesn't mean it isn't there." Cain responded.

"I'm just not ready to look for it yet!" Dawn shouted; her voice echoed throughout the desert wilderness.

"Come on guys," Ragnar interrupted. "We still have a few miles to travel before we get to Oasis. We have to get moving if we want to get there before nightfall."

Without a complaint, Dawn wiped the streams of water from her face, picked up her things, and continued behind Ragnar. Cain followed silently behind, his eyes peering downward into the dirt. After some time, he caught up to

Dawn and broke the dreadful quiet. "You know, if you want... I could teach you how to use magic."

Dawn dug her heels into the dirt and flipped toward him, glancing back and forth between Cain and Ragnar. "Do you think you actually could?" Her voice quivered.

"I think you could learn," Cain responded without hesitation. "I think you have some dormant magical abilities that you don't even know about. That flash of light we saw wasn't some anomaly. That was a blessing."

Dawn grasped her necklace. "If I had that kind of power, maybe I could have saved my family."

"Maybe," Cain sighed. "As servants of the Council, all reavers can use magic. To face what we do, we need it. But even so, I have still seen some awful things. Things that I couldn't have stopped, no matter what blessing I cast."

His demeanor had completely shifted. Just for a moment. Hardly enough of a moment for Dawn to notice, but she did. She asked the question that had been lingering in her mind, "What is it exactly that reavers do?"

Ragnar roared a laugh from up ahead, "You mean you don't know?"

Dawn replied, "Well, when I talked with my family, they both seemed to have different beliefs. My father said you are monster hunters. Dragons and such."

The reavers broke into an eruption of laughter. "Dragons?" Ragnar scoffed. "We specialize in hunting the big bad dragons?"

"Dragons are hardly even deadly compared to what we hunt." Cain stated, interrupting Ragnar. "Silly blind beasts they are. And the orcs have practically hunted them into extinction anyways. No, we hunt creatures from the Other called the Fallen. Demon creatures. Very deadly. The beast we just hunted near your village was called an anguis. A humanoid snake demon that rips apart its prey with its hands before feasting. Honestly, I wish dragons were the worst I had seen."

"Don't scare her, Cain," Ragnar said. "This is a reaver's job. We keep the world ignorant of the terrors we face. Would the world be a better place if they knew what we were saving them from?"

Dawn remembered her father's thoughts about the Fallen. "That can't be true. Demons aren't real… right?"

Cain's face fell. "You have heard of Moldolor?" He asked in a grim tone. Dawn nodded, fingering her necklace with dread. "The reason he was such a great threat to our world was because of the Fallen. He tried to harness the power of the demon king Seor to raise an army. We were lucky enough to stop him before he could complete the ritual to embody that power. It was close though."

Cain continued, "Fos sealed Seor and his fallen demons away in the Other a millennium ago. But when the red moon rises, the barrier between our world and the supernatural world becomes fragile. Some demons can slip through during these nights. It is our job to hunt the ones that do before they cause too much trouble."

As Cain spoke, the travellers came to the edge of a cliff overlooking a valley below. In the center of the valley was a magnificent desert city. "There it is!" Ragnar shouted. "The great city of Oasis!" They started down a dirt path that zigged and zagged across the side of the cliff. Powerful winds counteracted the intense heat of the afternoon sun. As Dawn peered out into the vast expanse toward Oasis, she noticed a towering fountain launching water up thirty or forty feet in the air. A grin crossed her face as they continued to descend.

4

The Guild

The travellers advanced towards the walls of the capital city of Quarrine. Stench of horses sitting in their stables overpowered their senses as cabbage farms dominated the land before them. Merchant carriages traversed the dusty dirt road between the fields. Standing at least four stories tall, the red rock walls of the city towered over the surrounding country. Soon they entered the magnificent city gates and made their way along the sandy paths of the city streets.

Walking through the brilliant city, they passed many inhabitants resting in the shaded areas beneath the canopies of the stone buildings. Their clothes were ratty and torn. Even after the events of the last few days, Dawn was better dressed than most of the Oasis citizens. Market stalls clustered around the town square in the city's center. The clamor of people buying and selling swept over Dawn like a sudden summer sandstorm. It was biting after the quiet of the past few days. The arrival of the travellers did not attract any curious gazes or any comments as they passed. Busy city life had enveloped the townspeople.

"Excuse me for a moment!" Cain shouted under the raucous noise of the crowd. "Oasis has some of the greatest spices in the world, and I need to replenish my stock."

Cain raced off into the crowd, leaving Dawn with Ragnar. A sweet looking boy, maybe eight years old, approached Dawn with arms wide open. "Mom!"

Stunned by a sudden embrace, Dawn peered around the market in a panic. "Excuse me, hon?" She patted the boy on his back. "I'm sorry, but I'm not your mother."

The boy released his embrace and glanced up at Dawn's face, tears welling in his eyes. Suddenly, a figure rushed past, crashing into Dawn as they pushed through the crowd. Dawn stumbled backwards, throwing her arms up to retain her balance. Once she regained her footing, she looked around to see that the boy had disappeared.

"I don't think so, kid!" Ragnar's voice echoed from a nearby alleyway. Dawn glanced over to find Ragnar holding a young man by the collar against a stone wall. "Hand it over."

The man pulled out an amulet and dropped it into Ragnar's giant paw. Instinctively, Dawn grasped for her own amulet, and realized that it was no longer on her person! She rushed to Ragnar, who released the thief down the alleyway.

"Keep an eye on your things around here," he stated, handing Dawn her necklace. "This marketplace is a paradise for thieves."

Dawn smiled up at Ragnar with gratitude, grasping the

amulet tightly in her hands. The string necklace had been cut clean with a knife, so she couldn't place it back around her neck. Ragnar smiled back at her, guiding her away from the bustle of the spice market.

One street over, Dawn paused to observe a strange commotion. A large group of peasants had gathered around a small wooden stage, where a man stood shouting down to the crowd. His voice was suppressed by the clamor of the market, but he spoke with enough authority that Dawn could still hear him clearly. "Let this be a reminder to anyone who crosses the Guild!"

Dawn approached the stage, leaving Ragnar to continue through the streets. She noticed a man kneeling with his head resting on a block. A menacing man stood nearby with a black mask over his face and a large axe in his hands. Dawn heard both cheers and concern from the bystanders. Shouts such as, "Let his head roll!" and "Leave him alone!" Dawn's heart raced, unsure of her feelings toward the supposed criminal. As the headsman approached the captive, Cain snatched Dawn's arm and yanked her away. "You don't need to be watching things like that," he directed, dragging her along.

A dark-skinned man sneaking through the crowds caught her attention. His eyes glimmered a bright blue and he wore a dark purple tunic with baggy white pants. While he snuck, he cut the coin purses of the onlookers, pocketing what must have been thousands of gold pieces. He looked up and made eye contact with Dawn after cutting his last purse, and slithered away into a nearby alley.

Cain pulled Dawn toward Ragnar, who was holding four bags of spices. "What do you think you are doing?" Cain grunted. "The last thing we need is to get mixed up with the Guild."

The three continued into the city until they found themselves at Ragnar's home. The roar of the marketplace had completely faded and dust had settled into a calm, crisp air. The home was a solid building made of stone; several stories tall. Rounded archways covered the oak doors, and an array of windows spread across the face of the marvelous structure. "You can both stay here for the night to rest up for your trip to The Citadel," Ragnar extended the offer with a gracious heart. "I can set you up with the supplies you need."

They entered and Dawn looked around the inside of Ragnar's mansion. Trophies and immaculate treasures hung on his walls. The furniture itself gleamed expensively. He lived alone, but his dinner table was set with silverware prepared for a host of guests. Dawn picked up a spoon and a cloud of dust exploded in the air, tickling her lungs.

Ragnar tossed a small chain to Dawn to replace the rope for her necklace. As she slid her amulet back around her neck, she noticed an emptiness in her stomach that Cain must have felt as well. "I think I am going to take Dawn to 'The Fountain' for a bite to eat." Cain stated to Ragnar.

"Don't cause too much trouble," Ragnar responded, picking up a large book and sinking into the comfort of a chair in the common room.

Cain laid a small bag down on a shelf near the front of the room and led Dawn out of the house and down some side streets of Oasis. The setting sun caused an orange glow to light up the sky. Shadows enveloped the city streets as they searched for their next meal. Cain led Dawn down a back alley where she saw a sign hanging out from above a rickety door. 'The Fountain' it read. "This is the place you are taking me?" Dawn asked.

Cain opened the door and waved Dawn inside. "This is some of the best food in the whole city. And I know good food! Don't be so quick to judge it by its looks."

Cain led them towards a corner table where they found their seat. There were many people scattered throughout the dirty room. The tables were splintered and weathered, though that did not keep the resident's spirits down; they sang songs together that roared throughout the tavern. Cain walked up to the bar to ask for drinks and a meal.

As he returned, Dawn couldn't help but speak, "I'm sorry about earlier," she said. "We didn't have very many encounters with the Guild back home. Although, the encounters we did have... they weren't exactly pleasant." Her voice trailed off.

"Hopefully we won't have any dealings with them while we are still here on Quarrine," Cain responded. "They are a dangerous lot. I wish the Council would take action and force them out already. But the Council has their own problems in the Citadel."

"Problems like what?" Dawn asked.

"After Ulumbra fell," Cain explained, "a new group called the Outriders took form. They want the same thing as Ulumbra, to remove the White Council from power, but they have much more radical views. The Outriders would like to see the whole world rid of magic. The larger they got, the more the Council has had to move out of Quarrine to reinforce the Citadel.

"And of course, space creates opportunity," Cain continued. "As the Council moved out, someone else had to move in."

"The Guild," Dawn concluded. An uncomfortable silence encumbered the table as Dawn peered around the room. Finally, she looked back to Cain. "What was in that bag you left behind at Ragnar's?"

"Just some things I am bringing home to the Citadel," Cain responded. "Reavers lead a dangerous life, looking for evil the way we do. It can be really easy to forget that life is a luxury. So, every time I survive an encounter with the beasts we hunt, I grab a souvenir to showcase in my home on Cirrane."

"What sort of souvenirs?" Dawn asked.

"Stones, bones, things of that sort. After one hunt, I took the sign off an abandoned building. 'The Safe house,' it was called. Had a horrific harpy infestation that had driven the people out of the area."

As Cain spoke, a delicious aroma filled the air. Dawn pointed her nose to the scent of curry over rice. The attendee brought their food over and Cain traded some coins. Dawn's mouth watered at the rich spice the chef was able to create for such a simple dish.

"I told you," Cain smiled, grasping the spoon on the table.

As they ate, Dawn overheard a conversation from some men sitting nearby. One man, who was wearing a leather outfit bedizened with red and orange jewels, was telling a story to the ones around him. "So, my cousin Barton is on his deathbed, dying of the Fever," he said. "His wife of forty years, she sits by his bedside waiting for the moment when he passes. While he lay there, he used his failing lungs to say a couple last things to his lovely wife. He tells her, 'Rose, after forty years, I have finally learned what you are to me.'

So, she asks him, 'What is that, my love?'

Barton tells her, 'When we met in Port Aurora, I had nothing. But still, you were always by my side. When we travelled all the way to Oasis, we lost all of our things on the road. Yet still, you were there. I worked in the fields and never got ahead, and there you were, still by my side. I finally earned enough to buy a shop and to partner with The Guild, and you stayed by my side. But! Then that shop burnt down, and The Guild turned away from me! But you! You were still there. And now, I am dying. I have nothing. And you are still right here next to me. Now I know. I know what you are to me.'

'Tell me, please!' She begs him.

And with his last breath, my cousin Barton turns to his wife, and he says, 'You are my jinx!'"

The group of men roared in laughter at the crass story. Dawn rolled her eyes, but couldn't help the grin on her face. Just then, the door slammed open, and some lackeys burst in holding a young man captive.

All the energy escaped the room. The sounds of singing faded into silence. The lackey spoke to the storyteller, "We found Nicholas sneaking through our vaults, Director Haze."

The director sighed, cutting into his plate of meat and taking a bite. Juice ran from his lips as he slowly chewed his meal. Not even bothering to glance up at the prisoner, he calmly spoke with food still filling his mouth. "What is the meaning of this, my dear Nicholas?"

Dawn noticed Cain's attention on the unfolding scene. His hand rested on the hilt of the blade at his hip.

"Don't make me ask twice, Nicky," Haze sang his words quietly. The hushed tone of his voice resounded in the silent tavern room.

"I...I... I'm sorry mister...Uhh, I mean Director! Director Haze. Sir," Nick stumbled over his words. "My... my family. We've just been struggling..."

"Come closer, Nick," Haze cut another piece of meat off his plate and pierced it with the fork in his other hand.

The Guild lackey pushed Nick forward and he fell at the feet of Haze's table. On his knees, he pleaded for his life. "Please. I just needed a little bit. For my family."

"You know, I *did* help you," Haze spoke as he took another bite of his meal. Food splattered out of his mouth as he spoke. "I gave you money, and *you* spent it. I gave you resources, and *you* used them up. I helped you. I helped your family. And this. This is how you repay me? By stealing from me? I thought we had become friends, Nick?"

Dawn squirmed in her chair pressing her back away from the Guild members. She could feel her heart beating in her ears as the goosebumps rose on her skin.

"Please have mercy, Director, sir," Nick whimpered. "Please..."

Haze slowly set his fork on the table and finished chewing the food in his mouth, wiping his face with an eloquent white tablecloth. "I am a man of mercy," he said. He turned in his chair toward the prisoner and placed the palm of his hand on the back of Nick's head, pulling the prisoner's head close to his own and leaving one hand palmed on the table. "But sometimes, the meaning of that word, mercy... It's different in my head than in other people's. See, I don't believe you live a good life. You don't provide for your family. You can't. You don't know how to get ahead. Even when you had friends that were willing to help. Still, you lead a miserable life."

Fast as lightning, Haze gripped his knife from the table and jabbed it into Nick's neck. Dawn gasped, nearly falling over in her seat. Haze bent down to whisper in Nick's ear, "I think ending your miserable life... I think that's mercy." Haze threw Nick's struggling body towards his lackey's. "Now... Well, now you don't have to suffer the fate that life brings to people like you," he said as he waved his subordinates away. Just as quickly as Nick had entered the tavern, he was gone.

Dawn sat staring; her jaw stuck open. Her vision blurred as the blood rushed to her head and her breathing sped up. Minutes passed, and soon the singing restarted, with residents banging their cups on the tables in cadence with one another as they chanted their drinking songs. Cain stood, pulling Dawn to her feet, and led her out of 'The Fountain'.

Cain rushed them down some streets until they were a ways from the tavern. "I am so sorry," he apologized. "I didn't expect anything like that to happen."

"I... I never knew!" Dawn searched in vain for her words. "He was so violent. And everyone else. They all just watched. No one did anything to help." She paused. "I... I didn't do anything to help."

Cain was quiet. He didn't have an answer. Maybe he could have helped the young man, but if he had, he would have put

Dawn's life in danger. "Sometimes the world isn't as black and white as you think. Sometimes there are grey areas."

"I'm not sure I can justify taking a life as a grey area," Dawn rebutted.

"You took the lives of those who attacked your village, right?" Cain asked.

Dawn peered down toward the street. "I was protecting my life, and my family's lives by taking theirs," she argued.

"That seems like a grey area to me," Cain said. "If I were to take the life of that man, Haze, the Guild director from the tavern, I would still be a killer. A man is still losing his life. But by taking his life I might be saving the lives of many. Who should get to decide? Who gets to draw the line? Is it ok to take the lives of those who seem to be evil? Or is all life sacred? Even the lives of those who do wrong." ***

"I feel like the answer should be obvious," Dawn replied. "But even though it's obvious, it doesn't seem easy."

"There is easy," Cain stated. "And then there is right."

The two continued to walk back toward Ragnar's house. Moonlight shone on the city while torches lined the streets. The roar of the market and trading from earlier in the day had quieted, and now, all Dawn could hear was the whisper of the wind.

Back at Ragnar's home they found the mansion lit up by red torchlight. Cain entered without a knock. Ragnar was sitting at a table in the living area, munching on some bread with one hand and wiping down a ceremonial looking blade with the other. When he heard the door, he turned to see his guests. "Geez!" He shouted. "It looks like you two just fought a ghost."

"We ran into an ugly scene with the Guild," Cain responded, hanging his grey hooded cloak on a coat rack. "Wasn't the most pleasant experience. I'll be glad to leave Oasis tomorrow and to get out of Quarrine for good."

"It may not be pretty all the time," Ragnar said, chewing his bread. "But Oasis will always be my home. Guild or no Guild."

Ragnar showed Dawn down a corridor lined with beautiful mirrors and paintings to what would be her room for the night. Setting her weapons and equipment on the bed, she looked around to examine her surroundings. A single window overlooked a garden outside, blossoming with brightly colored flowers glimmering in the torchlight. "Oasis always seemed to me like a beautiful escape from the scorching desert," Ragnar said to Dawn, looking out over the garden. "There is so much dead out there, so much desolation and wasteland. Oasis always seemed like a haven away from the outside world. The politics of the Citadel would never touch us, and we could just live our own beautiful lives here."

"That's what I thought my home was," Dawn murmured. "We were secluded and we felt safe. But we weren't prepared for the world when it finally reached us. None of us were. Except, maybe my dad."

"I had only met him the one time," Ragnar replied, "But your father seemed like a good guy." Dawn continued to gaze out the window as Ragnar noticed Cain walking down the hallway toward his room. "It might not be worth much, but you are in pretty good hands now."

Dawn couldn't explain it to herself, but she agreed. A sense of calm filled her body when she was with the reavers.

Even when things were going badly at the tavern, she trusted that she was safe as long as Cain was there with her.

As her mind wandered, she heard a crash from down the hall, followed by Cain's voice shouting, "Get back here!" She bolted out of the room where Ragnar had already caught the cause of the commotion. In his giant paws, a young dark man with bright blue eyes and a dark purple tunic attempted to wiggle himself away, terrified of the katze who held him captive.

"What are you doing here?" Ragnar shouted.

"Let me go, cat!" The invader screamed back, kicking against the hallway wall. "There's cat-nip in my front pocket. You can have all of it if you want!"

"I know you..." Dawn whispered under her breath as she stepped into the open space.

Ragnar slammed the man against the wall and growled in his face, "You have three seconds to tell me why you are in my house, or your life ends tonight."

"Wow," the intruder laughed. "Your place? Pretty big litter box." Ragnar smashed him against the wall one more time, and the young man paused his thrashing to respond to his interrogator. "Okay! Okay!" He paused to take a breath. "I am hiding. I thought I could hide here and not be seen, and then sneak out before anyone noticed."

With another ram against the wall, Ragnar screamed, "You're a liar! Thief!"

"No, please!" The man begged. Just then, three firm knocks came from the front door. The intruder's eyes flashed with intense fear. He gripped Ragnar's hands with fervor, "Please. I'm not here. Please. I beg you. I swear, I was just kidding about the litter box. A-a-and the cat-nip. Unless, of course, you are into that kind of thing? In which case I can definitely acquire some for you if that is what you..."

Ragnar threw his prisoner down the hallway towards Cain. "Shut him up," he commanded as he walked out toward the main room. "Everyone stay out of sight."

Cain dragged the intruder back to the end of the hallway and Dawn rushed back toward them to stay out of sight. "You were at the execution earlier today," the man said as he looked upon Dawn's face. Cain shook him to keep quiet. Annoyed, he continued, extending a hand out in courtesy. "The name is Krom."

Cain pulled a knife from a sheath on his ankle. "If you want to keep breathing, *Krom*, I would keep my mouth shut."

"OK! Geez!" Krom waved his hands in surrender. "I didn't realize I chose the uptight residence to take refuge in."

Ragnar looked out the front window to see a group of men gathered on the porch steps. Many of them held torches that lit up their armor and weapons. Some wore steel plate chest pieces, while others wore more elegant garments of clothing. Each of them was armed with military grade weapons.

As Ragnar clipped two hand axes on his hips, there were three more firm knocks on the solid oak. Exhaling a single breath, he unlocked and opened the door. He examined the man standing in front of him, and greeted him with cold courtesy, "Can I help you?"

"Yessir," the man said with a rough voice. "I am Captain

Grendel Greenwood, and we are with the Guild in Oasis. Is this the home of the reaver who goes by the name, Ragnar?"

"It is."

"Great. We are looking for a fugitive who our sources tell us is in this area of town. May I come inside and ask you a few questions? I understand reavers are protectors of the peace."

Ragnar glanced at the army standing outside his doorstep. "Of course," he grumbled. "Come right in."

Captain Greenwood gave a nod to the soldiers behind him, and entered Ragnar's home alone, shutting the door behind him. "You have a beautiful home, Ragnar. Please excuse my intrusion on your night. I know it's late, and I don't plan to be long."

Ragnar noticed Greenwood eyeing toward the back of the house, and pulled out a chair in the living area. "Please," he said, gesturing to the Guild captain to sit with him. "My home is always open."

"What the people of Oasis say about your hospitality is true," Captain Greenwood said, sitting in Ragnar's chair. "The sight of a katze such as yourself is enough to send a grown man running, yet here you are, being hospitable. More like a stuffed cat than a fearsome warrior."

Ragnar brushed the statement off, "May I offer you some wine while we talk?"

As Ragnar was in mid stride toward his wine shelf, the Guild captain grabbed him by the hand, revealing a tattoo on his forearm of a large cross with something set on top. "I am not much of a wine drinker, myself. But I will take some water if it is accessible?" With the request, Greenwood released Ragnar's arm, and pulled his sleeve back down.

"Of course, sir."

Ragnar grit his teeth as he walked over to pour two glasses of water. When he returned and sat in his seat, the captain began his conversation. "So, you have a reputation in Oasis as Ragnar the Wrecker. The Reaver of Oasis. I have come to know quite a bit about you from the rumors of the city people. They like to talk about anything that isn't their own meaningless lives. Now, I don't want to assume, but do you know much about me or the organization I work for?"

Ragnar took a drink of his water. "Of course," he said. "You are a part of the Guild. With the Council being pushed away from Quarrine after the war, the Guild has taken responsibility for establishing commerce and trade throughout the Wastes."

"Exactly!" Greenwood exclaimed. "So, you know of the Guild, but what about me and my team, specifically? Do you know who we are?"

"I'm sorry," Ragnar responded. "I have been on a mission in the west for a little over a week, and am a little out of the loop on some specifics."

"No need to apologize, katze," Greenwood said. "Let me explain. We are a team that has been labelled by the people as the Hunters. We have been tasked by the Guild director himself to find and destroy enemies of the Guild. This would include many sorcerers, thieves, revolutionaries, and the like. We hunt them down before they can cause any problems in our beautiful cities."

Ragnar took another drink of his water. "If that's the case..." he responded. "While it is a pleasure to have your company,

I am not sure why you have come here to my home. Unless you consider me one of these 'threats to the Guild'?"

Greenwood laughed. "Of course not! There are just a couple questions I have about your most recent mission to the west." He pulled out a small leather book from his breast pocket. "Some of our members saw you enter the city today and we have to get some information for our records. Do you happen to have some ink I can use?"

Ragnar fetched some ink and placed it on the table for the captain. "Thank you so much," Greenwood said. "Now, if you don't mind, what was the nature of your mission in these last weeks?"

Ragnar fidgeted nervously in his chair. "We were hunting a..."

"I apologize," Greenwood interrupted. "Who is 'we'?"

"My reaver captain and me," Ragnar responded. "We hunted a creature called an anguis in some ruins to the west."

The captain wrote down a couple thoughts in his book. "So, you walked on foot?"

Ragnar sighed. "No. We got horses from the stable outside the city. It was Fur's Stable."

Greenwood repeated Ragnar's words as he said them while copying down his account of the events. "So, you borrowed horses from Fur's Stable. Why, then, when you returned, did you return on foot?"

"The path grew too thick for mounts," Ragnar responded. "We tied them up at a village and continued on foot to our destination. When we returned to the village, the horses had been taken by raiders."

"I see. And do you recall the name of this village?" Greenwood stopped writing and glared into Ragnar's eyes.

Ragnar responded slowly, "I don't think this village had a name. It was quite small."

They stared at each other for a while, until Greenwood broke the tension by laughing and writing down Ragnar's answer. "Ahh, there are many of those out there, aren't there? Too many villages that aren't under any governance. If I had my way, I would make all villages and cities a part of the Guild's governance. That may just be a pipe dream though."

While the two were talking in the living area, Cain, Dawn, and Krom sat in the back of the house silently, listening in on the conversation happening just a few rooms away. As Dawn listened, she focused on the captain's voice.

Unable to contain her curiosity, Dawn inched into the hallway towards their room. Cain whispered at her to come back, but she was entranced. As she snuck past her room, she noticed men with torches outside her window surrounding the house, wielding longbows with arrows already nocked on the bowstrings. Goosebumps covered her body as she crept toward the end of the hallway.

"I am sure you have heard of the terrorist cult, Ulumbra, correct?" Greenwood carried on with his interview.

"I don't know much, only rumors," Ragnar replied.

"Let's hear what you have heard!" Greenwood seemed enthused. "Facts can be so misleading. The truth is so often hidden in the facts. Whereas rumors, true or false, can reveal so much."

"Well, Ulumbra was the militant group who caused the great war," Ragnar replied. "Led by the dark sorcerer Moldolor, he gathered an army who would help him rise to power to overthrow the governments of the White Islands. More specifically the White Council. They say he tried to harness the power of the dark god Seor, but he wasn't strong enough to hold that power and perished in the attempt."

"Yes, yes, yes. This is what the history books will say," Greenwood sighed disappointedly. "This is what the Council has told the people. But I want to hear the rumors!"

Ragnar paused, searching his mind for the right answer that may cut this conversation short. "There are rumors," he started, "that he didn't actually die." Greenwood reeled in his chair with a smile on his face. "That he actually imparted his power into something, an object or a person that was nearby when he died."

Greenwood clapped in excitement. "Thank you! My young reaver," he shouted. "Now, I can get to my reason for being here..."

As the two talked, Dawn peeked around the corner. The Guild Captain was facing away from her and she could see the whites of Ragnar's big green eyes.

Greenwood continued. "There are reports that have come to my attention. Reports that this 'object' or 'person', as you explained, could actually bring the dark sorcerer Moldolor back to life." Greenwood paused to take a drink of water before continuing. "We've also gotten reports that there is a village in the west that is home to Ulumbra conspirators who are attempting to find, and utilize this dark 'rumor' to bring back the great sorcerer and start a new war." Ragnar leaned back in his seat, clenching his fists. "I can't help but wonder," the captain continued, "if this is the same village you and your companion visited while you were on your mission."

As the Captain told his side of the story, Ragnar's focus shifted to Dawn watching from the hallway. Greenwood noticed his eyes wander to the back of the house, and turned to discover what had been distracting his host. Jumping up from his seat, he shouted out with his rough voice, "My dear! Please reveal yourself!"

Dawn inched out from the hallway. Ragnar rushed over, placing himself in between Dawn and the Guild captain. "This is my guest for the night," he said. "We met on the way back to Oasis."

"Is that right," Greenwood responded slowly. As he examined Dawn, his eyes caught sight of her necklace which hung loosely around her neck. "Well, I don't think I have any more questions for you, my friends. I have all the answers I need. If you don't mind, we are going to move on to our next destination."

As Greenwood rushed toward the door, Dawn shouted, "I know you!"

He halted, slowly turning his head to glance at the girl, an evil smile on his lips.

Dawn rushed forward past Ragnar, seizing a knife from the table nearby. Greenwood spun around and threw a chair into Dawn, sending her backward into her katze friend. The Guild captain grabbed the ink that was on the table and launched it at the front window, leaving a crack and a splatter of black for the outside world to see.

With a shout from the men outside and a blaring crash,

arrows cloaked in flame zoomed into the house through the windows, which were now shattering into pieces on the floor. Fire spread throughout Ragnar's magnificent home.

Ragnar threw Dawn back into the hallway, throwing the knife from her hands. Unsheathing his hand axe, he charged forward to take on Greenwood. The Guild Captain pulled out a longsword and a dagger and began to brawl with the reaver. Fire and smoke filled the room as the two swung, blow after blow, at each other with no sign of stopping.

Dawn watched the clash in the room, listening to the sounds of steel ringing in the air masked by the roar of the flames. She stepped forward to help her companion, but the fire had already spread too far. A beam from above crashed in between her and the ensuing fight. She turned and rushed back to her room to grab her weapons, and noticed her window had shattered and a Guild soldier was climbing inside with a sword in hand. The soldier's eyes met hers. She grabbed an oil lamp sitting on a desk. The man screamed and lunged forward just as Dawn hurled the lamp in his direction.

With a *CRASH*, the lamp made contact with the soldier's head, but it hardly slowed his approach. Bleeding, he swung his heavy longsword towards Dawn's head, but she ducked just in time. The sword lodged in the frame of the door where it splintered the wood, but with a push of his foot, the man kicked it free. He swung again at Dawn. One slash after another she rolled and dove out of the way. The smoke filled her lungs and every exertion of her body caused her to lose her breath.

Dawn jumped out of the way of one more sword swing, but this time the man followed through with a kick that sent her flying backward into the wall. He raised his sword one last time, but like a flash of lightning, Krom appeared between Dawn and her attacker with a short blade of his own. One quick parry, and Krom took out the offending swordsman.

Krom helped Dawn back to her feet. "The house is on fire, and you're taking a nap?" Krom laughed. "Come on! Your pals are already fighting their way out!" Dawn found a sword and slung her bow onto her back before following Krom down the hall.

In the main hall, splintering beams and melting plaster fell around them like acid rain from the engulfing fire. The billowing smoke was thick in their eyes and in their lungs. Dawn held her sword at the ready, knowing that an enemy could be right in front of her face. The smell of burning flesh overpowered the scent of blazing wood. With a flash in the firelight, Dawn saw a glimmer in front of her and swung her sword with all of her might.

Her steel struck another blade, but to her surprise, she heard a familiar voice, "Be careful where you swing that." Cain materialized and took her by the hand leading her and Krom toward an exit.

Screams drowned in the blaze of the inferno. The roaring beast of fire did not choose a side, good or evil, but instead devoured each person it encountered. Dawn felt cool at the touch of Cain's hand, as if a light breeze was blowing under the shade of a palm tree.

They found their way to the south side of the house, where the outer wall had crumbled and opened up into a dimly lit alleyway. Ragnar stood growling in the opening, drops of blood slipping from the blade of his axe. Bodies of soldiers lay on the floor beneath his massive frame. "We have to get out of the city," Cain said quietly. "Is there an exit route that isn't occupied by the Guild?"

Ragnar grunted with a scowl on his face. He glared toward Dawn and growled, "This is my home."

"Ragnar!" Cain shouted. "We can't stay here as enemies of the Guild. Is there any way out of the city?"

Krom shifted their attention towards himself with an answer, "I know a way."

The katze lunged toward Krom and clutched him by the collar of his purple tunic. "Why would we trust you?" He barked. "Thief!"

"I am in the same predicament as you!" Krom snapped back. "Like it or not, I am your best bet to get out of here. I have been running from the Guild for years, and I am still alive. Still have all my fingers too." He wiggled his fingers out in front of his face. "So, if you want to get out alive, I suggest you all follow me."

The rage in Ragnar's eyes burned hotter than the fire around them. He looked toward Cain, who gave a nod toward Krom, and with animosity, Ragnar let go of the thief. While Krom dusted off his shoulders, Cain asked, "Why do you care what happens to us?"

"You all saved my life tonight," he responded. "I may be a thief and a scoundrel, but I do still have some decency."

Krom led the group silently down alleyways toward the center of the city, until they came to the stage where the execution was held earlier that day. Underneath the stage, Krom opened a sewer grate and motioned the group down into stone caverns beneath the streets of the city. Krom grabbed a torch off the stone walls lighting up the streets and caught up with his new companions.

5

Wastes

Shadows flickered in the torchlight beneath the streets of Oasis. Cain snapped his fingers and produced a solid light from his hands that shone down the cavernous stone pathways. Krom looked over and scoffed, throwing his useless torch into the water flowing next to them. The sound of rushing water drowned out the whispers from the city above.

"These tunnels are a labyrinth," Krom said. "No one in their right mind would come down here of their own volition. Only the craziest of crazy. Because, if you don't know where you are going, you could be lost for days, maybe even end up as a rat's next meal!" As he spoke, Dawn heard the pitter-patter of little feet on the rocky floors. "Lucky for us, this isn't my first venture into crazy. Come on, this is the way to safety."

Krom started to lead the group down the passage, but

when he turned around, he noticed Ragnar had not followed. "I'm not going with you," the katze growled under his breath.

"Ragnar..." Cain spoke in a soft voice.

"Don't!" Ragnar lashed at his leader. "Don't even start. I don't need a lecture from you Cain. What I need right now is answers from her!" Ragnar pointed to Dawn.

Dawn gasped, "Me?"

"What was all that about!" Ragnar argued. He looked at Cain, but kept pointing to Dawn. "We stick our necks out for her, and she is part of that Ulumbra cult! You should have seen the captain's face when he saw her." He faced Dawn. "He recognized you, And you recognized him! Like you are the one he wanted this whole time. Like my home, and my life just burst into flames because you didn't have the decency to tell us the truth!"

Dawn mumbled under her breath, "I... I did know him." Cain and Krom both gasped. "His voice, I recognized it from the night my home was attacked. He was with the group that killed my family!"

"You told us it was raiders that attacked your village," Cain inquired.

"See," Ragnar looked down on Dawn. "We can't trust her. She has been in trouble with the Guild this whole time, and because of her dishonesty, now we are too. They weren't even looking for the thief. They were looking for her!"

"No!" Dawn shouted. "I swear, I had no idea it was the Guild that attacked my village. My family and I had no issues with the Guild. And we have nothing to do with Ulumbra. Or Moldolor."

"It doesn't matter," Krom interrupted the argument. "No

matter what happened in the past, we are all in the same situation now. We are all fugitives of the Guild, and we all need to escape the city."

Silence encased the passageway. Cain stepped toward Dawn. "The journey to the Citadel just got a lot harder. You know that right?"

Dawn frowned. "I know."

Cain nodded. "Then let's go," he said. "We have a long road ahead of us."

A low growl came from behind them. Ragnar glared at the three fugitives. "I'm not going." Cain looked back to him, but Ragnar continued, "I told you already. I'm not going to travel with her. This is my home. And if it's the Guild keeping me from staying here, then it's about time for the Guild to find a new residence."

"You know you can't go back up there, Ragnar," Cain said.

"I don't plan to," Ragnar replied. "Not yet at least. You're not going to want to come back through these sewers. I'm going to gather some friends to help me fight the Guild, and this will be where we'll operate from. If it is as hidden as the thief says, then we should be able to mount a successful assault from here."

Cain nodded and extended a hand to shake Ragnar's giant paw. "Until next time, friend," he said. Ragnar nodded, and started to walk away.

"I know this may be an emotional moment," Krom said, "But we really need to get moving to get into the wastelands before the sun comes up. We have to get a head start on the Guild or they will be right on our trail."

The trio marched down the cobblestone walkway

overlooking a flowing stream of water. The stale air combined with their tired, smoke filled lungs made each stride extremely exhausting. A black layer of dust covered Dawn's, now torn and weathered, light blue tunic. She looked around at her associates and noticed the same coating of soot on their clothes. Cain's face was plastered with the evidence of the house fire.

"I know this water isn't ideal," Dawn began, but she was quickly interrupted.

"Not ideal?" Krom laughed. "It's sewer water! Washing up here will leave us smelling worse than the fire did! And don't even think about drinking from that."

"I guess..." Dawn muttered under her breath.

After Krom led them through miles of tunnel and over some wooden bridges to cross over the filthy flow of murky water, they came to a narrow passageway. It seemed too small for most to be able to get through, but Krom insisted that this was the only way out into the wasteland. He dropped to his hands and knees and started to squeeze through the tight space. Cain followed him into the escape route.

Dawn hesitated. Her throat tightened. Her breathing began to quicken and her heart felt like it was beating out of her chest. "You have fought this far," she whispered to herself. "This is the least of the enemies you've faced." And without another thought, she followed her friends into the opening.

The moment she entered the pass, her mind immediately started to bounce like a rubber ball, considering ways back out into an open space. Her persistence kept her moving forward, keeping her eyes up to seek the light from Cain's hands which still illuminated the crawlspace. As she crawled, she thought she felt the stones surrounding her close in. Her stomach lurched, but she clenched her teeth to hold back the terror in her heart. She longed for the warmth of the desert sun and a cool breeze on her skin. "Just keep moving," she repeated to herself. "Just keep moving. Just keep moving. Just keep moving."

One movement after the next, she crawled forward. Her hands and knees ached from the rough stones she pressed against. When she finally felt a cool breeze on her face, her heart leapt. Her escape was in reach. *Just a little farther!*

At last, she exited the constricting tunnel and exhaled a sigh of relief. To her surprise, the cave that Krom had led them through seemed nowhere near Oasis. The mouth emerged in the middle of the Western Wastes.

"If you don't mind," Krom said, "we should close this passageway up so we can camp here safely. We are a ways away from Oasis and can probably use the rest before we continue."

Cain was hesitant. "You have brought us this far. Why journey with us more?"

Krom sighed, "I have been running for a long time, and it is a lonely business. I just want people to talk to."

Dawn couldn't hide a small smirk on her face. With all that she had been through, she was unsure if she would be able to relate with anyone ever again.

Cain placed his hand on the top of the entrance to the passageway, and released a surge of power. The ground shook for a second, and the rocks crumbled in on themselves. The group then gathered some sticks and kindling for a fire to shield them from the freezing desert. With a wave of his hand, Cain sent a blast of flame from his hands to light the shrubbery ablaze.

Dawn watched his movements with wonder. Each sway of his hand or snap of his fingers held so much power. More power than she had ever seen. Her father was an expert fighter, but he could never compete against a master sorcerer like Cain. She wondered if she would ever be able to compete with him.

Without another word towards each other, the three lay down to find some sleep. There were no sounds except the wind whispering across the desert plain. Dawn's stomach groaned, like a ball of hot lead had made its home there. She thought about Ragnar and how quickly he could turn his back on her. How quickly people could no longer be in her life.

She glanced over at her new friend, Krom, wondering if he would stay with her, or find his own way once he got what he wanted, whatever that may be. Her gaze made its way to Cain, who she couldn't explain why, but she trusted with her life.

Thoughts of her father made her heart slump. Instinctually she rubbed her eyes, but to her surprise they were dry. The tears were too stubborn to roll down her face.

Dawn closed her eyes, maybe to escape the reality of the world she lived in, but in her mind a war waged. She thought about Cammie, and how he thought he was ready to fight a real fight.

She thought back to the last day she saw her family, replaying each moment as if she could relive it. The conversations with Maron and her parents had started to become fuzzy. Words she wished she would have said had begun to replace the reality of the actual events of the day.

"Honey, is something on your mind?" a soft voice asked from nearby. Dawn inched her eyes open and noticed that she was standing in her village. She looked around to see who was speaking, and discovered her mother standing behind her. "You seem troubled."

"Mom!" Dawn bolted forward with arms open wide, seeking an embrace, but with a blink of her eyes, her mother had disappeared. "Mom?" She whimpered.

"She isn't here anymore, thanks to you," a familiar voice boomed in Dawn's mind, but when she searched, she couldn't see anyone nearby.

"Who's there?" Dawn muttered, her voice trembling. The sound of leaves crunched behind her, so she flipped around, only to find Cammie, sneaking between huts. "Cammie?" Dawn noticed his clothing was stained red, and his feet were leaving dark traces in the dirt behind him. He collapsed with a *THUMP*, and Dawn called out, "CAMMIE!" But his body faded into the wind.

"You couldn't save him either," the booming voice returned, but Dawn couldn't see anyone around her. "You couldn't save any of them. You failed."

"Show yourself!" Dawn screamed, drawing her sword and stumbling around her village. An orange glow shone from behind her, and when she turned around, she saw a blazing fire engulfing her home. Stumbling backwards away from the fire, she tripped, crashing to the ground. When she looked at what had caught her feet, Maron lay, staring back at her. His eyes were immobile and grey, yet still he spoke, "You are the reason they came, and you couldn't help us." His voice wasn't his own, but instead was the same booming voice that had spoken before.

Dawn screamed, crawling backwards until she found the wall of a hut. Maron stood up, his body destroyed by the raider's attack. As he stood, Dawn's mother and Cammie appeared, their bodies mangled, flames gnawing at their skin. They all approached Dawn, speaking in unison, "You did this. You did this."

Dawn clenched her eyes shut, clawing at her ears, screaming, "No! No! No!" Finally with a shout, she felt heat exude from her necklace, and there was a sudden silence. Dawn breathed heavily, unable to convince herself to open her eyes to see what had happened in the world around her.

"You're pathetic," the same booming voice spoke, but it no longer rang through her ears. Instead, the voice was speaking from in front of her. "And weak. I don't know how you've lasted this long on your own."

Dawn slowly opened her eyes. Standing in front of her was a silhouette with no clear features. Just a figure of black, overshadowed by a darkness radiating from within itself. "Are you scared?" The figure asked, taking a step forward toward Dawn.

A plethora of questions ran through Dawn's mind, but she couldn't find a way to form a question into words.

"You weren't enough," the silhouette said. "You couldn't save Cammie, and you murdered our mother!"

Dawn's mind stopped. "Our?" She questioned. The figure laughed a sinister laugh and stepped forward again. As it stepped, the shadows began to disappear, and Dawn saw the face of the thing standing in front of her. "You are..."

"I am you," the figure helped Dawn come to the realization. "It's a relief to finally speak with you. I have been worried about our wellbeing for some time now."

"I'm fine," Dawn said. The figure in front of her was like a reflection of her physical being, mixed together with her darkest, innermost thoughts. "I don't need help."

"You are a lot of things, Dawnie," the reflection said. "But you are not a liar. Why start now? Lying to yourself?"

"I have my friends now..."

"Friends?" The reflection laughed. "Heh. You are in over your head. Setting yourself up for heartache." Dawn sighed. "You must know by now that relationships are all temporary. Even the people closest to you are only in your life for a season. Your family is dead. Ragnar turned his back on you. You can't trust anyone but yourself." The reflection paused for a moment. "But you... You can't even trust yourself. Not after what you did to our mother."

"Stop!" Dawn screamed, tears streaming down her face. "What was I supposed to do? I wanted to do what was right by protecting Cammie. It was right. *I* was right. I was protecting him." Dawn paused to think, pulling her dark hair away from her face as it clung to her wet cheeks. "Everything went so wrong. It wasn't supposed to be like this."

"No. It wasn't," the reflection stated. "And now you cling to this man. This reaver. Like he will be able to help next time things go awry? I could have helped, you know. But you would rather rely on others. People who you can't trust. People who don't even trust you."

Dawn thought about Ragnar and the Guild captain's accusations about her family and Ulumbra. "I don't want to be alone..."

The reflection gazed down at her, and offered her hand. "You will never be alone again."

Dawn looked up and grabbed her reflection's hand. Suddenly a surge of energy flowed through her, but along with the energy she felt a hot rage rise up inside. Thinking about the events of the last week, and the abandonment of the katze just hours earlier made her angry enough to release a growl from the depths of her soul.

She jumped back up to her feet and let go of the reflection's hand. Peace enveloped her body again, and all the anger left like a bird being shooed away by unfriendly neighbors. "What was that?" Dawn asked.

The reflection laughed, "You didn't think that power like mine would come without a cost, did you?"

"I don't want to feel like that," Dawn said.

"So, you would rather be numb and weak?" Dawn didn't respond. "Fine! Enjoy the weakness of complacency!" The reflection's voice shifted to a booming shout that echoed through Dawn's mind. Shadows extended from the figure's body, creeping toward Dawn. A scream escaped Dawn's lips as she backed away from the terrifying reflection of herself. The booming voice reverberated throughout her mind. "Dawn. Dawn! DAWN!"

Dawn awoke to Krom shaking her vigorously. The

morning sun pierced the low hanging trees and warmed her skin. "Dawn! Are you ok? You were screaming."

Dawn looked around and saw Cain cooking breakfast around the fire. Her face started to feel hot, her cheeks shining a bright red. "Sorry," she said. "Bad dream I guess."

"I'll say! Do you want to talk about it?"

Krom's question sounded sincere, but the words of her reflection sat in the forefront of Dawn's mind. "That's ok," she said. "I'm ok."

The party ate the food that Cain prepared and started their journey to the east. "We should stay away from roads," Cain told them. "If we can travel parallel to the main road, maybe a mile off of it, then after a couple days we should make it to the Great Canyon Pass. With any luck, it will be clear of any Guild activity and we can cross with no trouble. That will take us directly to Port Aurora, where we will find our passage to Cirrane."

"That is a big 'if,'" Krom mocked. "The Guild is everywhere on Quarrine. What if they are stationed at the port?"

"That is a question for when we get there," Cain responded. "No use planning for a problem that may not even present itself."

The three continued through the wasteland, keeping away from the main road. Walking between the low hanging trees and staying in the cover of the shrubbery and increasingly large bushes, they felt comfortable. Their path was secluded from the civilized world.

After days of travel, while walking, Krom began to sway back and forth between the trees. His feet danced and stumbled both in a gracious and clumsy fashion. "Are you all right, Krom?" Dawn asked.

Krom continued to stumble around and began to moan. He danced over to a tree, but with a swift motion, he gripped a branch and flipped up into the leaves, finding a seat on the protruding piece of wood. "I think it's time for a break!" He shouted.

Dawn burst into laughter. "You are ridiculous!"

A grin spread across Krom's face, a light breeze blew from the east and he fell backwards to the ground. "Yeah," he groaned, lying on his back. "Definitely time for a break."

Dawn and Cain both erupted into a fit of laughter. "There is a stream just up ahead," Cain said. "Can you make it that far?"

"Aaawwwwooouuuugh," Krom whined. "Will you carry me?" Cain scoffed. "Come on! I'm not *that* heavy."

Cain waved his hand and suddenly Krom was thrown up in the air and to his feet. "I guess I can walk. Dang mages."

"You have a problem with mages?" Dawn asked as the group approached the stream.

"Just not a fan of magic in general," Krom responded. "Me and magic aren't really the best of friends."

"You aren't great at the whole, 'being friends' thing, are you?" Cain asked. "Mages *AND* the Guild? That can't just be bad luck." Cain found a bowl shaped stone to fill with water and heated it to a boil.

"They aren't exactly separate," Krom said. "My relationship with the Guild and my relationship with magic aren't necessarily opposed."

"What do you mean?" Dawn asked as she took off her shoes and dipped her feet in the cool flowing stream.

"It's a long story," Krom said. "Let's just say that I used to dabble in magic, but I made some pretty big mistakes, and those mistakes were pretty bad for my relationship with... uhh... Director Haze."

Cain paused, "Dark magic?"

Krom hung his head. "I said I don't want to talk about it. Not exactly proud of that season of my life."

Dawn could sense the tension in the air between her two companions. "What do you want in life?" She asked, changing the subject. "You couldn't have wanted to be a thief or dark mage your whole life. What is it you want to be? To do?"

Krom was surprised by the question. "I haven't thought much about it," he responded. "I wanted to be a part of the Guild for a long time. But now, I have been running for a long time. Always stressed about whether or not I am going to find food, or find a bed, or shelter, or be caught by the Guild. What I really want though... is to be bored."

"Bored?" Dawn asked.

"Yeah! I want nothing more than to have relief from the stress. I want to know what my next season will be and find rest. I am so tired of there always being... *Something*. War, poverty, rebellions, terrorists, famine, cults. What I want most is a calm, boring life."

Cain cooled the heated water with some magic and handed the bowl to the newest member of the party. "That is actually very admirable," he said. "So many people want a name. They want to be somebody, but end up making the world a worse place in the process. They don't care who they hurt on their way to becoming somebody of importance. There is power in being quiet, and content."

Krom took a drink of the water, and then handed the bowl off to Dawn to take a drink. "You still have to teach me how to do this," Dawn said to Cain after taking a drink of the freshly cleansed and cooled water.

"Get up," Cain commanded with a smile. "This will be your first magic lesson." Dawn jumped to her feet and rushed over to her mentor.

"Before you can use any magic, first you have to understand it," Cain explained. "Light magic is nothing more than a prayer to Fos. If you have the faith, he will respond by activating your innate, magical abilities and blessing you with power."

Cain continued, "But understanding that it is a prayer is not the only prerequisite. You also need to understand how much you can handle. Because each cast of a spell costs life force. If I were to cast too much for my body to handle, I would die. Magic can be dangerous in large doses."

"My father used to tell me something similar," Dawn said. "About knowing your limits."

"If that is going to be the first lesson," Krom interrupted. "Then shouldn't you warn her about dark magic?"

Cain glared at Krom. "Dark magic..." he sighed. "Dark magic is dangerous. It is a prayer as well, but not to Fos. It is a prayer to the Demon King, Seor. He has a different kind of trade off, though. Fos offers us magic in exchange for a portion of our current life force. This is something you can recover from. If I over exert myself, I can rest and regain my strength."

Cain continued, "Seor isn't so kind to just bless those who need something from him, though. His magic costs all of a person's life. While this may seem steep, he gives abilities that Fos won't. Unnatural abilities. Teleportation, conjuration, and the ability to play with time. Dark magic manipulates life, while white magic manipulates nature mostly."

"That doesn't make sense to me," Dawn inquired. "If it costs a life, wouldn't that mean that you would die if you cast the spell?"

"Not exactly," Cain said. "Dark sorcerers discovered the ability to drain the life force out of the things around them. The plants, animals, the earth beneath them. Some powerful sorcerers could even steal the power of another living person."

"And some skilled mages can store the power they drain for later," Krom interrupted again. "So they can have different lives to spend for many different uses of Seor's dark spells."

"That is enough about the dark forces though," Cain stated abruptly. "For you, let's try an easy spell. Ask Fos for the power to freeze the water left in the bowl."

Dawn closed her eyes. She had prayed before, but it had never felt so selfish. She had prayed for her family to stay safe during the cold winter months, or to find food during a hunt. Every time, though, she just felt silly. Not once had she heard an answer from this so-called god. Where was Fos when her family and friends needed her?

No, Dawn thought to herself. *I don't need any help to do this. I am powerful enough. I have this within me.*

Just then, a blast of icy cold escaped from her hand and encapsulated the bowl in front of her. "Whoa!" Krom shouted. "I have never seen anyone get it so fast!"

Dawn danced around, excitedly. "I knew I could do it! That hardly took any energy out of me at all!"

"Be careful," Cain warned. "If you waste your energy when it doesn't matter, you won't have the energy to fight when it does."

Not even this word of warning could dampen Dawn's spirits. Her smile was uncontrollable. "I think she has plenty to dance about," Krom laughed. He jumped toward her and started to kick his legs and wave his arms around crazily.

Dawn stopped, giving Krom an aggravated stare. "You ruined it," she laughed.

The group packed up their things and continued to travel. Every minute that passed, Dawn couldn't help but to think about her newly found abilities. "I am strong enough," she thought. "I have the power within myself to handle things on my own."

As the sun began to set, the trio talked about settling down for the night. While they looked for a good spot that had the benefit of nature's camouflage, Cain slowed them down and pointed through the trees. Dawn peered under the moonlit shrubbery and saw a strange figure rising out of the ground two hundred strides ahead of them. There was one shadowy beam extending vertically, and one beam placed in the center extending out horizontally.

The three slowly approached the mysterious shape, until Krom realized what it was, and stepped out into the light. "The Guild must have been here recently," he said, examining the body hanging on the cross standing before them.

Dawn examined the person hanging from the rugged pieces of lumber. "He's just a kid..." Her heart dropped in horror. When she looked up at the face of the young boy on the cross, all she could see was the face of Cammie. Except this boy was different. His face was dried up and empty. A husk of the life that used to reside inside. His eyes were hollow. Lifeless and void.

"This isn't the work of the Guild," Cain pondered.

"What do you know?" Krom sneered. "This is common around here."

"The Council needs to get involved," Cain ignored Krom, gazing at the lifeless boy upon the cross.

"The Council?" Krom mocked. "The White Council couldn't care less about anyone on Quarrine." Krom pointed up at the young boy, "I have seen *THIS* happening on Quarrine my entire life, and never has the Council ever done anything to keep the innocent people here safe. So, no. the Council isn't going to do anything. I don't put my hope in falsity."

"I am a servant of the Council!" Cain yelled. "You have no idea the terrors and monsters you have been saved from because of the reavers that the Council sends over here. You have never even seen true brutality. But this..."

"Don't tell me what I haven't seen!" Krom shouted. "If you

don't consider the torture and murder of this boy a brutality, then maybe you're the monster."

"Guys!" Dawn interrupted. "Let's get away from here and find a spot for camp. We are tired and irritable. We have been on the road for days, and need some rest."

The two men grunted, silently grinding their teeth. They moved away from the terrible scene and farther into the wilderness, where they could set up camp, and find their rest.

6

The Great Canyon Pass

Stars littered the midnight sky while the companions lay beneath. Dawn listened to the soft snore of her partners as she gazed upwards into the night. "Four hundred and thirty-eight." Her eyes grew heavy, but she dared not to shut them. "Four hundred and thirty-nine." She wouldn't give her past terrors a chance to return again, as they had before when she shut her eyes. Instead, she chose to count the speckled stars in the sky, humming a melody under her breath as she waited for the coming morning.

The frost covered rose
A reflection of Winter's grasp
The seed buried in snow
The condition of Springtime's task
Though the months seem cold
The harvest is coming
Though Death's sting is bold
True life is coming

The usefulness of Dawn's thoughts evaporated after some hours, her mind churning in the darkness like a runaway stallion. While her companions could embrace their dreams, she would not. The captain's face burned into her memory. He held her dreams in his pocket as if he paid her wages.

She crept to her feet, pulling her sword out from underneath the sack she used as a pillow. Stepping silently, she walked out of her companion's earshot and into a field of boulders and rocky terrain. She closed her eyes and drew her sword, imagining the face of Grendel Greenwood.

With the rising of the desert sun, Dawn's companions awoke to her lying in her place on the ground beside them, eyes wide open. They packed their things and made their way deeper into the wasteland. As they continued their journey westward, the scenery became less and less luscious. The desolate sea of orange and brown lost all the lively green that had brightened the landscape behind them.

Every few hours, a cloud of dust would kick up from the earth, making any forward progress impossible. Dawn and the others created masks out of spare pieces of cloth to cover their eyes when these dust storms would ambush them.

Streams became more and more of a luxury to the pilgrims. Each day that passed, the collective exhaustion of the group grew to new measures.

Dawn's energy wavered. Her mouth dried up and her breathing grew heavier after each step in the hot sand. When she reached to wipe the sweat from her brow, she found her skin dry; her body savoring the water inside. Her shoulders slumped and she dragged her feet along the path one step at a time.

Excitedly Cain yelled back to his two weary companions, "We made it!" Dawn's eyes grew large, and a burst of energy rushed through her limbs as she bolted onward to catch up with her mentor. Once she reached him, she discovered a cliff overlooking a magnificent canyon below. The ravines and rocks had been cut into wide open pathways dug out by a great river flowing through the center. Minerals within the rock walls glimmered red, orange and gold throughout the enormous spectacle.

Dawn stared in wonder. "No painting I have ever seen could do this justice," she mumbled to whoever might be listening.

As she spoke, a giant condor flew from one rim of the cliffs to another, with a huge crustacean in its talons. When the bird flapped its wings, a gust of wind buffeted the travellers, cooling Dawn's burnt skin. "That is what we don't want to encounter while we are here," Krom said as he finally caught up with his friends. "The creatures here aren't exactly friendly."

"We'll need to find the pass," Cain responded. "I would rather not take my chances with any of the beasts in the canyon."

Even the somber tone of her associates couldn't hamper the joy that filled Dawn's heart. The grin on her face was stubborn and her smile shone in the sun. Just the sound of the great river roaring and echoing off the walls of the canyon was enough to drown out their voices and lift her spirit.

Cain led the travellers back to the main road, searching for the entrance to the Great Canyon Pass. "It's a series of bridges," Krom explained to Dawn, "that lead travellers over the canyon. It should keep us safe from the creatures that reside down there in the depths. Between the beasts and the orcs, we don't want to be seen by any unfriendly eyes."

"Shh!" Cain hissed. "Quiet!"

Cain stopped at the top of a hill and crouched low to the ground. Dawn and Krom slowly approached, and Cain gestured them toward some rock formations nearby. Quarrelling voices reverberated over the crest of the hill.

"What do you mean there is a toll to access the pass?" A woman cried out. "My children and I have to get to the port. We don't have enough food to turn around and go back to Oasis!"

"Ma'am," a man's voice began, feigning polite courtesy. "This fund is helping the Hunters from the Guild in their search for fugitives on Quarrine. If I made an exception for you, I would have to allow everyone to pass, and that would just be unacceptable. I hope you understand."

"How am I supposed to understand?" The woman

screamed. "You are sentencing me and my children to death! Murderer!"

The sound of steel rang through the air as if a sheet of metal was sliding against leather. "Ma'am, if you don't have the proper funds, I am going to have to ask you to turn around before something bad happens. You wouldn't want your boys to have to live without a mother, would you?" As Dawn listened to the sobbing of the woman and her sons, Cain pulled her and Krom back down the hill and into the arid wilderness of the Western Wastes.

"Was that the Guild?" Krom asked. "When did they start taking a toll for the pass?"

"It doesn't matter," Cain said. "What matters now is that we need to get past them. Any ideas?"

"Is that the only way onto the pass?" Dawn asked.

"That's the only bridge," Krom answered. "It's the only entrance and it's guarded by those Hunters. There are multiple bridges that go on throughout the canyon, but the only way in from this side is right there." Krom pointed over the hill toward the entrance.

"We could skip the toll," Cain said, processing the thief's statement. Dawn could see Cain refining a plot in his mind. "We climb down to the first flat of the canyon, where we can wait and remain unseen. And when night falls, we climb back up to the bridge. Under the cover of night, we will be camouflaged by the darkness. If we make it far enough over the bridges..."

"They will never know we were even here!" Krom interrupted. "Man, where have you been all my life?"

The three moved toward the edge of the cliff, out of sight

of the bridge's entrance, and started to make their way down the face of the ravine. Once they had all found the flat, Dawn slumped against the rock wall of the canyon, waiting until the cover of night.

Afternoon progressed, and the sun had begun to set, Krom paced uneasily along the edge of the cliff. "Krom, sit down," Dawn said. "You're making me nervous."

"And wasting your energy!" Cain stated from across the flat.

Krom settled down next to Dawn. "I have been going through all the possible outcomes of tonight in my head," he said. "There are so many things that could go wrong!"

"We shouldn't have given you this much time to think things through," Dawn laughed. "Why are you so worried?"

"Were you not listening to me just now?" Krom asked. "So many things can go wrong! All it takes is one rock shifting and we are food for the birds. Big birds. Giant birds. With giant beaks! That can eat us in a single bite. There is danger on every side!"

"Except for right now," Dawn said. "Right now, we are safe. Something my father used to tell me, don't sacrifice your present on the altar of your future or your past. Be present in every moment. Don't waste this time we have now worrying about outcomes that may never even happen."

Krom grabbed a rock and drew lines in the dirt. "He sounds like a wise person. I'm sorry about what happened."

Dawn processed the apology. "It's ok. I am healing." She started to grin from ear to ear. "You know, this is the first time I have thought about my family without instantly feeling a sense of dread and mourning? I feel like I'm actually telling the truth. I really am healing!"

"That's great!" Krom exclaimed, though his smile faded quickly and he continued to trace over the line he had drawn in the dirt. "I guess I haven't gotten there yet."

"What are you healing from?" Dawn asked.

Krom sighed, "It wasn't very long ago. My parents died during the great war, when Ulumbra occupied Quarrine. I was nine at the time, and my little sister was six..."

"Little sister?" Dawn gasped. "I had no idea you had a sister."

"Yeah," Krom frowned. "We were all living in Port Aurora, and we were happy. The way you talk about your father, I had a similar relationship with my mother. Everything I know, at least all the honorable things, I learned from her." Krom paused, processing his thoughts. "I wish I had lived a life that represented her well. Instead, well... I followed after my uncle."

"Your uncle was a thief?" Dawn asked.

"Not exactly," Krom responded, throwing the rock into the vast canyon. "My uncle is a Guild captain."

Dawn's jaw dropped. "What? You can't be serious!"

Krom slumped in the place where he sat. "The Guild was fairly new when Ulumbra fell, but Uncle Haze always had a foot on the inside. Climbed the ranks as the Guild grew larger."

"Wait a second..." Dawn paused. "Haze. As in the Director? We saw him in Oasis. He murdered a helpless man in the middle of a tavern!"

"That's him," Krom continued to draw in the sand, this

time with his finger. "When my parents were killed, he took my sister and me into his care in Oasis. Taught us both everything about the Guild, though I never really connected with him. I guess that's why I tried so hard to make him proud. I did everything I could to make myself important in his eyes, but he never noticed. He never really cared about anyone except for Kathrine."

"Is Kathrine your sister?" Dawn asked.

Krom nodded, grabbing another rock to toss into the canyon. "The only thing we really had in common was how much we cared for her. I started to dabble in dark magic as a last effort to make a difference. An effort to be somebody worthwhile to the only parental figure I had in my life.

"But, like Cain told you the other day, the cost of dark magic is steep. It's dangerous. Seor isn't forgiving, and one mistake can cost a heavy toll. I thought I was alone, trying to adjust time and maybe bring myself back to a time where my parents were still around. I was focused on using the life force around me, maybe the earth, the plants in my home… I didn't know Kathrine was home…" Tears flowed down Krom's cheeks, unable to control his sobs. He buried his face into his hands. "I swear… I didn't know."

"Oh my gosh," Dawn mumbled under her breath. Krom pressed his face into Dawn's shoulder. "I am so sorry Krom. I had no idea."

Cain plodded over to the mourning friends. "There is darkness in all of our pasts," he said. "The trick isn't to live a life without blemish. It's how you move forward and mend the broken pieces."

Krom shot back up to look at Cain, tears still in his eyes. "I didn't realize you were listening."

"I am of the belief that the time we have here in this world is for one purpose," Cain said. "And that purpose is to heal. We are born into brokenness, and we spend each day mending ourselves."

Krom wiped the tears from his eyes. "What if you don't want to heal?" Dawn's eyes widened. "I deserve the punishment of living with this guilt. This pain I feel is the only connection I still have with her."

"You don't want her memory to always be painful," Dawn said. "That wouldn't be what she would want. She would want her memory to inspire joy. She would want you to remember the good times with her."

"Sometimes..." Krom paused to piece his words together in his mind. "Sometimes I'm not sure if it's all worth it. No matter what the relationship, even those who you love the most, it all ends eventually. And it always ends the same way. With pain, and heartache. Is it worth it? Is it worth all this pain?"

Cain knelt down and placed his hand on Krom's shoulder. "The reason it hurts so much is because it was worth it," he expressed under his breath. "Catch your breath. We have to get moving soon."

Dawn put her arm around Krom, squeezing him with an empathetic embrace. Now that she could see under his goofy exterior, the mask that he wore every day, she couldn't help but to feel the hurt with him. She had hoped that one day the wounds she held onto from her past would become scars, but Krom was living proof that some wounds may never heal.

Once Krom had calmed his mind, the three approached the edge of the safety of the landing where they waited. When Dawn glanced downward into the dark abyss below them, she felt a pain explode in her chest as her breath escaped her. It was an invisible force, ready to crush their bodies, and squeeze the life out of them.

Taking a final breath of confidence, the three grasped the rock wall and climbed over to the bridge. Every gust of wind threatened to blast them off the rocky precipice where they clung for their lives. With every movement, their hearts dropped, wary of the darkness below.

After minutes of climbing, Dawn finally saw their destination: the first bridge of the Great Canyon Pass. Her fingers stung, bitten by the cold desert air, combined with the freezing touch of the stones quickly caused her hands to become numb. Trusting her grip, she tried her best to follow the path and hand placements of her companions in front of her, but her reach was shorter than that of her friends.

Finally, with the wind continuing to freeze their outstretched limbs, the bridge loomed directly overhead. The end of the climb was in sight. Dawn peered around her at the canyon scenery, and the only thing bigger than the rims of granite peaks was the vast midnight sky, dotted with silver. Cain led the party up the face of the cliffs, slowly preparing each movement with precision and care.

Suddenly, a stone beneath Dawn's foot broke free, and crumbled down into the abyss. A small gasp left her lips as her arms flailed in the moonlight, reaching for the nearest stone shaft. With all of her strength, she grasped a single stone; all that remained to stop her from a seemingly endless fall. She dangled helplessly, the wind relentlessly working to blow her away.

"Dawn!" Krom shrieked down to her. "Hold on, I'm coming."

With a small yelp, Dawn swung her body and stretched out her free hand in an attempt to grasp anything sturdy, but with every endeavor her grip loosened. As each second passed her fingers continued to slip from the rugged rock. Krom hurried down the face of the cliff to help, but his scurried movements threw rubble down into Dawn's eyes.

Cain, staring down in horror, called out to Krom and Dawn, but neither of them acknowledged his voice. Then, with a burst of energy, he spoke some words under his breath, and waved his hand. Suddenly, an unyielding gust of wind surrounded his partners, blowing them off the wall and up into the air.

Dawn couldn't scream. There was no air left in her lungs to make any noise at all. Her eyes were welded shut and she felt her heart lump into her throat. But, to her surprise, she landed softly on something that felt like wood. Her eyes opened and she and Krom were both lying, unharmed, on the bridge.

She looked over and saw Cain climbing up onto the solid ground, but just past him there were three crosses along the road, illuminated by a flame light just a stone's throw away from where she stood. Dawn slowly walked toward the wooden torture devices, peering at the people hanging from the beams. One bore a woman, middle aged and weathered. Her clothes told the story of a life-long traveller.

Upon the other crosses hung two children. A boy and

a girl. They couldn't have experienced more than ten years in this world, yet already their life had been ripped away from them.

Dawn stared up at the three bodies, fists clenched and teeth grinding in her mouth. She glanced over to the orange glimmer with fire in her blood. A group of men sat around a flame. They ate together. Laughing. Singing.

Cain looked at Dawn, mouthing words to her, but she ignored him. Her vision narrowed. Her heart pounded until she could feel it in her ears.

THUD!

Suddenly, the singing stopped around the fire. An arrow pierced the heart of one of the men. He fell forward into the fire throwing sparks into the sky. Every eye turned toward the bridge, where Dawn stood in the open at the entrance of the bridge, bow in her hands and hate in her eyes. She drew another arrow.

Cain caught his breath, expelling a forceful gasp of air. "All lives," he whispered to himself. In a flash, he waved his hands and blasted a gust of wind at Dawn. Her bow flew out of her hands, launching her arrow into the night. She shot him a glare. Drawing her sword, she charged at the stunned soldiers.

Cain shot another blast of wind at Dawn, throwing her to the ground. With another quick motion he pulled air towards himself, dragging Dawn back to the bridge and the canyon.

Quickly, the soldiers stood to their feet, grabbing their own swords. Cain waved his hands at the ever-watchful eyes, and the orange flame flashed and expanded violently, engulfing the area between the soldiers and the bridge in a blazing fire. He quickly pivoted and rushed onto the bridge where Krom had helped Dawn find her way to her feet. Dawn took a step toward him to face their enemy, but he blasted her backwards again. "Go!" He yelled at them.

As he yelled, a bolt of lightning flashed by their faces and crashed into the rocky cliffside ahead. Looking back, they caught sight of one of the soldiers with electricity emanating from his fingertips. The soldier waved his hands around, pulling the spreading fire towards himself until each flame had consolidated into a single ball above his head. In a flash the ball exploded, sending lightning into every direction; crashing into the sides of the canyon and soldiers alike. Quickly, the attacker shot another bolt at the travellers, but Cain met it with a magical blast of his own. The two bursts of energy exploded as they collided, whipping up a storm of dust and smoke.

Under the cover of dust, Cain rushed to Dawn and Krom who had already started to sprint across the bridge to the other side of the ravine. Not even the roar of the great river beneath them could mask the beating of the encroaching footsteps of their pursuers. They reached the other side of the overpass and continued their escape into the array of bridges extending over the Great Canyon.

Dawn peered behind them to find the soldiers in fast pursuit. Their eyes shone a disturbing amber under the dark night, piercing through the darkness. Every movement they made was swift and effortless, like leaves blowing in the wind. She felt the screaming of her lungs and the will of her muscles going farther beyond what any exercise could ever demand.

Cain leaned over to try and collapse the bridge behind them, but he was too late. As he sent the burst of energy from his hands, their pursuers leaped over the newly created gap between the falling bridge and the cliffside, finding solid ground. Dawn and Krom turned to catch sight of the spectacle, but Cain reprimanded them in an instant. "Run!"

Kicking up dust, they dashed in the opposite direction until they found the next bridge overlooking the coming valley. When Dawn turned to check on her mentor, she saw flashes of light emanating throughout the darkness. Bursts of cool air, followed by blasts of intense heat. Cain was using all of his magical power to keep the oncoming threats from reaching them. Fire, ice, and lightning flared in the dark, desolate desert around them. One blast of energy after another, Dawn watched wide eyed. Finally, Cain expelled a blast from his hands towards the feet of his opponents, sending them flying backwards so he could make his escape.

As he approached his companions, he screeched, "Why do you keep stopping?" The three of them rushed across the wooden platforms strung together with ropes with no intentions of looking back. With every stride, the bridge swayed from side to side, hampering their balance as they raced to the other side.

Just then, a violent quake shook the earth, and Dawn felt her footing give way as the planks beneath her feet descended into the darkness below. All at once, the scenery blurred and the dull desert colors swirled and blended together like a bad mixture of paint. She lunged forward to grab hold of the tearing rope in front of her before she was overcome by the pull of gravity. Whipping through the air, the rope threw her body into the face of the cliff, the bridge collapsing into the canyon below.

Dawn looked down to see that her companions were also holding onto the ropes and hanging from the cliffside. Standing on the rim of the opposite canyon face, the soldiers stood with fire emerging from their fingers and a scowl on their faces.

"We have to jump!" Dawn heard Cain call out from below.

"What!" Krom responded. "That's suicide! It's too long of a fall!"

"You have to trust me!" Cain shouted back.

Dawn's mind raced through every possible outcome, most of them in her mind ending in death. Even though she gazed down into the endless darkness, Cain's voice soothed her. She closed her eyes, and began to count out loud, "One."

"No, wait!" Krom yelled up to her. "It's too far!"

The soldiers started to emit more energy from their hands, chanting something under their breath.

"Two!"

"Dawn, think this through!"

"THREE!"

Dawn pushed off the wall with her feet and released her grip. Even though she fell, it didn't seem like she was falling very fast. As if some force had caught her and was lowering her slowly to the ground.

Krom screamed after her, "Dawn!" His adrenaline was flowing too much for tears to fall. As he called out to her, a lightning bolt zipped past his head and exploded into the cliffside, blasting him down into the dark ravine.

With a soft *THUD,* they both hit the ground, discovering that Cain had already lowered himself into the crevice. The mage lifted them both off the rocky surface and rushed them into cover where their attackers could no longer see them. Cain pressed his finger to his lips, silencing his companions and listening for the pounding footsteps of pursuers. After some time, he led the others farther into the canyon and away from any bridges looming overhead.

"I told you that this wouldn't end well!" Krom scowled as they traversed the shadowy canyon. His head swiveled, quickly turning one way to the other. "I knew we would end up down here."

"It's not ideal," Cain said, "but now this is our only choice. Even if we found our way back up, the pass will be crawling with the Guild. If we stay together and watch each other's backs, we will make it to the other side."

"How do you know that? Do you even know the way out?" Krom asked with a glare.

"It has been many years since the last time I travelled through the canyon, but my memory is better than most," Cain responded.

"I trust him," Dawn stated.

"Why?" Krom asked. "Why would you ever trust this man? He has only ever led you into disaster."

"His plan would have worked," Dawn quivered. "If it wasn't for me."

Cain looked at Dawn softly. "You're right," he said. "You

messed up, Dawn. People are dead because of you. The man you killed had a family. You are going to have to live with that for the rest of your life."

Dawn gazed into the dirt beneath her. She was no better than the bandits who killed her family. She left a family without a brother, or a father.

But they killed that woman and her kids, she thought.

"But for now, we move," Cain continued. "We take the effort it would take to regret, and use that energy to move forward. And we don't stop until we are out of the canyon. We can't afford to stay in one place for too long. We can rest once we escape."

7

Danger on Every Side

As the group followed Cain, Dawn noticed a limp in his walk, as if each step was a negotiation rather than an order. "Cain," Dawn began, "Are you alright?"

"I'm fine," he responded coldly. He turned to face her with remorse written on his face. "Do you remember what I told you about the cost of magic?"

"I do."

"Keeping us alive tonight has cost me quite a bit. Sometimes the price of life is pretty high. I will be fine though. I just need to recover my strength."

Even though Cain seemed confident, Dawn couldn't help herself but to worry. She had already lost so much; she couldn't lose one of her only remaining friends. She watched every time he stumbled, ready to tend his wounds, if there were any.

"*You caused this,*" a voice in her head boomed.

As they walked, the sun peeked over the tops of the rocky cliffs, glimmering against the quartz inside the canyon walls. The beauty of the magnificent canyon felt different while they were within the dangerous depths. "There's a touch of grey for every shade of blue," she whispered to herself.

"What was that?" Krom asked.

"Oh, something my mother used to say to me," Dawn replied. "There's a touch of grey for every shade of blue. It means that no matter how beautiful something is, there is pain somewhere in it. Like this canyon. It is beautiful, but it is dangerous at the same time."

"Both of your parents sound like great people," Cain said back to her. "I wish I could have known them."

"Yeah," Dawn said, watching her feet as she kicked a pebble down the rocky path. "They had so many nuggets of wisdom that they would say all the time. Just little phrases that have stuck with me throughout my life."

"Like what?" Krom asked as the sun continued to rise higher into the sky.

"Oh, I don't know," Dawn answered. "One time my father told me, 'So much of our joy depends on how we see the world.'" Dawn attempted a deep voice to imitate her father's. "We can be staring at our shadow and see only darkness, and not realize that if we are staring at a shadow, then the sun is right behind us, illuminating our lives."

"Oh," Krom said with a chuckle. "I like that! Did he come up with that himself?"

"I doubt it," Dawn responded. "He had been all over the world before I was born and he settled down. He probably heard it from a dark elf in Ardglas or something."

"Doesn't really sound like something a dark elf would say," Cain quipped. "They actually quite enjoy the shadows. They thrive in them."

"You know what I mean," Dawn scoffed. "He heard it from someone, somewhere, which probably wasn't even on Quarrine. Could have been Cirrane. Could have even been the Fauns in Napora. I don..."

As Dawn spoke, the thundering whoosh of flapping wings echoed off the canyon walls. The travellers rushed to the cover of a nearby rock formation, eyes scanning the sky. With another flap of its wings, a giant red condor zipped across the blue canvas overhead. The gust of wind that flooded the canyon nearly blew the companions off their feet, and just as quickly as they had heard the beast; it was nowhere to be seen.

"Gotta say," Krom started, "I want to turn around and see the sun down here, but it seems like every time we turn around there is danger."

"You're right," Cain said. "Let's keep moving. The sooner we get out of here, the better."

After a few hours, Dawn heard the roar of the Great River flowing in the distance. As they turned a corner, the sight of the rushing water made her eyes beam. She had forgotten how dry her mouth had become. Darting into the refreshing stream, she cupped her hands to splash water into her mouth.

The water flowed so clear that they could see the smoothness of the rocks underneath. While Dawn and Cain cooled themselves off in the river, Krom found a dying tree nearby to use as target practice for some knife throwing. He possessed many knives, and each of them had a different weight distribution. Not knives meant for throwing, but he didn't want that to hold him back.

"This must be what Ragnar was always talking about," Cain said, his feet soaking in the stream. His two friends gazed toward him with interest. "He was always talking about Oasis being a haven away from the wasteland. This must be how he felt whenever he returned home. A breath of fresh air, and a drink of cold water."

"I don't know," Krom replied, tossing a knife into the dying tree. "This may feel like a haven, but everything around can kill us. It is still dangerous, no matter how refreshing."

"Well, so is Oasis," Dawn said. "It seemed nice, but that's where the Guild is based. Was never really the safest place to be in the first place."

"Worth fighting for though," Cain said. "Maybe even worth dying for, to him."

"I guess we look at the beauty in the negative spaces," Krom said. "The world is evil, but there are still pockets of good hiding around."

Dawn glanced up at Krom, "Do you really believe that?"

Krom shrugged, tossing one final knife into the mangled tree. "It sounds nice. But just because something sounds good doesn't mean it's true. Like you said, everything beautiful has an imperfection."

"That's only one way to look at it," Cain responded slowly. "That also means that every imperfection has its own version of beauty."

"That makes it sound better than it really is," Krom laughed.

After filling up their water pouches, they continued

traversing the dreary canyon. Cain led them through seemingly insignificant passageways that opened up into even larger ravines that, to Dawn's untrained eye, looked mostly the same as the previous corridors. A feeling of dread flooded her mind, a sense of disorientation that she hadn't felt since she first left Boar's Head Cave. She quickened her pace to catch up to her guide.

With the sun shining bright in the midday sky, the travellers trudged along more slowly, stopping every few minutes to take a drink from their slowly depleting pouches. Heat licked their sunburnt faces and coiled around their limbs like a great hot-blooded serpent. Their urgency had faded into the sunlight, as this was no weather to hurry in.

Turning a corner and passing into a clearing, Dawn spotted orange and grey hills scattered throughout the opening. Lizards scurried to find shelter in the shadows of nearby rocks where the sand was not hot enough to roast them, but there was no shade large enough for anything of substantial size. Dawn shaded her eyes with her hands and peered across the cleared canyon passage.

A fishy smell amplified by the stale air filled the opening. Cain slowed his pace, stepping forward silently to listen to the noises around. "What is it?" Dawn asked.

As she spoke, the sound of small stones rolling down the orange hills echoed between the canyon walls. The travellers stopped in their tracks. "I have a bad feeling," Cain mumbled.

Rocks abruptly crumbled all around them and the earth shook violently. The hill on which Dawn was standing rose from the ground, throwing Dawn from her feet. When she looked up, a giant crab emerged, shaking sand off its amber shell. She jumped back to her feet and peered around the canyon floor to notice more than a dozen other crabs rising from their slumber.

As Dawn scanned the nesting area frantically for her friends, her heart fell, spotting them on the other side of the giant den of crabs. She called out to them, but her voice drowned in the rumble of the monsters. Massive claws swung towards Dawn's body. She tried to duck out of the way, but was struck in the side, sending her flying through the air and into the dirt.

Gasping, Dawn jumped back to her feet as quickly as she could, wincing with every painful movement. Her legs shook as if they couldn't support the weight of her body, though her head was the only part of her that felt heavy. As another claw closed in on her for an uninvited embrace, she unsheathed her sword and swung it in front of her, slicing through a piece of the creature's pincer. A sharp shriek resounded off the walls, silenced by the rampaging beasts frenzying around them.

Flashes of ice coated in lightning lit up the already bright midday valley. When Dawn looked, she noticed that Cain had not even drawn a weapon, but was relying solely on his magical abilities to fight off his nearby foes. Distracted by her companion's fighting strategy, a pincer hammered Dawn's blade out of her hands. She stumbled back into the rocky wall, staring up at her attacker's disgusting foaming mouth, thumping both claws into the ground in a rage. The creature charged toward her, but she jumped out of the way just in time and the crab pummeled into the canyon wall.

Rocks exploded down the side of the ravine, crashing all around the brawlers. Dawn noticed an opening in the wall that could lead her to safety and rushed inside. The narrow passage walls felt as if they were closing in around her. As her mind wandered to claustrophobic thoughts, the earth shook and the rugged canyon walls collapsed around her. The crab attempted to follow her into her hiding place, but its giant body just dragged against the rocky walls until it was completely overcome by the stones falling around it.

Dawn raced farther and farther into the passageway, her legs nearly crumbling with each step. She knew she was breathing, but the air just wasn't going in, as if her lungs had been enveloped in a metallic casing. She choked on the thick desert air, clouded by the dust of crumbling rock. Even in the shadows of the enclosing walls, the sun reminded Dawn of its presence by exhaling warm breaths down her neck, smothering her like the pelt of an animal.

Dawn couldn't tell if she had been running for minutes or hours. All she knew was that her legs felt like jelly and each breath she inhaled was harder and harder to take. Her pace slowed to a stop and she slumped against the wall of the canyon, peering in every direction for signs of jeopardy.

Panic welled up inside her like a series of explosions from within her abdomen. Tension grew in her face and limbs, her mind replaying the events of the last few weeks. Her breathing became more rapid, shallower. She recalled Cain's belief in Fos, and his faith that he is being watched over by a power that is greater than he is, a being that supplies him with his own power. Suddenly, Dawn spoke out loud, "Fos, I need help."

She listened intently, but there was no answer. "Fos, please. I need you right now."

Her lungs tightened and she grasped at her chest, her hand grazing her amulet. Seconds later she curled tightly into a ball, her only movement being the trembling in her limbs and the salty tears darkening her sleeves. "Fos, please answer me."

There she sat, unaware of the progressing afternoon until, like the sun that lit up the desert sky, the feelings of angst had finally passed. She opened her eyes to the soft night sky, gazing at the stars sprinkled throughout. Though she could still feel each of her breaths rasping in her throat as if she was sick, her heartbeat had slowed.

Her calm couldn't last though. A noise like a rock crumbling away rang throughout the passageway. Aside from Dawn's wheezing, there was silence in the canyon.

Dawn stared unblinking toward the end of the narrow passageway. A growl resounded off the walls, followed by a low noisy sniffing. The ground rattled and a raspy breathing filled the air. Great scaly claws emerged from around the corner, accompanied by a large reptilian head slithering out of the shadows. Wings extended from the creature's backside. The dragon rolled its neck toward Dawn and bellowed under the moonlight.

Dawn silently made her way to her feet, and slowly crept backwards away from the blind beast. Carefully, she chose her foot placements, finding the spots with the least debris to place her steps. She strode steadily, but the dragon approached with haste. A long, slimy tongue slapped around like a whip, searching the areas ahead for signs of its prey. Dawn watched the beast breathe, the dust on the canyon floor flying up in a whirlwind with each exhale.

With the mixture of dust and her already raspy breathing,

a tickle took shape in her throat. She attempted to hold her breath until the itch had subsided, but it was to no avail. Unable to contain it any more, she exhaled a forceful cough into the cold night air. The dragon's head snapped in her direction, and a shot of smoke expelled from its nostrils.

Dawn's heart stopped, her eyes wide and trembling. Quickly she bolted away back where she came. Crashing footsteps rattled the earth and rubble around her. She reached for her sword, but there was no hilt for her to grasp. A roar bellowed from the depths of the dragon's being, startling Dawn into the rocks behind her.

She pressed her body up against the wall of the canyon and held her breath again, more silent than she had ever been. Yellow and brown scales sparkled in the moonlight right in front of her face, with a monstrous head sniffing around her for signs of life. Warm breath engulfed Dawn's quivering body. She thought back to her lesson in magic. Focusing on the energy flowing through her, she tried to summon the power to strike the creature. She thought to herself, *If Fos won't answer, then I can still do this on my own.*

She held out her hand, but all she could feel was the warm breath of the great dragon. Clenching her fists, her nails dug into her palms. Cold shivers ran through her body, trembling against the rock wall behind her.

Nothing worked.

As Dawn focused, to her surprise, the dragon squealed in agony, crashing backwards down the passageway. Nothing had come from her body though. No magic, or powerful force. A bronze coated bolt protruded from the top of the rampaging creature's head. High pitched chuckles resonated within the canyon walls, as goblins crawled down the rocks like a swarm of ants. Arrows fired in every direction from the tiny treacherous demons. Dawn lay down as flat as she could to not be struck by a stray.

The dragon crashed into the walls and flapped its wings in an attempt to escape the clutches of the little monsters, but it was too late. Goblins swarmed around the beast with blades in their hands, cutting away at its scaly exterior.

When the sound of arrows whizzing through the air had slowed, Dawn jumped up to escape the commotion of the canyon dwellers. Noisy chatter rang through her ears, and three goblins quickly stopped her with short spears pointed up at her chest. They clacked at Dawn in a language that was foreign to her; all she could do was raise her arms and plea for mercy.

Just then, a loud voice spoke and silenced all the goblins. A deep and menacing voice. Definitely not like the creatures threatening her now. When the voice spoke, Dawn's captors lowered their spears and cursed under their breath.

Dawn turned around to see a large orc standing before her. His skin was a dark green mixed with a brutish brown, covered in scars and paint. In his hands were two scimitars, dripping with the blood of his latest victim. Dawn shuddered under his shadow.

"Who are you?"

The orc's voice was deep and gravelly. His accent made him difficult to understand, but eventually Dawn pieced his question together. "My name," she spoke slowly. "Is Dawn."

"Bleh!" The orc grunted, spitting on the ground by Dawn's

feet. He belligerently gave orders to the goblins in another language, and suddenly Dawn felt iron around her wrists and chains dangling by her feet. She shouted, but the orc turned around, pushing Dawn to the ground. "Human girl," he said. "Get human chains."

Dawn's palms sweat as adrenaline pumped through her body again. She thought to Cain and Krom, wondering if they had even gotten out of the crab's nesting place alive. And if they had, were they in a better situation than she was now? Before her mind could get too far away from her own situation, reality pulled on her chains to walk with the herd of goblins. The iron bit at her wrists, and she was alone again.

8

Imprisoned

Stars speckled the midnight sky like ten thousand fireflies scattered across a black canvas. Dawn stared up at the beautiful painting of creation as chains dangled around her feet. Goblins shoved around her, pushing her forward faster and faster, as if they were escaping a pursuer.

Grunting loudly, the orc captain barked orders in his brutish native tongue to the Goblin gang. The creatures chattered back at their leader, but after a fierce shout, they settled again.

A funky, ill-scented perfume wafted through the air and penetrated Dawn's nostrils. The overpowering stench conjured images in her mind of corpses rotting in the dark pits of The Other. Her stomach lurched and her eyes watered, but her captors paid no notice. They had already become accustomed to the foul smell.

After walking for what felt like miles, the company entered the blackness of a cave puncturing into the wall of the canyon. It sloped downward into the depths of the earth, until all hope of coming back out to gaze at the glittering night sky had been abandoned.

Small, loose stones littered the floor, which combined with the ankle chains caused Dawn to tumble as they walked. The orc captain quickly gripped her arm tight enough to bruise and yanked her back to her feet. "You stay up," he growled. "Or you stay down."

The cavern wormed its way half a mile into the mountain. Its general shape was ovoid. Giant stalactites extended from the ceilings arching a hundred feet over their heads. An orange glimmer shone from deep within the cave; at last, they came upon a great orcish city buried deep within the mountain.

Calling this city a kingdom would be like calling a muddy potato world class cuisine. There were very few functioning roads and the population seemed malnourished and disheveled. They lived in wooden huts with gaping holes in the poorly constructed walls. Roofs were not a necessity to the inhabitants, which made sense in Dawn's mind because of the shelter from the weather of the outside world.

Everything seemed so dull compared to Oasis. No extravagant gems lining the roads. No high climbing towers. Just dirty homes alongside dirty pathways carved into the side of the mountain.

On the other side of the city, a series of caves extended even deeper into the mountain, with prison cells dug into the walls. The captain ripped Dawn's clothes away from her and dressed her in raggedy orcish prison garb. Dawn squirmed, protesting her independence and attempting to acquire some privacy, but the Orc wouldn't allow it. At a glance, the captain saw the necklace hanging from her neck, and with one swift motion he ripped it away from her.

Screaming, Dawn grasped desperately for her father's gift. Rage erupted from her body and she swung violently at the brutish thief. Her mind went blank and her vision narrowed as if nothing else mattered in the world, but she stood no chance against the giant orc that stood in front of her. With one solid smack, he knocked her against the wall, and Dawn lost consciousness.

Slowly, Dawn tried to open her eyes, but they were glued shut. Her body ached and her limbs were too heavy to move. "Hey!" She shouted. "That's my necklace! Give it back!"

"Well, look who's awake," Dawn heard another voice from nearby. Forcing her eyes open with nothing but sheer will, she peered around to find a cold, damp cell enclosed by iron bars. Across the passageway on the other side of the cave there was another cell with an orc sitting slouched against the wall of his chamber. "You know you're not getting that necklace back, right?"

"What do you know?" Dawn snapped. "Who even are you?"

"Hmph. That fiery personality might not last so long in here," the orc responded. "Especially if you're not willing to make friends."

"You want to be my friend?" Dawn retorted. "Why should I trust you? You are in prison. You're a criminal."

"Is that right, human girl?" The orc laughed. "And why are you in that cell? Are *you* a criminal?"

Dawn paused, unable to give an answer.

"Oh," the orc leaned forward with a smile, focusing his attention on his fellow prisoner. "Maybe I misjudged you. I didn't expect someone of your... Stature... To actually *be* a criminal. I guess with that fiery personality though, it's not too far-fetched." He slouched back into his lazy position against the wall.

"I'm not wanted by orcs!" Dawn yelled, gripping the iron bars of her cell. She heard her voice echo through the halls of the prison and quieted down, leaning back into the rock wall behind her. "I shouldn't be here. This is all a big mistake. I just..." She paused, tears welling up in her eyes. "I just want my necklace back."

"And there it is!" The orc declared. "That fiery passion, already extinguished. Didn't last very long."

"What do you want from me?" Dawn shot back.

The orc laughed from his cell. "Oh, silly human. Always thinking there has to be a motive. Always a destination. Can I not just have a casual conversation with a friend?"

"What makes you think I want to be friends with you?"

"Well, you could have stopped this conversation at any point, but you haven't," the orc replied. "That means one of two things, my girl. Either you have a hidden motive in this conversation. Or you actually do want me to be your friend." The orc looked over at the girl weeping across the cave from him, silently suffering. "Is this your first time?"

Dawn wiped the tears from her face with the beige sleeve of her prison rags. Unable to force another word from her mouth, she nodded solemnly toward her new acquaintance.

The orc studied her. "I'm not sure that's true." Dawn jerked her head up with a scowl on her face. "There is more than one kind of prison, girl. It seems that yours has followed you for some time now."

Dawn's scowl turned to remorse and she gazed back into the dirt, wrapping her arms around her knees.

"Hey," the orc started again. "My name is Gromoth."

Dawn looked back up at the other prisoner. "I'm Dawn."

"Humans have strange names," Gromoth laughed. "It's nice, but it's strange." Gromoth paused for a second before raising the question that plagued his mind. "So, Dawn, why do you care so much about that necklace of yours?"

"It was a gift from my father," Dawn responded. "It's all I have left of him."

Gromoth scratched his head. "That's not true either." Dawn reeled back in shock. "Your father will always be with you. The spirits of the dead live on through us. Every living being has two deaths in this world. The first is when you breathe your last breath. The second is when your name is spoken for the last time. It is your responsibility to help your father live on. Not just remember him with some silly necklace."

Dawn agreed with Gromoth, but couldn't vocalize it. There was a yearning within her gut that felt broken, and when she wore the amulet, the shattered pieces of her soul felt mended.

Silence coated the prison for the rest of the night. Gromoth's snoring echoed throughout the caverns, keeping Dawn from some much-needed sleep. Torches lining the walls outside her cell illuminated her temporary home as if it were midday, even though there were no windows. No openings to the outside world. Her brain constantly searched for a signal, a repressed memory, that her companions were safe.

Hours passed, and goblins swarmed the hallways, clanging steel weapons against the iron bars of the cells. One came through and placed a small ration of food inside Dawn's room: nothing but a slice of bread and a chunk of burnt meat. Cain would have scoffed at the lack of any seasoning. Disgusting as it tasted, Dawn scarfed it down quickly, savoring each bite.

A large orc approached her cell and inserted a key into the lock holding the bars closed. "To the pit!" He grunted at Dawn, grabbing her tight by the arm and pulling her down the oblong hallway. They entered a huge cavern. Bats flew back and forth across the dimly lit ceiling, which extended so high into the canyon that Dawn couldn't even see it. The dark void looming overhead set a lump in her throat.

Many orcs in the same beige prison garb worked in the cavern with pickaxes in their hands, pounding away at the solid walls. Dawn wondered why the prisoners didn't use the tools they were given to try and escape, but she noticed goblins wielding bows standing on a ledge surrounding the pit.

Dawn's escort shoved her forward and threw a pickaxe at her feet. "You stop working, you stop eating." Without another word, her aggressor turned and left her to her new labor.

Dawn studied the mining pits, and the prisoners who spent their time there. Many of them slumped their shoulders and sluggishly pushed wheelbarrows. The emptiness of the cavern had leaked into their minds and contaminated their spirits.

Walking toward the walls, Dawn felt every eye in the mine shift on her. Suddenly, she was very aware that she was the only human in this prison. A lone trespasser in an enclosed society.

Her stomach shifted uneasily. She noticed, as she dragged the mining tool behind her, that her free hand was hugging herself, pinching into the skin around her waist. Even when she released herself, her hand fiddled with the cloth of her outfit, as if in a constant need of reassurance. Her eyes flickered to the walls of the cave where just days ago she had been on the outside, admiring the beauty of creation. Now, instead of awestruck wonder, she was filled with dread.

"They're staring at you," a familiar voice echoed inside her head. Dawn peered to the working Orcs, sensing their unfriendly eyes. Goosebumps shot up and down her skin like an army of ants storming the gates of her body. "Surrounded by enemies. I told you your friends wouldn't be around for long."

"No," Dawn whispered to herself. "No. Stop it."

"Poor Dawn. Once again, all alone."

"Stop!"

Just then, a hand grasped Dawn's shoulder. Swinging the pickaxe through the air, Dawn released a scream that curdled the blood of every prisoner in the mine. "NO! NO! NO!" Her eyes were clenched shut as she slashed through the air at her invisible enemy.

"Dawn!" She opened her eyes and noticed Gromoth on

the ground in front of her, with sweat dripping from his forehead from dodging her wild blows. "Are you alright?"

She dropped the pickaxe and fell into the dirt, tears rolling down her face. "I'm so alone."

"There are all these orcs here," Gromoth stated. "You aren't alone."

"I may be surrounded, but I am alone," Dawn replied. She wiped the tears from her cheek. "Surrounded by strangers. I had nothing left to lose, but still, somehow, I lost it. I fell even farther into the pit. Into this pit!" She grabbed a rock and hurled it against the cavern wall.

"I thought we weren't strangers anymore?" Gromoth smiled.

"Hey!" One of the jailers barked as he approached the two prisoners with a whip in his hand. "Back to work! No breaks!"

Gromoth stood to his feet and clenched his fists. "Give her a break. It's her first time in the pits."

"No breaks!"

The jailer raised his whip, and Dawn heard a sigh come from Gromoth's lips. Before the lashes could crack in the air, Gromoth jumped out of the way, quicker than lightning, and reached his hand out to grasp the rope. With a single yank, the opposing orc was pulled into the dirt, and the whip was no longer in his possession. Scowling with hatred, the orc lifted his head and pulled himself back to his feet, raising one hand into the air. "Goblins!"

Armed creatures lining the rim of the cavern drew back on their bows, waiting for a signal to fire. All across the pit, the other prisoners rushed to find whatever cover they could, though nowhere was safe from the on looking archers.

Gromoth dropped the whip, and raised his hands in surrender, mumbling in his native orcish language. Scanning him intently, the jailer eventually lowered his hand slowly, and the archers eased the tension in their bowstrings. Dawn glanced at Gromoth, then at the jailer, and then back to Gromoth. "What are they going to do?"

"To you?" Gromoth whispered. "Nothing."

Dawn's muscles felt cold. "What about you?"

"You don't need to worry about me," Gromoth stated. "We aren't friends, remember?"

Dawn's heart sank. Shackles clasped around Gromoth's wrists and he was led down a tunnel that Dawn had not seen before, the whipping rooms, and quickly he was gone.

Stubbornly, she picked up her pickaxe, and started swinging into the side of the cavern, losing track of the hours that were passing. One swing after another, she would wipe the sweat from her brow, and then swing again. Blisters formed on her previously soft hands. Finally, there was a shout from behind her, and all of the prisoners walked back to their prisons where they would find bland food, and rest.

Dawn gazed into the empty cell across from hers. The silence emanating through the halls that night was deafening. She longed for the rumble of a snore from the orc who could have been her friend, her only friend, in this forsaken place.

"Everyone who tries to help you just suffers," the same familiar voice had returned inside her head.

"I didn't ask for help," Dawn replied.

"Oh?" The voice said. "You didn't vocalize it, but you did ask. You would be dead if it weren't for Gromoth. You would be dead if it weren't for Cain. For Krom. Even Ragnar.

And now each one of them, because of you, their lives are in flames."

"No," Dawn mumbled to herself. "No. No. No. They chose to help. They chose this journey. They chose their own path."

Days passed in that lonely place, and Dawn did her best to keep discreet. To just comply. Prisoners were treated worse than cattle, or pigs. They were fed rations only enough to keep them from starving to death and it was the same meager fare every day. Pickaxes swinging through the air into the hard, rocky mountain, searching for coal. If they didn't work hard enough, they were whipped. If they blundered, they were whipped. And nothing could save someone who tried to escape. Prisoners would go to the whipping rooms, and when they returned, their backs were bloody masses of open flesh; fearful testaments for the other prisoners.

"But they are alive," Dawn always whispered to herself, as she swung her pickaxe over her head, glancing at the beaten victims. "Still alive."

The days stretched out like a road through the sand, with barren landscape on either side. Most prisoners wandered the mines, taking steps as if they wished each was their last. Their skin had been broken so many times that their bodies were gnarled maps of pain.

The despair of the prisoners was like a plague. With each orc whose spirit had withered and depleted, the more infectious the communal suffering became. Prisoners who hadn't even gone to the whipping posts dragged their feet; their passion ripped away from their hearts.

One boy, an orc of twelve years, worked nearby Dawn most days. He was smaller than the other prisoners, and couldn't make as much progress in the mines because of his small frame. It didn't take long until he was curled into a weeping ball in the dirt, his spirit broken.

"Back to work!" The jailer shouted, approaching with a whip in hand. "No breaks!"

Without remorse, the jailer snapped the whip and slashed the boy's legs. Writhing in pain, the boy shrieked, curdling the blood of the other prisoners. Dawn gnashed her teeth, white knuckles grasping her rusty pickaxe. As the jailer readied his arm again, a white-hot rage filled her body, and her vision went dark. As if time hadn't passed, she felt drops like a warm rain shower her skin.

Finally, once her vision had returned, she saw the carnage that she had caused. The body of the jailer lay mangled on the floor, and her axe dripping with blood. The boy pressed his back up against the rock wall, distancing himself from the monster that stood before him. Dawn peered upwards and the Goblins had set their sights on the scene unfolding, readying their bows to shoot.

"Stop!" A giant orc was standing across the mine, holding a fist in the air. "The human lives!"

Lowering their bows, the goblins snarled under their breath. The giant orc strode quickly over to Dawn, and clutched her arm. His grip was so tight, she felt like he would pull her shoulder out of its socket. Blood dripped down her fingertips as he led her into the whipping tunnel.

"Thank you," Dawn said to her captor. He glanced down at her with furrowed eyes. "For saving my life."

"Hmph," he grunted. "By the time we done with you, you wish I didn't."

Red pools stained the dirt path where the jailer pulled Dawn. Smells of copper and iron lingered in the stale air, diluted by the overpowering scent of rot. The odor stung like thorns in Dawn's nose, weighing down her lungs as if they were filling with sand.

Weathered wooden posts scattered throughout the cave, with iron chains hanging like arms from their bodies, ready to detain anyone they could grasp. "No..." Dawn whispered to herself under her breath, slowly hyperventilating. "No, I have to keep going. I have to!"

"Quiet!" The orc yelled as he shoved her to the ground, shackling her to a whipping post. "Your punishment will come soon enough." Without another word, he was gone.

Uncontrollable tears flowed from Dawn's eyes, but it was more than just crying. It was the kind of sobbing that comes from a person who has been drained of all hope. Grit dug into her knees as the palpable pain flowed from her soul. Her breathing was ragged, pulling helplessly against the chains that confined her. There was nothing left. Nobody left. No reason to fight anymore.

"Hmph. Didn't think I would see you again, girl." Dawn peered up at a whipping post that was positioned a ways down the cave, where Gromoth knelt in a pool of his own blood. "I'm glad to see you. Though the current circumstances aren't exactly ideal." He coughed as he spoke, gasping for air as if his lungs wouldn't cooperate with his mind.

"You're alive!" Dawn yelped. "They have been torturing you this whole time?"

"I'm not exactly - *Cough Cough* - someone that they want

dead," Gromoth wheezed, struggling to find his breath. "It's my worry - *Cough* - for you as well." He hacked until he could spit the blood that was filling his throat out into the dirt.

"I don't understand..." Dawn said. "Are we special somehow?"

Gromoth burst into laughter until his cough reminded him that joy brought him pain. "Well, for starters, you are a human. You are too valuable to them to kill. They would rather use you as a bargaining piece and get something from the surrounding human cities. The Guild specifically."

Dawn sighed, unsure of what to say. She couldn't compel her lips to move. As if she were stuck underwater, everything seemed to slow and warble.

"Even though they want you alive," Gromoth said. "They don't really care too much what condition you are in. I am sorry."

Dawn gazed up at the orc prisoner, "What about you? Why haven't they killed you?"

"Well, I know things they want to know," Gromoth answered. "Humans don't know much about the goings on in the mountains, do they?"

Voices echoed from further in the cave, grunting in a grumbled Orcish tongue. Gromoth squirmed in his shackles, pulling on the post that constrained him. Suddenly, he lifted his head, and his heavy eyes locked with Dawn's. "I'm sorry."

An Orc, accompanied by two hyperactive Goblins, trotted into Dawn's vision. The Goblins danced around and laughed sadistically, waving around whips and crusty wooden planks. The trio walked past Gromoth and entered Dawn's new prison. The orc ripped the wooden plank out of the goblin's hands and leaned to one side, pressing the weapon into the stone floor beneath them. "What is your name, human?"

Dawn glared up at her captor, "Why do you care?"

Swiftly, the orc swished the plank through the air and smacked Dawn on her hip. She cried out in pain as she wrenched to her side.

"I ask once more," the orc stated. "What is your name?"

"Dawn," she exhaled heavily, still writhing from the smack on her hip.

"Good," the orc reassured her. "Where do you come from?" He leaned again against his weapon.

Dawn sat quietly, contemplating how much she should tell the jailer. The orc groaned, and waved the board through the air again, this time crashing into Dawn's shoulder. Gromoth shouted, "Stop! human bodies can't handle the abuse that an orc's body can!" But the orc paid no mind, shouting over him.

"Do you get how this works?" The orc demanded. "We ask. You answer. Where do you come from?"

"Oasis!" Dawn shrieked.

The goblins chuckled from the open tunnel around them, their snickers echoing down the hall. Dawn heard a disappointed sigh from Gromoth, as if she had just let him down.

The jailer laughed. "There are other humans that would pay a pretty price for your head, girl from Oasis." Dawn shifted uncomfortably in the gravel beneath her, pointed stones digging into her knees. "Just your head. Nothing attached."

"No!" Gromoth shouted.

The orc reached his hand out and ripped the whip from his goblin companions, creeping behind the constrained girl. Without hesitation, the whip split into the back of Dawn's head, reaching its fingers around and tearing through the skin on the left side of her cheek.

Again, the jailer pulled back and slashed into her back, ripping through her prison garb and tearing her skin. One crack after another, her captor lashed at his prisoner without sympathy. The goblins laughed and danced around them heartlessly as Dawn sunk into the pool of her own blood.

With each lash from the torturous weapon, the pain dulled. The sharp, bleeding sting faded as Dawn's vision blurred. Breathing became unbearable, as the air in her lungs became cold, and heavy. As if there was a thick fog filling the air.

Her head slumped. Her knees dug deeper into the pointed stones beneath her. Nothing held her body up except the post tied to her hands. All her strength faded, and a black curtain fell over her eyes.

Just then, a crash resounded from further in the tunnel. The orc jailer paused to glance in the direction of the ruckus, but before he could respond, an arrow had been released into his gut. Seconds later, another followed to find his neck, and he collapsed into the blood-stained dirt.

The goblins fell quickly after, unable to even see where the attack was coming from. Once the sadistic jailers had been neutralized, a tall, slender orc woman ran into the torture chambers and cut Gromoth loose from his restraints. "Sorry it took so long," the woman said. "This one was difficult to find a way in."

"I only care that you found us," Gromoth responded. "Thank you, Dura."

Dura handed Gromoth an unlabeled bottle which he drank swiftly. Glancing back at Dawn, who hadn't moved since the commotion had started, she asked, "They got a human?"

"Not just any human," Gromoth responded, taking a blade from his companion and cutting Dawn's shackles loose.

Dura examined the lifeless girl carefully. "You can't mean…"

"I do. This is the one the Hunters have been looking for. We can't leave her here."

With a quick gesture toward two orc companions that Dura brought with her, they grabbed Dawn and navigated their way out of the prison.

9

Civil War

The orcs moved swiftly through the tunnels, navigating the terrain like it was their home. The impish goblins attempting to swarm the insurgents stood no chance, and were quickly cut down as the invaders powered through the prison caves.

Bodies of guards and prisoners alike lay scattered across the floor. The stench of iron and rot filled the air, even stronger than before. Fresh blood had a different smell than the stale crusted blood they were used to. Even though the smell wasn't as rancid, it made one's gut churn all the same because fresh blood hinted at immediate danger.

Dawn's eyes wavered from attentive to dazed every few seconds, unable to comprehend the events taking place. In her mind, she was still being tortured, and dragged off to another holding cell to await her fate.

Gromoth led fearlessly through the prison, like his body

was in pristine condition. Dura's concoction had taken full effect, numbing his muscles for the time being. Though the scars and lesions from the whip were permanent reminders of the Hell he had endured, the pain had left him. Only his purpose remained: to free the tortured souls of this quarry, and get this human to safety.

As they approached the orc city, the party had regained much of the troop that Dura had brought to mount this rescue operation, along with seventy orc prisoners. The city had been evacuated and in front of them stood a squadron of jailers, orcs and goblins alike, prepared to halt the prisoner's escape.

"We can't let you go," the orc captain quivered, drawing his sword from the sheath on his hip.

Gromoth laughed. "Do you think you, Agru of the Staren Tribe, can stop us?" Gromoth walked forward slowly with his sword already drawn. "Our bodies are cages for a spirit you cannot touch. You hold your power over those whose eyes have dimmed, submissive to your abuse. But you hate those whose eyes burn with the knowledge of your inferiority. True orcs feel love. They feel integrity. But you?" Gromoth pointed his blade at the shivering soldier. "You are neither. You and your mindless followers are empty shells. Pretending to be alive. This is the end for you. You are a snake who has run out of venom, yet still holds on hoping to defeat its enemy. But we are lions. And our spirits do not bear one single mark from your whips."

Agru gnashed his teeth, pointing his sword towards the rebellion as a signal for his squadron to charge. With swift strikes and well-placed arrows, the jailers stood no chance against their oncoming enemy. Gromoth and his warriors were like wind, ruthless but untouchable. Finally, Agru kneeled wounded, surrounded by the bleeding bodies of his subordinates.

Gromoth walked next to him, pressing his blade into the captain's chin, lifting his head to see his eyes. "Now it is your eyes that have dimmed, captain." Before Agru could respond, Gromoth slashed quickly at his neck, extracting the remaining life from his body.

The orcs swiftly moved through the caves until reaching the exit and could see the starry sky above the Great Canyon. Travelling in shadows and dark corridors, the dark of night helped them to maneuver away from their enemy's territory.

The cool desert air stabbed like nails into Dawn's shredded back, reinvigorating her mind back to reality. She clenched her jaw shut to keep from screaming in pain. As her shock faded, the deep burning returned as if her entire body had been stripped of its skin.

The party delved into another cave across the canyon. Down the twists and turns of the passage, they finally approached their own village. Dawn glanced frantically between huts and rock walls, seeking something that could help sooth her from this incredible pain. Gromoth rushed her to the hut of a healer who tended to her wounds.

"Tara! She needs immediate help, please!" Gromoth yelled, as he lay Dawn face down on a table.

The elderly orc woman swiftly cut away the remnants of the prison garb left on Dawn's back. "You not gon' like this, hon," she apologized. "But we has to disinfect."

As Dawn lay in tears on the table, clenching her fists as

if that would alleviate the pain, Tara mixed together salt and water. Pouring the mixture over the wounds, Dawn couldn't hold back the scream anymore. Every gash stung with the salt penetrating every cell that should have been protected by smooth skin but now laid open and raw.

Tara grabbed a cloth and rolled it up for Gromoth to place in Dawn's mouth. "The whip was poison," she said in a thick Orcish accent. "We have to burn the infection." She grabbed a metal plate attached to a rod and stuck it in the fire burning in the center of the room.

Gromoth gently placed the cloth in Dawn's mouth. "Don't fight passing out. It may make this whole process easier."

Dawn spit the cloth out of her mouth, "Why are you not in this much pain? You were whipped for days!"

Gromoth raised the cloth back to Dawn's mouth. "Don't worry about that now. We can talk when you are feeling better."

Without remorse, Tara removed the metal rod from the flame and pressed it into Dawn's back. The scream that emerged from the tortured soul could have given the most hardened warriors nightmares. Quickly the shriek faded, and Dawn dimmed out of consciousness.

Hours passed, and finally Dawn could open her eyes again. Peering around the room, anxiety flooded her mind. She jumped out of the bed where she lay, leaping toward a door across the chamber, but she quickly tumbled back to the floor, overwhelmed by the soreness and pains that encompassed her body. Slowly she pulled herself back to her feet, groaning softly under her breath and hobbled towards the exit.

Peeking outside, Dawn examined the village around her. Scattered throughout the rocky cave, orc children played together, tossing stones back and forth while their parents watched from a distance. It seemed like there were rules to the madness she witnessed, but her groggy mind made it difficult to comprehend.

"Dawn!" Gromoth emerged from around a corner, extending his arms out in joy. "You are up early! How are you feeling?"

Dawn stumbled toward him, holding onto the walls of the surrounding homes for support. Her legs were still shaky. "I feel like I am in a dream. Like physically I am here, but the rest of me is somewhere else."

"You have been through a lot," Gromoth said. "But you're safe here. Welcome to Thradak Village! Let me show you around."

Cocooned in the body of earth, the village nestled safely away from the dangers of the world. Dawn's blood returned to a comfortable warmth. The overpowering scent of decay of the previous days had been replaced by the smell of water running over smooth stones. Dawn was reminded of the first rain of autumn, when the dry rock finally received welcome moisture.

Gromoth led her slowly around the shanties and huts built against the sides of the cavern. Groups of orc children dashed around carelessly, unaware of the dangers of the world. Dogs jumped and ran with the kids, barking playfully together.

"The dogs are the pups of our war dogs," Gromoth said. "If we want to stand a chance to defend against Grumuk, we need to have a military presence too."

"Grumuk?" Dawn asked, leaning over to scratch the head of one particularly playful pup.

Gromoth laughed. "You're serious?"

Dawn glanced up blankly at her rescuer, not speaking a word.

"I forgot that humans are ignorant to the goings on in the mountains," Gromoth sighed.

"I was pretty sheltered until just recently," Dawn responded, pushing the pup off to go and play with the rest of the beasts. "I'm not a good representation of all humans."

"Hmph. Well, at least you're honest." Gromoth responded. "There is a civil war happening down here. Between the followers of Grumuk, and our tribe, the Riders of Thradak. Grumuk is a chieftain who has gathered followers that believe orcs and goblins are superior to the other races in the world. The katze, humans, even elves.

"And while I don't think I disagree with him there," he laughed. "Some have taken this superiority to believe that they should be the dominant race. Grumuk had planned to organize an army to take all of Quarrine and enslave the other races."

"That's awful!" Dawn shouted. "How can they do that?"

"That is what my father, Thradak, said," Gromoth answered. "He was a counselor to Grumuk when he had taken power. And when Grumuk had brought his plan for war to his counselors, my father was the only one who was willing to speak out against him."

Gromoth continued to lead Dawn through the village, surrounded by the playful inhabitants. "This of course did not go over well. My father became an outspoken voice against the chief. He gained followers and started to take a stand against Grumuk. Violent outbreaks against Grumuk became more and more common, until finally, Grumuk had enough. He sent an elite hit squad to kill my father in the night, and succeeded."

"I am so sorry, Gromoth," Dawn's voice was soft and comforting.

Gromoth grunted under his breath. "He was a good man. His death was the catalyst that began the Riders of Thradak. And while they were fairly self-sustaining, they needed a leader."

"Who better than the son of the activist himself?" Dawn concluded. "That's why they didn't just kill you when you stood up for me in prison."

"You got it," Gromoth stated.

"Well, even with the danger lurking around the corner, this place feels so great!" Dawn noted. "I don't know how one tribe of orcs can be so evil, and then a few miles away there can be a place like this."

"What do you mean?" Gromoth asked.

"Well," Dawn answered. "I grew up hearing about the orcs from the mountains and just how barbaric they were. How orcs were all violent savages and I should avoid them at all times. And my encounter with Grumuk's tribe and that mineshaft and even your story just now kind of confirmed everything I had heard." Gromoth's head dropped in disappointment. "But then I meet you, and I am seeing this place. It's so different from the stories!"

"That's funny," Gromoth laughed. "Orcs believe the same about humans." Dawn's eyes furrowed in confusion. "We hear about the Guild. An organization who makes its money through fear and torture, yet it is the main form of government in Quarrine. Completely run by humans. Does that constitute all humans?"

"I guess you have a point," Dawn responded.

"You never hear about the good things in our world," Gromoth continued. "You don't hear about the ones who feed the hungry. You don't hear stories about the orcs that lived a quiet life; we only hear stories about the terror. About the cruel kings and queens. The warriors who slaughtered thousands in the name of their race, or their country, or their city. All for honor. That is the problem in doing the right thing. No one wants to hear about it. No one cares."

"It's like we need drama," Dawn realized. "As if life isn't dramatic enough."

Around a corner was a stream flowing through the cave. Children and adults alike flocked to the cool water; the only water Dawn had seen on the inside of the mountains. Dura stood at a table nearby, scanning maps littered with figures and orcish symbols. Tiny cuts speckled her face, with one large scar on the left side extending from her eyebrow to her chin. Dawn hadn't noticed the wounds of this fierce warrior the night before when the looming threat of death hung over their heads.

"Dura, take a break for once!" Gromoth shouted, helping Dawn over to a chair near the table.

"You know I can't," she responded without looking up from her maps.

"Why not?" Gromoth laughed, picking up a stone to toss

into the stream. "Even the most loyal warriors need a day to rest."

As Gromoth was speaking, a boy approached Dawn from the stream, cupping his hands together to create a makeshift box. He released his grip into Dawn's lap and revealed many beautiful smooth stones, hand-picked from the stream. "Thank you," he said to her. "You saved my life."

Dawn responded with an appreciative nod and an uncontrollable smile, recognizing the boy from the prior day. He giggled and scurried away, laughing with the other children playing in the stream.

"That is why I can't stop," Dura smiled. "There are more children like that being tortured nearby every day. We can't just let them suffer."

"And you can't help them if you run yourself dry," Gromoth stated, handing Dawn a small sack to hold the child's gift. "We will find the way into the other mines. But today we have victory! Today, we celebrate!"

Gromoth grabbed Dura around the shoulder and yanked her away from the map. He placed one hand around her waist, and with the other he grasped her hand, swiftly spinning his reluctant partner. Dawn giggled, watching the two orcs swinging each other through the cave.

Without noticing, another orc snuck up to Dawn and placed his hand softly on her shoulder. Nearly jumping out of her skin, she whipped around, practically plummeting out of her chair. "Sorry!" The orc apologized. "I don't mean to scare! I just want to introduce myself to the human. My name... Aron."

Dawn caught her breath, slowing her heart rate. "Sorry,"

she responded. "I guess I am just a little on edge. My name is Dawn."

"My son say... you save his life... in prison," Aron said with tears welling up in his eyes. His speech was stuttered and slow, but Dawn could piece together his sentences. "I would love... to serve you lunch today? If you wish."

"Oh, that isn't necessary!" Dawn stated. The orc father's face fell at her words. "Just knowing he is ok is payment enough."

"We gladly accept your offer, Aron," Gromoth interrupted, halting his dance to join the conversation. "Go and prepare. We will only be a few minutes."

Aron grinned from ear to ear and raced off to grab his son and prepare the food in his home. Dawn peered at Gromoth dumbfoundedly, "What was that about?"

"Don't be so quick to dismiss another culture, girl," Gromoth smiled. "It's a great respect for orcs to be invited over for a meal. It is also very dishonorable when someone refuses..."

Dawn gasped. "I had no idea!"

"You're welcome," Gromoth laughed. "Now you get a chance to experience some real orc hospitality, too! Get some real food in your belly."

Dawn hadn't even realized, but after mentioning food, she noticed her stomach rumbling. She could remember her last meal, and it had been too long ago. She hoped Aron cooked better than those goblin jailers who had been feeding her throughout her time in prison.

After a few minutes, Gromoth helped Dawn out of her chair, and led her and Dura to the home of their hosts. Dura tried to protest, but Dawn could tell that when Gromoth spoke, things happened. Even a woman as tough as Dura couldn't dissuade him once his mind was set.

Aron's home stood like a raggedy old farmhouse. If the wind from outside were to reach into the cave, the shack would likely fall. The painted exterior had faded to a dull red. Gromoth pulled the door open, listening past the creek of the wood. "Hello!" He shouted, awaiting Aron's welcome into his home.

"Come in! Come in!" Aron's voice could be heard from around a corner.

The roof sagged, like a loaf of bread taken out of the oven too early. Though the home was beaten and shabby, Dawn felt comfortable. A feeling she hadn't felt about a place since she left her home. It wasn't perfect, in fact it was far from it. But to these people it was safe, and it was home. To them, nothing was better.

As they walked into the kitchen, the table had already been set. Six plates and six stone chairs. The table was the nicest thing in the entire house. Something that was only used on occasion, like fine china.

"Please, sit," Aron requested, pulling out a chair for Dawn. "You know my son, Wen?" Aron gestured toward his son, who was helping cook the meat in the oven. The same boy from the river and from the prison. He turned toward Dawn and gave a sheepish smile, but quickly spun away again. Soon, the plates were served and the feast that Aron and his son had prepared was placed in front of Dawn and her friends.

Dawn indulged, eating more than she thought was possible. It was delicious! The creamy soup, mossy green with islands of orange floating beneath the broth, warmed her belly. A handsome fish dish prepared by Wen followed. The trout lay on a silver platter garnished with green herbs that Dawn didn't recognize, but enjoyed the flavor. This dish was supplemented by a side of mussels. Their black shells lay open, the beige insides spilling out - sickening, yet enticing. Dawn had never tried them before. They felt horrible on her tongue, slippery and nasty, but they tasted pleasantly of the ocean without an overwhelming aroma of fish.

"The stream in this cave runs to the ocean," Dura explained. "If you were to follow it, it would almost take you right to Port Aurora."

"That is actually where I am headed!" Dawn exclaimed. "I didn't realize I was still on track to my destination."

The thought of her companions entered her mind. It had now been weeks since she had seen Cain or Krom. Battling with the crabs had escaped her thoughts for some time, but now that she had found safety again, she found herself meditating on the welfare of her friends.

Without even thinking, she reached for her necklace, but it wasn't there, and terror overcame her. Thoughts continued to accelerate in her head. Faster and faster. She wanted them to slow so she could breathe, but they wouldn't. Her heart hammered like a rabbit thumping the floor with its foot.

She abruptly jumped up from the table. "I need to help them!" She shouted, startling the dinner guests and hosts alike. Wen secluded himself into a corner, awaiting what may come next.

"I lost everything!" she continued to shout. "It's all gone!"

Gromoth leaped from the table to subdue the frantic

human, keeping her hands away from anything that could harm herself or their hosts. Dura stood and laid her hand on her sword, unsure of Dawn's next action.

Dawn's words flowed from her mouth like a geyser, with important key phrases missing, creating fragments of incoherent sentences. She talked like she didn't have the time to say what she needed to, thoughts jumping from one concept to another. All her fears came tumbling out, unchecked by her brain, like some sort of mental freefall.

Gromoth tried to gently calm her, but his words bounced off her like a hard and heavy rain. Dawn grasped Gromoth's tunic with white knuckles, asking over and over again, "Are they ok?" She screamed their names. "Cain! Krom! Are they ok?"

He continually responded with an overtly sincere, "Yes." His voice was dull. Calm. Collected. A wet blanket to smother the flames of Dawn's panic.

Tears and frantic words slowly became a soft sniffling. Silence encumbered the small orc home. Gromoth's voice remained as warm as the late spring. "I think it is time for us to go."

Dawn nodded. Wiping her eyes, she stood and thanked her hosts. Unsure what just unfolded in front of them, Aron and his son bowed, and silently showed their guests to the door.

Gromoth led Dawn toward another house with the same feel of Aron's home. Faded and tattered. As they entered the home, Dawn asked the question that had been lingering in her mind, "How are you so calm?"

Gromoth glanced toward her bewildered, but Dura burst

into laughter. "Don't even try to pass it off like you aren't the most undisturbed person in these caves. You keep everyone calm. You always have."

Gromoth shrugged his shoulders. "Life is hard enough. It doesn't need my help making mountains out of molehills. We all see the craggy mountain of ice when we are afraid, or we're maxed out emotionally... So instead of that high drama, just breathe... Let your energy come down to something softer... Then breathe a few more times and watch that big 'ol scary hill become something a little more friendly. It's all about perception, really. The only thing you can ever truly control is yourself, and that's something you can learn."

Gromoth placed his arm around Dawn's shoulder, pulling her close. "It is important to love everyone, and that includes yourself. Lay yourself down through the panic if you must. Imagine your breath is keeping a leaf afloat, or that you're meditating on the moon... whatever works... Calm always returns. Self-respect grows. Self-control emerges. You gain liberty and maturity with empathy and greater self-reflection. We must be the calm mentors our people look toward for guidance, the keepers of deep wisdom and infinite love... that's what we should develop into... the kind of person every kid is blessed to be loved by. That is motivation enough for me."

Dawn frowned, reaching again for her absent amulet. Inhaling one large breath, she pictured the leaf, steadily floating in her vision. Slowly exhaling, she saw the leaf lift into the air, and leisurely find its way back down. One more steady breath, and she had calmed again.

"You keep grasping at your neck," Dura noticed. "What for?"

"I just..." Dawn paused briefly. "I have lost a lot of things over the last month, and I feel like I have lost myself."

"It's that necklace, isn't it?" Gromoth asked. Peering toward the ground, Dawn nodded her head. Dura and Gromoth locked eyes, and turned back towards their human companion. "I think we may know what happened to it."

Dawn's eyes flashed at them, "What?"

Gromoth laughed. "Grumuk and his tribe are pretty predictable when it comes to their offerings. Chances are your necklace went straight to Kytas."

"Kytas?" Dawn asked.

"You really are fresh, aren't you?" Gromoth laughed. "Kytas is the Titan of Quarrine. Essentially a god. Don't they teach humans anything?"

"The only gods I am aware of," Dawn responded, "are Fos and Seor."

"Hmph," Gromoth grunted. "Even when humans do teach ancient enlightenments, they only teach half. The titans are how Fos defeated Seor in the Great Reckoning, a millennium ago. When the demon armies of Seor had finally been suppressed back into The Other, Fos split his essence into 3 different beings. While any of these extraordinary beings were on any of the three outer islands, Seor and his minions would be sealed to The Other, unable to return to this world. Of course, when the red moon rises, Seor's power grows and some of his minions are able to break through. Those creatures are amply hunted and destroyed."

Dawn scoffed in disbelief. "How could there be a god here on Quarrine, and nobody knows about it?"

"Let's say you discovered a god. And that god offered you protection and power in order to keep his secret. Would you betray his trust? Most people pass off these teachings the same way you did. Just religious mumbo jumbo. Something that can't be proved. But being an orc who lives in the canyon, I have seen it."

"You've seen it..." Dawn speculated.

Gromoth nodded.

Dawn pondered for a couple seconds before asking the question on her mind, "If you know where this titan is, could you take me to him?"

Gromoth paused, contemplating the request. "You care that much about this necklace. To steal from a god?" Dawn gazed at the floor silently, slumping against the wall of the shack.

"I like you Dawn," he said. "I like your heart, and I like your spirit. I don't want you to get in over your head."

As if the life that was just breathed into her had been squeezed out of her gut, Dawn sat apathetically on the floor. Her silent thoughts screamed in her mind.

"I will take you to Kytas," Gromoth finally yielded, a grin escaping his mouth.

Dawn's eyes beamed. "Really? Thank you so much!" She leapt off the ground in a fit of joy. "Things can finally start going back to normal!"

Dura glanced over at Gromoth with uneasy eyes, communicating a clear message without ever speaking a word, "This is a bad idea."

10

Through the Dark

Icy blasts laced with lightning flashed across the clear midday sky. Giant crabs stomped throughout the canyon in a fury, unaware of the damage they were causing. Cain glanced over to see Dawn scamper into an alley, a colossal crab tracking her closely.

He rushed toward her, but the beast swung a claw into his gut, sending him flying into the rock wall. Doubling over, he felt his mouth fill with the coppery tang of blood. Something like fire shot through his veins, and suddenly a bright light exploded from his hands, ending the life of one monster.

Krom waved his sword and danced under the feet of the beasts, scanning for an escape route. His head buzzed unproductively, crabs closing in from every side. Their bloodcurdling snarls made his hair stand on end. The canyon floor was a lethal playground for the brawlers.

As Dawn broke free into the narrow canyon pass, Krom

noticed a small hole in the rock wall nearby. A perfect place to find cover from the monsters. He rushed through the destruction caused by the rampaging beasts, seeking out his exhausted partner.

Cain continued to exude blasts from his hands, never drawing his sword. His trust in his abilities was evident, but his energy quickly drained. Life left his body like a water pouch pouring out its contents into the dirt. Fire that once flowed through his veins cooled into an icy numbness. Dark clouds circled his vision until the only thing he could hear was his own heartbeat. His breath came in ragged, shallow gasps; each one splintering in his lungs. Until finally, all he saw was black.

Seconds passed, and he heard the snarls of the creatures attacking him. Were they swarming him? That is what he expected, but for some reason he felt no pain. The sounds of battle faded until all he heard was a familiar voice. "You're gonna be ok. Don't give up just yet."

Eventually, his eyes opened to a fire inside a cave. He rested, cocooned within the body of earth feeling the rock under his back. On the other side of the flames sat Krom, skinning a rat to prepare it for dinner. "What happened?" Cain groaned, massaging his head and finding his way to a seated position.

Krom jumped, "Woah! You scared me. I didn't know when you were going to wake up."

"Sorry," Cain laughed. "So, what happened? How did we get here?"

"This cave was the only safe way out of that awful nesting ground," Krom responded. "You were running yourself dry using your magic, but I was able to get you in here. The crabs tried to follow us in and ended up collapsing the cave's entrance, but at least we were safe. I thought I was too late though. You have been out cold for a few days now."

In the darkness of the cave, Cain felt his blood return to a comfortable warmth. His lungs still ached like a rose bush had pressed up against his insides, but he was healing. "Have you ever experienced your energy being drained, Krom?"

Krom stopped preparing the meal, shaking his head.

"It isn't like what most people say. Most people think it is just becoming weak. Losing our strength. Like any older person experiences before they pass into The Other from their age. But that isn't true." Cain shuddered, gazing into the emptiness of the cave around them. "No, not at all. It's the feeling of being squeezed dry until everything within you is gone. Stolen away. Like all the blood inside has evacuated your body, but your heart still beats. Pumping, but there is nothing to pump. And the whole time you are gasping for air, even though it's not what your body needs." Cain glanced back up to Krom's fearful eyes. "You don't need air. You need life."

Krom shuddered uncomfortably. "Why would you do that to yourself?"

"I needed to save the people around me," Cain sighed.

Krom paused, "You mean Dawn, huh?" Cain nodded. "Why do you care so much for one girl? Enough to go through something like that?"

Cain pondered the question, "I don't really know," he responded honestly. "I never really thought much about it. I guess she just reminds me of my son."

Krom studied the broken reaver sitting across the fire. "I recognize that tone of voice. A little too well. He isn't around anymore, huh?

Cain shook his head, choking back the tears that welled up in his eyes.

"You don't need to tell me," Krom said, "But you should talk to somebody. I know you and I aren't the greatest of friends, but maybe once we find Dawn again, you could talk to her?"

"I don't want to put any more weight on her already troubled soul," Cain responded in frustration. "She carries the weight of the world on her shoulders already! She wants to do what is right for everyone else, and doesn't care what that means for herself. That is exactly what killed my Roy. I won't put that same weight on her!"

Krom stood to his feet and moved slowly around the fire, placing his arm around the sobbing man. "I'm sorry for your loss, Cain."

Wiping away tears from his eyes, Cain noticed the rodent in Krom's hands. "You haven't been eating rats for the last few days, have you?"

Krom skewered the rodent and held the bare meat over the flame in front of them. "Meat is meat my friend," he laughed. "And I never say no to a meal."

Cain scoffed. "Are you even seasoning them?"

"I don't know how to do anything like that!"

Cain reached into his bag and removed a small pouch, extending out his hand to receive the skewered rat from Krom. Quickly, he seasoned the animal in the expensive gourmet salt, and handed their meal back to Krom.

"Don't burn it, now!" Cain laughed. "If you can't handle the cooking, you let me do it."

Krom glared across the fire, holding the skewer over the flickering flame. As his partner cooked the rodent, Cain noticed stones and algae around the cave that had faded in color, bland and lifeless. "Oh no."

"What is that?" Krom asked nervously. "I've seen quite a bit in my life, but I've never seen anything like that."

Sweat pooled under Cain's brow and dampened his back. His experience as a reaver was often a blessing, but at this point his knowledge was a curse. "This is dark magic."

Krom stopped in his tracks, "No, no, no. We hardly have the energy to defend ourselves against the rats down here, let alone a mage."

"Not just any mage," Cain's tone sent a chill down Krom's spine. "I had heard tales of a witch that has been hiding here in the canyon since the war, but I didn't think it was true."

Krom slowly pulled the rat out of the fire. "You are more powerful than this witch though, right?" He pleaded.

"I don't know," Cain shuttered. "Definitely not right now. Not in my current state."

"Gah!" Krom growled. "I hate this! I hate it. I hate it. I hate it!"

Once the rat was cooked to perfection, Krom split it with his blade to share with his partner. "I must admit," Krom stated, mouth full of the delicious meat. "I have missed your expert touch on the meals the last few days!" They shared a brief smile before continuing to chomp down on the rodent.

The men wandered the cave for days, pushing farther and farther into the heart of the mountain every day. There was no way out except to go farther in. No route back to the outside world. The crabs made sure of that. Their only chance was to keep pushing forward, hoping that they found the sunlight before this creature found them. With each new campsite they noticed more and more discolored scenery, until finally they travelled into a burrow that was completely lifeless. Even when they built a fire, it only illuminated different shades of grey.

"I wish we could go the opposite direction," Cain's anxiety was difficult to hide. "We seem to be getting closer and closer to whatever is causing this... blight." As he spoke, a low gurgle, followed by a scream erupted from deeper within the cave. It was a strangled cry of someone in mortal terror. A haunted scream.

Around the corner the bodies of three of the soldiers who had chased them into the canyon lay lifeless. Their colorless eyes lay open, and their skin had lost all pigment. Cain kneeled and began pulling their bags off their back, starting a fire in the room with the snap of his fingers. "We'd better not sleep tonight."

Flickering flame light rebounded off the grey cave walls. Even the air seemed lifeless within the dark corridor. Calm, like when the wind halts before the hurricane rolls in. Krom's ears sharpened to every tiny noise nearby. Every loose stone rattling was a monster. Each aroma that wafted in made his brain jump to the most fearsome beasts and his body prepared itself for flight, or fight.

If he was honest with himself, neither fight or flight would likely be his actual response. More likely he would just freeze under pressure. Other people, he could handle. Warriors or

Guild thugs were simple. But even with a recovering reaver under his care, he had never fought against the supernatural. He had no idea how he would react. For now, the only thing to do was sit on the moist rock, water seeping into his pants. Waiting. Breathing. Watching.

Cain lay on his back with his eyes shut, picking dirt from his fingernails. His breathing was slow. Calm almost. "What are we going to do?" Krom asked in a hushed, but urgent voice.

"About what?" Cain didn't even open his eyes to respond.

Krom grit his teeth. "About that... thing! We can't just... not sleep!" He pointed to the lifeless husks lying nearby. "But whatever did this is around here somewhere. Somewhere close."

"Closer than you realize," Cain stated.

Krom's blood chilled. "And you are just sitting there, picking at your nails?"

"You need to rest, Krom."

"Don't tell me what to do!" Krom screamed. "What are you going to do? How are we going to get out of this?"

"Quiet..." Cain's eyes shot open.

Krom opened his mouth, ready to shout again, but the sound of rolling stones shoved his voice right back down into his throat. Cain sat up, rolling onto his knees and sniffing the air. Out of the darkness of the cave ahead came a stench. Not the sickly odor of decay, but a foul reek as if unnamable filth had piled in the shadows, now making its way toward the travellers. Krom laid his hand on the hilt of his blade, but Cain scoffed. "That isn't going to help us now." With the wave of his hand, Cain extinguished the fire and darkness flooded the room.

Krom pressed himself against the wall behind him, avoiding whatever could lie in the shadows ahead. It could have been morning on the outside, but he would never know. The impenetrable dark was so dense; it felt as if he were drowning. It seemed like the darkness breathed blindness into his eyes and into his mind. All memory of color and forms of light faded out of thought.

Estranged footsteps approached in the pitch-black corridor. Slow, creeping footsteps, pressing into dirt and rock. A long, gurgling hiss resounded throughout the passage; startling and horrible in the heavy silence. Krom squinted in an attempt to see whatever monstrosity approached, but the dense blackness veiled the beast. Still as a stone he waited, the stench of filth in his nostrils, waiting for something he couldn't know.

He held his breath, listening intently to the low exhale of this unknown threat. It was right there. Right in front of him. If he just reached out his arm, the cover of shadow would have no more use, and he would have been discovered. Warmth radiated from the foul-smelling beast. Was it sulfur?

Krom had no time to linger on the thought. Suddenly, a flash of light emanated in the room, blinding both Krom and the creature. He could hear the voice of Cain shouting from ahead, "Run! Now!"

Without hesitation, Krom's feet began to move. His sight hadn't returned, but that didn't matter. All he could do was escape from the low gurgling shrieks of the monster. As he ran, the floor lowered steeply. Every step he descended lower and lower into the abyss of the dreaded canyon. He could hear Cain striding with him, but their hunter was also close behind. Blinded momentarily, but not defeated. Still bent on death.

As they ran deeper and deeper into the tunnel, a red glow illuminated the tunnel in a dim, menacing smolder, as if the cave itself was inside a furnace. Their steps slowed, until finally they were forced into a sluggish walk, every pace forward more difficult than the last. Their feet felt like they were encased in lead.

Soon it was too much to bear, and even with their stalker approaching from behind, Krom lost his footing and fell forward into the rocks.

"No, Krom!" Cain shouted, reaching out his hand. "Today is not your day. Fight until your last breath."

Fighting off fear and calling on all of his remaining strength and resolution, Krom pulled himself up to his feet, forcing his limbs to move. Screeches echoed from behind, pushing them forward. One step. Then another. And then another. Until finally, the red glow softened, and the weight removed from their limbs.

When Krom looked back over his shoulder, he saw it, a ghoulish creature, almost insect-like in shape. Its grey, mangled face nearly distracted from the multitude of decrepit human arms and hands protruding from all sides of its long body. With hatred in its eyes, it approached, snarling with each step.

"Enough!" Cain shouted, and he shot a bolt of lightning into the tunnel, crashing into the side of the foul creature.

Squealing in pain, the creature fell into the dirt, almost exactly where Krom had fallen before. Suddenly, as if with a mind of its own, the ground began to shake and the crumbling earth swallowed the beast.

Red glow faded into more colorless shadow, and darkness engulfed the passage yet again. Cain snapped his fingers, and a bright light shone in his hand. The smell had faded, but the fear and dread lingered in the corridor.

"I thought…" Krom stuttered. "I th…thought you said you c…c… couldn't beat it?"

"I can't," Cain stated, pushing Krom forward down the winding path. "Keep going. We don't stop until we're out."

They walked briskly down the sloped pathway. Cain's light flickered with each step, slowly fading with his energy. Krom watched his limp grow more extreme the farther they travelled. "Cain, do you need to rest for a second?"

Cain responded slowly, forcing the words from his throat. "I… I'm fine. Keep your eyes up."

As they walked, Krom peered to each corner of the cave around them. Even with Cain's dim light, there were too many nooks and crannies to truly keep your eyes open for everything. The shadowy corners could easily hide on looking creatures or monsters, and the thought chilled his blood.

Something like a wind blew through the lifeless tunnel, ruffling his tunic and biting at his skin. He thought he heard a voice, low and grumbling, resound from the cave behind, so he whipped his head around.

Nothing.

He didn't believe it. He couldn't. He knew what he heard. The rush of wind couldn't have been natural in the cave so far underground. Just because there was nothing there now, doesn't mean there never was.

Closer and louder this time, the same dark, rumbling voice filled his head. "Soooo... Much... Fear." The voice transformed, shifting into a shrill squawk. "Are you afraid to die?"

Suddenly, decaying arms erupted from the ground. Hundreds of hands grabbing hold of their legs, pulling the travellers down into the pits of the forsaken canyon.

Krom shouted ahead to Cain, reaching for his sword in its sheath, "What is this?"

He hacked away at the arms one at a time, making no progress in freeing himself. Every time he cut one arm away, two more would grab him. It felt like they were pulling the life out of him, sucking him into the underworld one drop of blood at a time.

The earth shook violently and Krom's feet sunk into the dirt, pulled inch by inch by the decomposing hands. His passion quickly faded; energy exhausted. He dropped his sword, accepting the fate that had been waiting for him since that awful day with his sister. This is what he deserved.

Deeper into the damp ground the hands pulled him, until finally his head was beneath the dirt. He expected it to be like holding his breath underwater, but this was nothing even close. As if an enemy had a knife to his throat, commanding his heart to stop beating. Of course, it will continue to beat. And just like his heart continues on, his lungs will inhale whether it's clean air or grainy dirt and rubble. "Is Cain suffering the same fate?" Krom thought. "Or has his magic saved him from this torment? He doesn't deserve a death like this. He was a good man."

Abruptly, like a hand rescuing Krom from his fate, an unnatural white light pierced through the dirt into his eyes. Several beams emerged around him, growing larger and larger until finally he was no longer submerged in the earth. The dirt had shifted and blown away, and Krom was falling. To where, he couldn't know. But his breath had returned.

Rubble and debris flew through the air around the fighters. Shards of rock and sections of the mountain exploded into every direction. The bright burst of energy opened the cave to the dangers of the outside world, illuminating the dark tunnel with the midday sun.

With a *THUD*, the fall came to an abrupt end. Krom peered around the newly formed battleground. Pale, bleak sun rays glittered among the newly exposed quartz of the deep mountain cavern. Decaying arms and bodies of several different demonic monsters littered the burrow. "Had these beasts all been in the tunnel with us?" Krom asked himself. He continued to look around the shaft to find Cain lying face down, writhing in pain on the floor. *Better than dead,* he thought.

But there she was. Right behind Cain she stood, seemingly unharmed from the blast and the fall. She was beautiful, but in an eerie way. Her pale skin contrasted her dark black cloak. Her waist long hair lay against her body. She hadn't been touched by the dust storm and debris from the explosion. As if there were a force field that kept her safe. Her glowing bright orange eyes shifted in his direction. Adrenaline flooded Krom's system, pumping and beating, trying to find an escape from this awful scenario. "Even now, still afraid." Her lips didn't move, but her voice echoed in his mind.

In a puff of smoke, she vanished. Krom shuddered, timidly peering all around. "Pathetic." She was nowhere to be found, but Krom couldn't remove her utterance from his mind. He could taste the saliva thickening in the back of his throat, beads of sweat trickling from his brow.

"Run," another voice spoke from across the tunnel. Krom gazed over to make eye contact with Cain, finding his way to his feet. "Run!"

A gust filled the room, and Krom was blasted through the air, jetting backwards into the still crumbling stone walls. His vision blurred. Running his hand against the back of his head, he felt a warm, wet substance flowing from his skull.

"I expected beings with so much innate power like yourselves to be a bit more difficult to drain," the witch reappeared in the center of the burrow. "Though, your suffering is better than a meal to me."

Slowly, the sadist raised her arms as a red glow radiated from within her being. Cain shot a waning blast of ice toward her, but she easily deflected it. Suddenly, a smoldering orange and maroon portal erupted from nowhere, exhaling an evil energy from within. Fear, anger, pain, and darkness filled Krom's heart.

White eyes glowed from within the portal. Whatever the dead eyes were attached to was tall, for these eyes were twice the height of the witch. Hissing and gurgling noises resounded in the room, engulfed by the screaming of the portal itself. A giant creature, snake-like in appearance, but with a humanoid, demonic upper body emerged from the hellish pit. Six arms extended from its monstrous upper torso, and its twisting, snaking tail whipped behind it.

Evil, lifeless white eyes glared over at Cain. To this creature, he was nothing but meat. A meal to tide it over until the next, and it was starving. A crack like a whip sounded as the brute demon pivoted toward the depleted mage.

Krom watched in horror, unsure of what could possibly make such noises in this world. There was nothing. This ungodly creature was like nothing he had ever experienced. Cain's grunts as he weaved in and out of danger were silenced by the hellscape around them. The demon reared up, spinning in circles, and roaring in frustration. It pounded the dirt and stone.

In the hectic distraction of this demon, the witch had focused her eyes on the mage fighting for his life. She laughed, seemingly refreshed by the visceral fright in her victims.

Krom pulled his knife from its sheath. Standing to his feet, all it took was one fluid motion. He raised his arm over his head and flung his weapon forward. It flew, end over end, through the air. One slip, and the opportunity was gone. It couldn't have taken more than a single second for the knife to find its target, but the time elapsing felt like an eternity.

Then, the knife met flesh. Even a being as powerful as this one was made only of soft, pudgy skin and organs. No amount of magic can bring a person back to life after a blade pierces their heart. Suddenly, the glow stopped, and the portal shut like an eyelid, leaving a dark, sticky residue beneath. The witch fell to her knees, and then swiftly to the ground without a word.

That was enough to shift the attention of the creature

toward the new corpse in the burrow. That was all Cain needed. He leapt forward into the monster, and shoved his blade into its neck. It sank deep and the demon screamed, flailing and thrashing through the tunnel, until finally it lay dead in the dirt.

"What in the world was that," Krom exhaled a sigh of relief, limping over to Cain.

"That," Cain responded, pulling his blade free from the beast. "Is what we call an 'anguis'. A demon from The Other. Very dangerous. Ragnar and I just hunted one in the west before we met Dawn. Though, that witch shouldn't have been able to summon a portal like that. Not with a titan on Quarrine."

Krom stared out into the open sky. "I can't believe we are able to see the sky again. I didn't think we ever would!"

Cain nodded in agreement. "That explosion couldn't have come at a better time. It's funny. A similar thing happened on that day with Ragnar too..." Cain paused, peering out into the canyon outside. Suddenly bolting away and climbing up the loose dirt and gravel, he wheeled back toward the exhausted Krom. "It was Dawn!"

11

Kytas

Just hours earlier, tucked tightly into blankets, sleep pooled Dawn's eyelids. The wooden buildings in the mountain were filled with the soft sounds of Orcs snoozing, without a care. All, except for Dura and Gromoth, who paced back and forth in the main room of Dawn's guest house.

"This human will be the death of you," Dura said coldly.

"You say this like I am acting any different now than I have acted before," Gromoth responded. "Would I not do the same for any of the young orc boys in our tribe?"

Dura was quiet for a moment, finding the correct words to counter. "Those are orcs, Gromoth. We all risk our lives for our own kind. What good does it do us to risk our lives for this one human girl?"

Gromoth's eyes narrowed, his voice lowering almost to a growl. "Every movement starts with one. This one human girl is important. Unless you are beginning to turn away from my father's ideals?"

"No... It's just..."

"I won't hear any more of it, Dura." Gromoth growled. "Her life matters just as much as mine. And right now, she needs our help finding herself again. I believe we can help her do that."

"And what if we lose you in the process?"

Gromoth slowed his speech. "Then it will be a worthy sacrifice."

Soon, the sound of children filled the streets again, signaling that morning had come. Torches were lit to simulate sunlight. Stretching her arms, Dawn leapt out of bed and ran to find Gromoth, unaware of the wounds that had plagued her the last few days.

She found her guide preparing satchels and equipping blades to his waist. "You may want something for protection as well," he stated.

Dawn peered at him quizzically, "I guess it isn't a safe road?"

Gromoth laughed. "The road itself is safe enough. It's the destination you should be worried about."

Dawn gazed into the floor, rethinking her decision. No, this was right. She couldn't express it in words, but the amulet was more than just important to her. Losing it felt like she had lost herself.

"I will take a sword," Dawn affirmed. "And a bow if you have one."

"The bows we have might be a little too heavy for you,"

Gromoth chortled. "Built more for orcs than a petite human girl."

Dawn shrugged, equipping a blade on her waist and a dagger on her ankle. Dura exited a hut nearby with another orc woman of similar stature. "Good luck out there, Gromoth," the stranger said.

"We don't need luck," Gromoth responded, placing his hand on the hilt of his blade. "Dawn, this is Dina. Dura's sister. They are the fiercest warriors in Quarrine."

Dawn reached her hand out to greet Dina, but Dina ignored her kind gesture. "Nice to finally meet you, Dawn," she sneered. "You are... smaller than I expected."

Dawn only stood inches shorter than the woman, but she felt as if she was a child gazing up at *REAL* adults. There wasn't much difference, but Dina towered over her with a calm arrogance. It was disguised as confidence, but it couldn't fool Dawn.

Grabbing two torches off the wall and handing one to Dawn, Gromoth led his human companion away from the Thradak village and down multiple cavernous pathways that narrowed in size the farther they travelled. Quickly, the stony surroundings grew rough. The environment was no longer an inhabitable city, but now a dangerous wilderness. The cave had morphed into a jungle of rock and dirt.

Suddenly, Gromoth stopped in his tracks and held a finger to his lips. Dawn could feel her heart lump into her throat. Just feet ahead of them, a giant centipede slithered across the rough cave floor. Normal centipedes were small and harmless, but this one could crush Dawn with just one of its giant legs.

Just then, Dawn's foot slipped and the sound of the rocks crumbling beneath her echoed throughout the cavern. When she looked back up at the giant insect, it was already aware of her presence, and had started to charge toward them. Gromoth drew his sword, readying himself for battle. But before the predator could cover the distance between them, a large stinger appeared out of nowhere, striking the centipede in the side of its disgusting outer shell.

The insect released a sharp shriek, turning towards the new enemy; a western canyon scorpion. Knowing the danger of the battle that was about to happen between these two monsters, Gromoth slid his blade back into its sheath, grabbed Dawn by the arm, and snuck around the ensuing conflict. Soon, the only remnants of the encounter were the echoes of the beasts' cries fading with distance.

"How can you live in these caves with so much danger around every corner?" Dawn asked quietly. "I would never be able to sleep knowing that a few miles away there are creatures like that."

"Those creatures aren't the monsters in these caves," Gromoth answered. "I wish they were the only things we had to deal with."

"You are more afraid of the other orcs than you are of that giant centipede?"

"Yes." Gromoth held no reserve for his disdain. "These creatures are just trying to survive. They hunt because they are hungry. They kill only to eat. Sometimes, if we encroach on their territory, they will protect their families. Are they evil for that? Grumuk and his tribe aren't starving, yet they still hunt us. They weren't in danger from the outside world, yet they still planned to enslave and murder the other races. They are the monsters. The ones that should have a conscience, but choose not to use it. The ones who know the difference between right and wrong, and choose to do wrong anyways."

"What if to them, they are right?" Dawn asked. "What if we are actually in the wrong?"

"You know that isn't true," Gromoth replied. "You don't have to believe in a higher power, or be well educated, or be born into privilege to know that some things are right and some things are wrong. They know what they are doing is bad. They just don't care. 'A necessary evil,' they call it. And that is terrifying."

As much as Dawn hated it, she knew he was right. Even as sheltered as she had been her whole life, she knew the difference between right and wrong. The first time she took a life, even though it was in defense of herself and her family, it had made her sick. She knew that life had value, even the lives of those who were wicked. She was born with the innate sense of good and evil, and had to fight against her instincts to act in corruption.

The travellers continued into the depths of the caverns. Light from Gromoth's torch glimmered against the stalagmites protruding from the floor. Dawn noticed small gems on the ground, hidden amongst the quartz in the cave's foundation.

"We are getting close," Gromoth whispered. They came to a slope, descending into the dark abyss of the grotto. "If you continue down this slope, and take a left when the road forks, you will find yourself in Kytas' lair." Dawn nodded and tightened her grip on her torch. Before she could take a step forward, Gromoth grabbed her arm. "Be careful. In my experience, the gods aren't very forgiving."

Dawn gazed into Gromoth's caring eyes, turned toward her destination, then spiraled back to face him. "Will you be here when I return?" With a broken smile, he nodded, and Dawn descended into the darkness of the cavern below.

The darkness of the cave seemed to suck the light from her torch. Gleam from Gromoth's flame disappeared as Dawn rounded the corner. Her steps were quieter than smoke on a gentle wind.

A grand door suddenly shone ahead of her, laced with sparkling jewels and lined with glowing golden threads. She pressed against the fixture and it slowly swung open, creaking loudly into the emptiness of the cavern.

Once inside, Dawn felt a surge of energy from her head to her toes. Unsure if it arose from proximity to the gold and exquisite stones piled throughout the room, or knowing that she was close to having her precious necklace back in her possession. Torchlight glimmered in the reflection of the gold pieces. The gold lay as still as a corpse, but it seemed to dance with the flames. Mounds of treasure were piled as high as Dawn's head, offerings from the orc tribes.

How could a part of Fos be so greedy? Dawn thought to herself. *What does a god need with gold?*

Quickly she diverted her thoughts to the task at hand: finding her necklace. It should have stood out among the gold and bright colors of the gems being a silver chain and pendant, but Dawn had underestimated the fortune that was housed in Kytas' dwelling. She dug through the top layer of the mounds nearby, not knowing how long she might be searching.

Suddenly, a thundering voice boomed throughout the cave. "Who are you? And why are you here?"

Dawn fell backwards into a pile of treasure, dropping her torch into the gold, smothering her only source of light. A blaze flashed throughout the room, and flames engulfed the walls surrounding the god's treasure. Dawn slowly found her way back to her feet, peering around the room.

Perched on a throne in the center of the room sat a dark silhouette wrapped in golden armor. Orange eyes glowed from underneath an exorbitant crown on his head, reminding Dawn of ancient kings of the desert kingdoms. In one hand the being held a staff with an orb set on the tip, and the other sat encased in a golden glove. Shining snake-like creatures slithered up the engraved throne as if they were a part of the design themselves.

Dawn's eyes widened in awe. The magnificent sight hadn't been in the room before; at least she hadn't noticed something so glorious before the voice had spoken. Was this the majesty of Fos?

"You aren't an orc," Kytas' voice boomed once again. "What is your purpose being here?"

"I..." Dawn stuttered under the magnificent being. "I lost something. Something important to me. And a friend told me you could help me in finding it."

"You haven't lost just anything," Kytas responded. "You

have lost yourself. You have been lost for a long time. Why, only now, are you searching?"

Dawn continued probing for her amulet as she responded to the god. "I don't know what you are talking about."

Kytas roared in laughter, shaking the cavern around them "Is your necklace really that important to you?"

Astonished, Dawn jolted her eyes up to the being on the throne. "How did you know?"

"Why does it matter so much to you?"

"It is the last thing I have from my father," Dawn responded. "When I wear it, I feel complete."

"You don't truly understand the truth behind your words," Kytas chuckled.

Dawn's heart raced and anger filled her soul. She glared up at the glamorous god-like figure.

"Do you really think having your amulet back will complete you?" Kytas asked.

Quickly the rage turned to sadness, and tears welled up in Dawn's eyes. "I don't know," she sniffled. "I... I really don't know."

Kytas studied the young girl carefully for a period, examining the authenticity of her tears. "You may not always have the objects that make you feel whole. You need to come to terms with yourself first."

Just then, a wind like a hurricane roared through the throne room. Violent whirlwinds of shadows extinguished the flames surrounding the room. Suddenly, standing in front of Dawn was a silhouette with no clear features. Just a figure of black, overshadowed by a darkness radiating from within itself.

Then, that same familiar voice boomed throughout the cavern. That haunting voice from her dreams, from her visions. "What do you think you know about me?"

Flames reignited around the room. Beginning to resemble human features, Dawn gazed into the abyssal darkness of the figure like looking into a mirror; a shadow reflecting back at her.

"So, you have finished hiding your true self?" Kytas reclined backwards on his throne.

Dawn stood silently, awestruck at the fantastical scene.

"I have never been in hiding. We have always been complete. Never separate." As the shadow spoke, Dawn could feel her chest resonating as if the words were coming from within herself.

"Do you speak for the both of you?" Kytas asked.

With a snickering laugh from the shadow floating in the center of the room, the flames flickered again in another whirlwind, softer than the last. "You think she can speak for herself? She needs me. On her own, she is weak."

"Wait!" Dawn finally mustered the courage to raise her voice, but she was engulfed by the booming voices of the other beings.

"Do you really believe your wholeness has already come?" Kytas asked again calmly, turning to Dawn as if he was ready to listen to her remarks.

But the reflection's patience was cut short. "We have been fine our entire life! I have always protected her when she needed it. We don't need the help of Fos or his Titans any more today than we did yesterday."

"Hmph," Kytas grunted, leaning downwards on his throne.

Suddenly, Dawn could see her amulet in his hands. Had it been at his feet this whole time? "I guess you don't need this then, do you?" Without waiting for a response, the godlike being stood to his feet and placed the necklace around his neck.

Abruptly, the shadowy reflection distorted like she was fading away, and the whirlwind reappeared, carrying her through the air like a spirit. A low rumbling growl resonated inside the chamber, and suddenly the shadow was standing on the god's throne, raising a translucent sword into the air to strike down her enemy.

Like lightning, Kytas flashed to the other side of the room, pounding his staff into the floor. Rattled by the shifting floor and the storm of weather that raged around, Dawn cowered and bolted to a nearby pile of treasure to take cover. Though fear flowed like energy into her veins, she also couldn't help but to gnash her teeth and clench her fists in rage.

Suddenly, as the magnificent beings flew around the room, Dawn stood to her feet. Both of these entities held a place in her soul that she couldn't explain, even to herself. The fear that coursed through her body wasn't for her own safety, but for the safety of the two engaging parties. She rushed up the pile of treasure, watching the gods whisk around the room, thunderous clangs resounding every few seconds when the two would finally clash.

"Stop..." Dawn said, following the skirmish with her eyes. "That's enough."

To no avail. The shadow creature and the god continued their brawl. Gold and gems flew into the air as they whizzed by.

Dawn noticed the necklace around Kytas' neck began to glow. A radiating white light that seemed to overpower the flames encasing the room.

"Enough!"

Something like a fire welled up inside her. It wasn't rage, but passion. The same electricity that she felt inside herself when she first used magic resurfaced. With a flick of her hands, she extended her arms out and grabbed a hold of the two beings attempting to fly past her.

"ENOUGH!"

As Dawn gripped the two magnificent entities, her necklace erupted in light. Her eyes began to glow, and radiance exploded from her, shaking the foundations of the throne room and the earth below. Kytas' eyes shifted suddenly from an arrogant power to a fearful regret. For the first time, he was scared.

The shadowy reflection formed into Dawn's being as if they were becoming one, until the silhouette had disappeared entirely from the room. With a glorious flash, the jewel around Kytas' neck burned brighter than the midday sun, Dawn's eyes following suit to match with the amulet. Heat radiated from within and without Dawn, yet she felt like a cool breeze had engulfed her. The light grew and grew, until nothing could be seen anymore.

Just as fast as the light came, it dimmed. Kytas was gone, and the desert sun was illuminating the once dark throne room. Pieces of fallen rock covered the piles of treasure throughout the room, and Dawn passed out of consciousness with her amulet freshly snug around her neck.

12

Exodus

The bright light flashed in the cave where Gromoth waited. Energy emanating from the throne room knocked him backwards into the dirt. "What the..." he whispered to himself, gazing toward what used to be a tunnel veering toward the chamber of a god.

He watched and waited, unaware of passing time. It must have been a while, because he heard the voice of his people approaching from behind. "What was that?"

"I don't know," Gromoth responded. The question had come from Dina, but there were many Thradak soldiers with her.

"That blast of light nearly blew a tunnel directly to the village!" Dina shouted.

Dura caught up with the rest of the soldiers that had found Gromoth. "We immediately readied ourselves and rushed this way when we saw it. Are you ok?" Her eyes locked onto the hobbling orc captain.

"I haven't seen any movement come from Kytas' chambers," Gromoth said, staring downward to the newly illuminated throne room. He shifted his gaze to Dura, his glossy eyes quivering. "She has to be alive, right?"

Dura slowly treaded to her companion, placing her hands on his shoulder. "Let's go find out. Together."

Led by Dina, with Dura and Gromoth close behind, the troop marched forward cautiously. Even though they lived with a god at their backdoor, never had they experienced anything so otherworldly. The fallen rock was difficult to traverse, but it couldn't prevent their progress. Weapons drawn, they trudged along, ready for whatever awaited them.

The treacherous canyon sky shone brightly on them. Dina kept her eyes peeled upward, watching for the great birds that made their home within the dangerous walls. She already had an arrow nocked, ready for the worst.

The blast had embedded gold and silver into the walls. Shards of the great door littered the passage. Gromoth scanned the once great room, and there she was. Lying on her side in the center of the room. Dawn was completely alone. Kytas was nowhere to be seen. He rushed over to her, checking for any signs of life. She mumbled something incoherent under her breath, but could not force her eyes to open.

"She is still breathing..." Gromoth whispered to himself. "She is alive! And Kytas is gone!" He gazed back toward Dura. "We have to get her back to Tara."

"What happened to Kytas?" Dina asked hesitantly.

Dura finished the thought that everyone in the room had been thinking. "She didn't... kill him... did she?"

"I don't know," Gromoth responded. "But that explosion has definitely drawn attention to this spot, and we can't just leave her here..."

Rolling stones echoed in the newly formed burrow, catching the attention of every orc soldier inside. They watched the top of the hill leading into the open canyon, readying their weapons and awaiting whatever creature stalked them. Gromoth could hear his own breath beneath the cover of the wind.

Suddenly, two human men leapt over the crest of the hill with blades in hand. One man was of a darker complexion, wielding a blade in one hand and a knife in another. The other man was a weathered mage, but it seemed like magic was currently difficult for him. They locked their attention on the unconscious girl in the middle of the room. "Let her go!"

Quickly, the men rushed the troop of orcs, ready to draw blood. Before they could make contact with each other, Dawn had surprisingly found her way to her knees, screaming with all of her being, "STOP!"

The entire room froze, both orcs and humans alike. Dawn pushed against her knees, attempting to stand to her feet. If she had only tried once, she would have failed. But she was stubborn. Headstrong. Finally, once she was standing, she stumbled toward the humans, falling into their arms. "I am so glad you are ok," she sobbed aloud, tears soaking the men's dirty tunics. She turned toward the orcs. "Gromoth, meet Cain and Krom. My friends, and travel companions."

The blades may have been sheathed, but tension still lingered among the troupe. Krom and Gromoth helped Dawn walk through the tunnel back to the Thradak village, while Dina and Dura were alert for enemies.

Back in the village, everything had changed. The playful spirit of the inhabitants left the caves with the coming of the sunlight. Every orc that lived side by side with Gromoth stood outside their homes, disoriented and gazing towards the approaching crowd.

"Aron," Gromoth snapped, spotting the father in the crowd. "Start gathering the tribe. The captains will make a decision about our next move, but we can't stay here any longer."

Aron sent orcs back to their homes to pack their things and prepare for the road. "The road may be long," he said to them. "Bring only what possessions you need."

Gromoth led the company into his hut, setting Dawn down on a stone stool. As Cain and Krom made their way inside the building, Dina stepped in their way, placing her hand on Cain's chest. "You think you are going to be a part of this conversation, human?"

"Dina!" Gromoth shouted. "The next move we make is important, and can be crucial to our relationship with the humans. Let them in." Hesitantly lowering her arm, Dina glared at the humans as they stepped by her to stand near Dawn. The sun may have been shining on the village, but the room felt cold as ice. "Good," Gromoth calmed himself. "Now, what is our next move?"

"We have been making our way toward Port Aurora," Cain replied. "In order to find passage to the Citadel."

"How does that help us?" Dina snapped.

Dura added on to her sister's remark. "Aurora is a human city. Orcs would never be allowed to enter."

"I don't know if that is true," Cain responded. "I am a reaver, and my word holds some weight with the authorities in the world."

"Are you saying you could find the Thradak tribe a new home at the port?" Gromoth asked.

"I can't make any promises," Cain stated. "But I can definitely try."

Dina scoffed under her breath, rolling her eyes away from the humans.

"This sounds like a bad idea, Gromoth," Dura vocalized her sister's not so silent remark. "We can't base the future of our tribe on the word of some human, who can't even promise this will work."

"Do you have a better idea?" Gromoth asked.

"We find a new home where our people will be safe!" Dura shouted. "A place where we can rebuild. *Inside* the canyon. And continue the work we have started here."

"That isn't moving anything forward!" Gromoth contested. "We have been fighting this fight for too long. If anything, it has only gotten worse. This human offers us an opportunity to take a leap forward into the future. Into progress. Into equality. Into orcs and humans being able to live in peace with one another."

"What if his word isn't worth as much as you say?" Dura's cold words pierced Dawn's soul.

"What if it is?" Gromoth slowed his speech, affirming the finality of his decision.

Dina stormed out of the hut, slamming the splintered wooden door behind her. Dura followed, but while she had the door in her hand, she turned toward Gromoth. "My counsel used to mean something to you." Without another word, she exited the hut to go prepare her things.

"Will that be a problem?" Krom asked solemnly.

"They will come to their senses," Gromoth responded. "They just need time." He turned his attention to Cain, who was resting in the corner of the room. "We can trust you, right?"

Dawn opened her mouth to speak, but Cain held up his hand, silencing her. "I promise, I will do everything I can."

Gromoth bared his gritty orcish teeth into a smile and clapped his hands together. "Then let's get ready to go. We will leave in one hour."

Sometimes an hour can seem like a lifetime, but to Dawn this hour was just minutes. Like ants, the tribe scurried between the rustic buildings preparing for the journey ahead. Children and adults alike wore their entire lives on their backs in bags and rucksacks. Dura and Dina removed themselves from the group, but still they prepared for the road by equipping the war dogs with satchels and saddles for those who had the skill to ride.

Soon, thousands of orcs flowed out of the cave. Gromoth led the tribe with his soldiers in the front. The riders travelled along the sides of the pack as protection. Dawn walked along in the middle of the pack with Cain and Krom, chatting with Aron and his son as they trekked onwards. Dura and Dina were nowhere to be found. She expected that they went on ahead to scout the road.

Orcs knew the canyon better than anyone else. Gromoth led the tribe with purpose, swiftly escorting his people to safety. Night quickly approached, and setting up camp while still within the dangers of the canyon was not an option for him. The birds and the isopods would have been bad enough, but the things he had seen in the depths of the canyon wrought terror in his heart.

Heaviness in the air increased, weighing on the hearts of the people. Dark clouds overtook them, a somber canopy with great billowing edges. Their chatter slowed and quieted until finally the entire tribe was silent. Waiting. Watching.

Once the sun went down, a blood red moon rose shining through the smoky haze. The peaks of the canyon walls concealed themselves inside the pillow of nature's camouflage. Gromoth led them over streams and hills, through the shadowy passages of what he once called home. No longer.

Cain strode forward to the front of the pack, goosebumps now lining the skin of his forearms. His eyes scanned the dark alleyways they passed, watching for any signs of unnatural movement. He approached behind Gromoth, never averting his eyes from their surroundings. "We need to move faster," Cain's voice trembled. "The red moon brings many terrible things."

"I know this, human," Gromoth sneered. "We can only move as quickly as our slowest members. They aren't soldiers ready for orders. They are children. And families."

"And the children and families aren't safe here," Cain shot back under his breath, returning to the middle of the pack.

Silence pressed on their ears as they glided through the foggy landscape. Each pilgrim could hardly see ten feet in front of themselves. With their eyesight impeded, new scenes seemed to loom suddenly in the oncoming darkness. They strode deeper and deeper into the murky underbelly of the Quarrine wasteland, their eyes wide, gazing into the eerie grey mist of the shadows beyond.

Finally, seeing the signs of green grass and shrubbery through the opaque clouds, Gromoth spotted the exit of the Great Canyon. A collective sigh of relief fell upon the entire tribe. They quickly maneuvered through the passage to find themselves in an open field of browning grass, with the weathered rock and sand now lying behind them.

Swift as sparrows, the tribe set up tents and fires to prepare themselves for the night to come. Even though the scenery had changed, the deadly desert nights were still enough to freeze the most hardened of warriors. Cain and Dawn wandered the campground assisting in lighting fires with their use of magic. Even in his weakened state, it only took Cain a snap of a finger, but Dawn was beginning to catch on. By the time they were finished, she was almost as fast as her teacher.

Krom found himself playing a dice game with some of the orc men, gambling simple things that they had brought in their packs: pots, pans, clothes, and the like. A roar of spirit and joy enveloped the fields and echoed in the passage behind them. Whatever fear that had overcome them in the canyon had been flushed out by hope and freedom.

For all except Gromoth. While watching Krom play his game, Dawn noticed him sitting alone at the edge of the camp, carving a stick into little pieces with a pocket blade. She approached and sat next to him on a nearby stump. "It's not like you to be so removed from the fun of your people."

"We have known each other for a few weeks, and all of a sudden you know me?" Gromoth laughed.

"You knew more about me the day we met than I knew about myself," Dawn responded. Silence fell between them, until Dawn decided to ask the question in her heart. "What is going on with you?"

Gromoth sighed. "I have just led my people away from the home they have known their whole lives. The Canyon was where I was born. Where my father was born." He gazed into Dawn's eyes. "What if this was never my father's plan for us? Am I making the right choice? Not just for me, but for my people?"

Cain's comforting voice sounded from behind them. "Let the past pass. The future is coming whether you are ready for it or not. Like the sun that rises in the morning, tomorrow is coming. Lean into the new. Your people will be thankful for it in the future."

"I wish it were that easy," Gromoth grumbled.

"I don't know much," Dawn said, "but I do know that you can trust Cain with your life, and with the lives of your tribe."

"This is not the end," Cain interjected. "Only the beginning."

As they spoke, Dawn noticed a figure approaching from the east, riding a war dog. It trotted slowly, almost as though it were sneaking its way into the camp.

"Dina?"

13

At the Gates

The morning came like a thief. The orcs packed up the tents, the dice games, everything, and loaded it all into their packs. They extinguished the fires, and marched ahead into the day.

They saw no signs of any living thing except birds. The rolling fields did nothing to hide the group's movement, but that was fine because there was nothing to hide from. Just wide plains of dying grass and dust whipping through the air.

Earlier the canyon walls seemed hostile, as if they were harboring secret eyes within the stone crevices. It seemed an impenetrable fortress, impossible to escape. Now the walls didn't seem so bad. On the plain the tribe was exposed and unprotected from enemies that may be watching. Just the thought sent shivers down Dawn's spine, even the hair on her neck stood on end. She couldn't shake the feeling that someone was watching them. More precisely, watching her. She grasped her amulet and sank into the crowd.

Days turned into nights, and the tribe would set up camp again. While the orcs partied and played in the wilderness, Dawn watched along the edge of the camp scanning the darkness for signs of danger lurking within. Never did she see any enemies, but every night she spotted Dina riding back through the shadows.

She must be scouting ahead for the next day's travels, Dawn thought to herself. Still, she couldn't shake the unease growing in the pit of her stomach, which felt like acid boiling away her insides.

On the third day, before the sun rose, Gromoth sounded the morning alarm to awaken the tribe; orc children sprinting through the camp crashing pots together. It wasn't subtle, but it was effective. Within minutes, everyone was awake and tearing down their portion of the campsite.

As the troupe continued their trek to the port, Cain pulled Dawn and Krom toward the front of the pack. They found themselves walking alongside Gromoth. "We should be arriving today if we keep this pace," Cain said.

"That is only the beginning of our trials," Gromoth stated grimly. "So far, this journey seems all too simple for my liking."

"When we arrive, allow me to move ahead to speak with the guards and Lord Artimus," Cain explained his plan in detail, ignoring the orc's hesitation. "Don't approach the city too closely, or they will think they are being attacked, and there will be no turning back. We don't want to start a war today."

Gromoth nodded in agreement. The weather was grey and overcast, the brisk winds of winter having descended upon them. Children wrapped themselves in blankets and bundled up in multiple layers of clothing. The sun, shielded by clouds, cast long, dark shadows over the plains.

Soon they approached a series of great hills. They were a patchwork of green with hues of dying grass to deep forest green, made more varied by the shadows of clouds playing across the earth below. Each hill had a path that led the tribe up to the summit and back down into the valley below.

Dina took her dog and rode ahead, perching herself atop the final hill and scouting out the land ahead. Quickly, she spun around and drove back to the pack. As she approached, they could all see the terror in her eyes.

"We must stop!" She cried out. "It is a battlefield ahead!"

"What do you mean?" Gromoth inquired.

"There must have been a great battle," Dina stated. "Leading up to the gates of the port are hundreds of dead bodies. Orcs and humans alike. It's a graveyard."

Gromoth held up a closed fist, and suddenly the tribe halted their progress. Dawn could hear whispers travel across the grass. "What do we do now?" Krom whimpered.

"We move forward with our plan," Cain sternly stated, glancing over to Gromoth. "You and the tribe stay back here while Krom, Dawn, and I go to inquire what has happened."

"You expect for us to just wait here while you jaunt along to safety and warmth?" Dina shouted.

"Dina, quiet," Gromoth retorted.

"No!" She shouted even louder, her voice echoing across the plains. "I don't care if everyone can hear me! This human is trying to get the better of us, and you are doing nothing about it! Your people are freezing, Gromoth!"

"This human has brought us this far…"

"No! We brought *THEM* this far! And what have they done for us?"

"What do you suggest we do, Dina?" Gromoth asked, raising his voice to a level Dawn had not yet heard from him. "Would you like to kill them?" Krom and Dawn both recoiled from the suggestion. "We must put our trust in them, and I will not turn away now. The only way to earn trust is to give it. This is the only way."

As Gromoth spoke, Dura approached from the back of the pack on her own war dog. "What is this about? Why have we stopped?"

"Ask them," Dina responded coldly, flipping around toward the back of the pack. "That city should belong to us. And the longer we wait, the more our people suffer under the rule of those murderous humans."

"Leave us!" Gromoth commanded, silencing all the whispers of the tribe. He marched up to the war dog, unconcerned as it snarled and bared its teeth. "If that is what you truly believe, then you have no place in this tribe. Leave."

Without hesitation, Dina kicked her boot against the dog's hind and galloped off into the distance. Dura gazed after her, glancing back and forth between Gromoth and Dina. Finally, she raced off to catch her sister.

"Don't let me down, reaver." Gromoth turned toward Cain with a sickening grimace.

Gromoth hiked down toward the tribe, beginning the process of setting up camp. The humans glanced at each other and commenced their journey toward the top of the hill. Unaware of what lay on the other side, the trek seemed to take forever, every step weighing more than the last. Their feet sunk deep into the soft earth and cold wind bit at their faces, blowing harder the higher they ascended.

When they had finally reached the crest of the hill, Dawn beheld the sight in the valley. Bodies. Hundreds of bodies, piled upon one another. Men were laboring to clear away the carnage, but not much progress had yet been made. Making their way down to the battlefield, Dawn carefully stepped over the corpses. Stomach acid stung at her throat. Rain fell on the weary travellers, loosely masking the reek of decay.

Each carcass screamed of the battle that preceded, but silence lay over the stained dead grass. Dawn's mind wandered to the mothers and fathers, brothers and sisters who waited in vain. Each of these soldiers had been so innocent once. Telling stories and laughing with their friends at silly tales. Now, they just lay as a feast for the crows, a bitter winter wind brushing their flooded faces.

"Stop right there!" One of the laborers drew a blade as they approached the gates. "State your business!"

Cain raised his hands in surrender. "We are reavers in need of passage to the Citadel. We need to speak with your Lord, Lord Artimus."

The laborers huddled to discuss the strangers on the threshold to their city. Their mistrust was well placed, considering the carnage just outside their gates. A familiar voice echoed in Dawn's mind, "Why should they trust you? You lead the enemy to their doorstep."

"They aren't enemies," Dawn whispered under her breath. Cain glanced toward her, but quickly turned back to their potential hosts.

Finally, the huddle broke, and one man called out to the travellers, "We will grant you entry to our city, but first you must lay down your weapons."

Dawn and Krom both gazed toward Cain, who nodded in agreement. One piece at a time they removed their equipment, laying it all at the feet of the laborers and guards. Krom, however, held onto one small blade which was still attached to his ankle, hidden under the cloth of his pants.

Obliviously, the guards nodded at each other and guided the companions into the city, sliding their own weapons into the safety of their sheaths. Outside the gates, rugged crosses bunched in groups of three stood guard, each decorated with a lifeless warrior hanging from the beams. As the gates opened, Dawn saw her first glimpse of Port Aurora. On most days, the city would be a sight to behold. Merchants and vagabonds would travel from all over Quarrine as it was the only port city on the eastern coast. If someone wanted access to Cirrane and the Citadel, they would have to go through the port.

Now, as Dawn walked through the empty streets, she saw nothing of the wonder this city could bring. The pouring rain amplified the despair clouding each avenue. Other than the patrolling guards on duty, not a single soul greeted them. Gusts of bitter wind wound between the well-built wooden buildings. The taste of salt in the air was diluted in the heavy rain. Water poured off the burgundy roof shingles, puddling on the rustic beige brick lining the road.

As they rounded a corner, Dawn noticed boxes and crates in the alleyways leading closer to the docks. On the crates were strange markings concealed by maroon stains. Some of them brandished a winged horse, while others held the same mark she had seen many times before; a teardrop atop a cross. Suddenly, her amulet felt heavy around her neck, as if it were draining her energy as she walked between the buildings.

"You aren't safe here," Dawn heard the voice speak in her mind. "No one is safe."

Dawn glanced back and forth around her. The more she searched, the more crates she noticed with the teardrop label. Then she started to see the same symbol displayed on doors and walls, everywhere. Rain water washed away scarlet stains from the streets, revealing the same emblems. They were surrounded.

"Here we are," the guard stopped at a stone building at the edge of the water. The doors stood tall and glamorous, large oaken slabs decorated in steel trimmings. "Only one may enter to speak with our Lord. Reaver, please follow me."

As Cain followed the guard into the building, Dawn glanced to the roof of the capitol building, where a large horn was nestled inside a stone chamber, ready to sound at the sign of attack from the coast. She trembled in her boots. The voice in her mind continued to speak to her, warnings of impending doom. "You are in danger," the voice repeated.

She had no reason to believe the voice now. That part of her was angry. Pessimistic. Hateful. Even fearful. That wasn't what Dawn wanted to be in her life, but still she had an urge in her bones to flee. Her eyes scanned the city for escape routes and hiding places, readying for the worst scenario.

Dawn closed her eyes, concentrating on her breath. Breathe in.... and out. Slow. Steady. Easing her heart beat. Sedating her mind.

When she opened her eyes, the rain stopped. Not a break in the clouds, but the drops had actually suspended midair. The wind ceased to blow, but Dawn and Krom were both very aware of their conditions.

"What is happening?" Krom whimpered, looking at Dawn. "Did you do this? Is this your magic?"

"I... I don't know," Dawn replied.

* * *

As Dina ran off, Dura followed her sister across the plains until they were both out of sight of the rest of the tribe. Thick fog like honey engulfed the valley. As if she were being pursued by a predator, Dina rode into the wilderness of Quarrine. Soon, trees and rock formations made it difficult for Dura to follow. She could hardly keep track of her sister's trek through the region. The fog sucked the color out of the world. It grasped her heart like ice. As she approached, she nearly called out again. An unfamiliar voice, rough and heavy, speaking in the cold wilderness confirmed her darkening thoughts. "Things are going according to plan, then?"

Dura dismounted her dog and crept to a looming rock nearby. She couldn't see much, but Dina's voice was unmistakable. "The girl and her friends will be alone soon," she said. "It's just a matter of time now."

Before Dura could identify the other two shadowy figures standing with Dina, she jumped back onto her dog and raced as fast as she could to the tribe.

Water began falling from the sky with purpose. Normally, the droplets were lazy, as if there was nothing better to do than fall from their home in the clouds above. But this time, each drop carried a sense of malice. An army of challengers hampering the progress Dura was making across the fields. But with each drop, the fog dissipated.

Still, she rushed back, until she stumbled into the battlefield that had immobilized the tribe. Black clouds in the dark sky had flooded the graveyard below. Though the grass looked normal, each squishy step told a different story. The soft earth below swallowed her dog's feet, nearly tripping over himself.

Suddenly, as if a curtain were being lifted from her eyes, the bodies began to disappear, evaporating into the air. One at a time, until the field was clear of any hindrances, the massacre faded out of sight. Dura watched in astonishment as the facade vanished from her eyes, but she quickly pulled herself together and rode back to the tribe. That was the proof she needed. There was something else at work here. Something unnatural.

***

Hooded figures rounded the corner of the capitol building. Disguised as Guild Hunters, their hoods bore the same teardrop emblem that had littered the city. Dawn and Krom were quickly surrounded by these menacing strangers.

Krom kneeled down for his knife. "This isn't good," he whispered to Dawn. "They must have been waiting for us."

Dawn focused on the power she summoned all that time ago in the wilderness. Her latent magical powers. She held out her hands, and concentrated.

But there was no time. The Hunters descended on them at lightning speed, brandishing their own blades in an attempt to cut down the travellers. Krom parried what he could with his knife, but he couldn't hold back the attack. As one foe swung his blade, another shot a blast of dark magic at his feet, sending him flying back into the stone wall of the capitol building.

Dawn ducked and dodged the best she could, but she was no match. She fell on the slick brick pathway, her head slamming against the pavement. A sudden rush of pain jolted throughout her body. She could feel the scabs and scars on her back reopen and the blood run down her skin. She touched the back of her head feeling the wound left by the stone floor. Her tongue tasted of blood.

Opening her eyes, she couldn't see anything except shapes and colors. Beams of color and light flashed through her vision. *Is this the end?* She thought. *Was all of the fighting for nothing?*

"Get up!" A muffled voice shouted. It was a man's voice, but not one she recognized. Suddenly, her mind snapped back into focus, and she heard it again. "You need to get up now!"

Her vision cleared and she saw two humans had joined the fight. Their blood-stained weapons glimmered as they slashed into the hooded enemies. Dawn glanced next to her.

The blade of a departed foe lay within reach. She gripped it and stood to her feet, readying herself for her adversary.

One by one, the hooded figures fell to the newly invigorated party. Krom jumped back into action, and their new colleagues used their own magic to counteract the dark mages. As the Hunters were eliminated, their bodies evaporated into a fine dust. Rain released from its suspended state.

When all threats had finally been terminated, Dawn gazed upon their rescuers. Two human warriors, a man and a woman. The man's intimidating physique reminded her of Ragnar. He wore loose fitting rags and was equipped with nothing but one of the largest swords Dawn had ever seen. The woman donned heavy blue armor, and carried a long steel spear and shield.

With a single hand the man swung the weight of the massive blade up onto his shoulder, resting it on a leather insignia featuring a winged horse. From his towering height he peered down at Dawn with his dark brown eyes and spoke with a booming deep voice. "The port is no longer safe."

Krom readied his blade, untrusting of the strangers. "Who are you?"

"Ephras!" the woman called out, glancing over to the hulking man and paying no attention to Krom's question. "We have to get moving."

The man looked down at Krom with a comforting smile. "I am Ephras and this is Kaela. We are peacekeepers from the Citadel investigating the movements of the cult Ulumbra. We tracked them here." Dawn recalled the words of the Guild Captain from Oasis regarding Ulumbra. "Where is Cain?" Ephras continued. "He had sent for us to meet him here."

Just the mention of her mentor's name blasted lightning through Dawn's body, and without another word, she bolted up the stairs leading to the capitol building doors. With her companions behind her, she launched her body against the solid oak doors, breaking them open with a blast of energy that discharged from deep within her. Inside and up multiple sets of stairs they ran to find Cain, holding a blade against the throat of a vulture of man that lay on the floor. The man's face shifted into different shapes, taking the form of multiple personas uncontrollably.

Dawn's unexpected entrance pulled Cain's attention toward the front door, and the shape shifter kicked at Cain's feet, knocking him to the ground with him.

"Get away from him!" A scream exploded from Dawn. Without even thinking, fiery beams shot from her hands, electricity emanating throughout the flow of her magic. The man flew backwards into the window behind him, crashing through to the brick streets below.

Suddenly, the sound of rain rebounding off the roof was silenced, as if the clouds had cleared. Dawn ran over to Cain, pulling on his hand to help him to his feet. He glanced at the peacekeepers who had found his way up the stairs. "Ephras! Kaela! I am glad to see you here."

"It feels like it has been ages, my friend," Ephras responded, hugging the exhausted reaver.

Shouts echoed from outside the building doors. Kaela readied her spear atop her shield and stared towards the front doors. "Ephras!" She shouted. "No time for snuggles. We gotta go!"

Before any other words could be said, the doors were

blasted off their hinges, hurled and twisted on the ground. All about, stone, cracked and splintered into countless jagged shards, exploded from the walls around the doors and piled into ruinous heaps. Hundreds of hooded soldiers now stood at the doorstep, charging in one at a time with weapons drawn. Ephras and Kaela stormed to the ruin in a flash of steel and magic, slowing the flood of enemies.

Dawn jumped to her feet to help the fighters, but Cain tugged on her arm. "If we can sound the Coastal Horn on the roof," he stated. "Maybe it will signal Gromoth and the orcs to rush in and help us."

Leaving the peacekeepers to hold the front door from the flood of attackers, Dawn, Krom, and Cain ran to the back of the room to a set of stairs guiding them upwards into the building. As they climbed, Krom glanced outside to see Guild Hunters climbing up the walls of the building and into the windows. They picked up their pace up the stairs.

Suddenly, rushing down from the roof were more Hunters with blades in hand. Krom tossed his knife upward into one of the attacker's throats, sending him tumbling down the stairs. They jumped over his rolling body, Krom retrieving his knife, and charged the oncoming threat head-on. Dawn and Cain flashed their steel seamlessly, fighting like a single mind in two separate bodies. When Cain needed assistance, Dawn was already there, and when Dawn overextended herself, Cain was prepared to watch her back.

Soon, they reached the roof, glancing passed a crowd of enemies to see their target. Cain searched within himself for energy to simplify their fight, but he was still so tired from the excursion of the previous weeks. He grasped his sword tightly, shoulder to shoulder with Dawn and Krom.

The Hunters charged them with determination, but to no avail. Like one sword, the three travellers cut down their opponents with ease. One at a time the Hunters fell to the experienced blades.

Soon, their enemies were few. Cain shouted to Krom, "Move forward! Sound the horn. We got this back here."

Krom quickly averted himself to the outskirts of the battle, jumping and dancing between ledges and un-maneuverable obstacles. He moved with comfort, avoiding the blows of any enemies who would give him chase.

Dawn and Cain continued to fight in sync with each other. As Dawn waved her sword, Cain would defend her exposed body.

"There you are, girl!" A rough, deep voice shouted from behind them.

Dawn turned to see Greenwood climbing up onto the roof of the building. In one hand he wielded a longsword, and in the other was a short hatchet. Fire burned from within her, her eyes glimmering with hate. She rushed toward the Guild captain, leaving her mentor behind.

"Dawn!" Cain called, but she didn't hear him. The noises of the world around her had silenced, and all she heard was a ringing in her ears, along with the memories of her family's voices.

She rushed forward, slamming her sword into the man, but he had brought up his own sword to defend, swinging his axe around at Dawn's head. She dropped to the floor, out of the way of the axe. But Greenwood didn't stop. He slashed down at her with his sword, then his axe, cycling through his choices of weapon as Dawn rolled out of the way as quickly as she could. Each time the captain's metal struck the ground, the sharp ringing of steel upon rock blared into Dawn's ears. Finally, she avoided one last strike and kicked upward into the captain's chest, throwing him backwards into the barrier that kept him from falling off the roof of the building.

Dawn jumped to her feet, but as she found her footing, her eyesight had blurred. "Everywhere you go, Dawn," the same familiar voice whispered in her ear. A strange force in her body forced her head to turn. She watched Cain, struggling among the fighters she had left him to. Suddenly, an arrow flew through the air, striking Cain in the shoulder, dropping him to his knees. He looked to Dawn with sadness in his eyes before collapsing into the rubble beneath him.

"NO!" She screamed, energy blazing to life from within her. She extended out her arms and lightning flashed in front of her, striking down each of the Hunters that were descending on Cain's body. Bodies flew from the roof in each direction until it was only Dawn and Greenwood still standing.

"What are you?" Greenwood trembled as she turned to him. Her eyes had glossed over, rage filling her. Electricity emanated from her fingertips and around her sword.

She stepped toward Greenwood with ill intent. A menacing smirk drew across her face. The captain, in a blind burst of hope, rushed forward, but Dawn shouted one last time, another bolt blasting from her person. It made contact with Greenwood and shot him over the ledge of the building, plummeting to the streets below.

Quickly Dawn came back to her senses. She clenched her

eyes shut in an attempt to see clearly, stumbling over her own feet. When finally she forced her eyes open, it was as if she was seeing double. She gazed absently at the body of one of the Hunters who had been cut down before, pressing her eyes shut again. When she reopened them, the body lying in front of her had transformed into that of her mother's, a silhouette like a reflection standing over her.

"You did this," Dawn's own voice came out from the silhouette. "Cain too. Chaos surrounds you. Death follows you."

"Stop," Dawn mumbled, glaring at the shadow standing in front of her. The battle below had completely escaped her consciousness.

"There are no coincidences."

"No!" Energy radiated around Dawn like a fire. Darkness descended on the city, as if the sun and moon were obliterated from the sky.

"Dawn," the reflection calmly spoke.

"Why are you following me?" Dawn shouted, though her lips never moved. "What do you want from me?"

"Dawn, you can't get rid of me," the reflection said. "As much as you can't get rid of your shadow. You don't always see me, but I am always there."

Just then, a horn blared from the other side of the rooftop, snapping Dawn back into reality. Her reflection burst into a blaze of fire and the sky filled with light once again. She clenched the hilt of her sword and pushed herself back up, eyeing the body of her mentor. She rushed to him, checking his pulse for signs of life. To her relief, she felt the thumps of a weak heartbeat, still pumping the blood through his veins.

Krom sounded the horn again, waiting for a response

from the army waiting outside. One more time, and finally the sound of an orc horn blared from the walls of the city, the roar of an invading army rushing into the streets like rushing water.

"Cain!" Dawn shouted, shaking her companion in an attempt to return to consciousness. "Cain, just hold on! You can't go! Not now!

Krom rushed to her side, watching Cain's chest rise and fall at slower and slower rates. "What happened?" He asked.

Before she could answer, a blaze of light burst from the street up to the rooftop, and suddenly, Greenwood stood in front of them again. Except he wasn't the same. His body was mangled and his face contorted. "It won't be that easy, girl," his voice gargled beneath the blood that filled his lungs.

Before Krom or Dawn could respond, fire exploded from Greenwood's hands, blasting towards the companions. Krom tackled Dawn, as the heat flashed past their bodies. The blasts crashed into the side of the building next door, and unnaturally engulfed the brick and stone walls.

Dawn grasped Cain's cloak and pulled him out of the open. She glanced up, but two more fire blasts had already discharged from their nemesis. She grasped the cloth on Krom's back and rolled them as fast as she could out of their trajectory and behind a wall nearby. Krom quickly jumped up, yanking Dawn to her feet.

Krom threw his knife towards the zombie of a man. The blade stopped in the air, a strange aura emanating around it. Abruptly, the steel blade exploded, launching shrapnel in every direction.

"That won't work on me, boy!" The captain snarled.

Dawn's breathing intensified, stumbling along the wall to find cover behind a table. "Fos, help me now," she whispered to herself with her eyes closed. "I need you now."

Just then, a light shone from her fingertips. Warmth came over her body, though she couldn't stop shivering. Without thinking, she jumped up. Her arm shot out toward the monster. Waves of lightning exploded out of her palms, crashing into the walls of the surrounding buildings.

One single bolt launched into the mangled captain, blasting him back to the floor behind him. Dawn strode toward the sorcerer. The aura emanating around her lit the city like a star lighting up the night sky. When she looked at her hands, it seemed as if they were shining bright and engulfed in shadow at the same time.

The man gazed up at Dawn, grinding his teeth and clenching his fists. As Dawn readied another magical blast, the captain jumped up, prepared for the attack. Flashes of lightning strobed through the sky, but every bit of the energy sucked up into the hands of the sorcerer, who released his own shockwave, shaking the very foundation of the building.

Dawn flew backwards into the wall, crashing through the stone and tumbling down the stairs leading back down into the capitol building. Stopping her descent, Ephras stood and caught her in his giant arms, lifting her back to her feet. Behind him followed Kaela and a squad of orcs, leaving a slew of enemy bodies in the foyer. Ephras and Kaela pressed on up the stairs with weapons drawn. They glared at the sorcerer standing on the other side of the rooftop. Gromoth and the Thradak tribe flooded onto the roof next, stamping over the bodies of the enemies who lay dead, Dura storming in behind them on her war dog.

Greenwood snarled, gathering energy in his hands. Suddenly, a flare erupted behind the dark sorcerer, and there stood a tall, pale woman. Her black hair hung down past her waist and covered her dark, menacing eyes. She wore no hood, but instead a dark purple and black cloak. Her dress seemed to have life of its own as it wavered in the wind, though Dawn couldn't feel even a breeze in the cool coastal air. The air had died and lay still upon the city.

"Finally, I see your face," the woman spoke with an air of elegance, staring down at Dawn.

The witch peered across the rooftop, sneering at the reunited companions. "We are done here, Greenwood," she commanded. "We know when we have been beaten." She waved her hands, and a rush of heavy wind blew across the rooftop. A flash of light, and as quickly as she had appeared, her and the Guild captain vanished.

14

Seabound

Dawn rushed over to Cain, kneeling on the stone roof. He still drew breath, but each inhale was weaker than the last. Ephras strode over and grasped the arrow that had pierced his shoulder. "Poison. He is in danger."

Dawn gazed up at her new companion with tears welling up in her eyes. "Can you save him?"

"Here? No," Ephras responded. "I have medicine on my ship that could return his strength and slow the poison, but he needs Citadel medicine."

Ephras draped Cain over his shoulder and carried him down the stairs and toward the docks of the port city. A small sack slipped from Cain's person, catching Dawn's attention. Dawn collected the bag and peered within, seeing four small stones, smooth to the touch, nestled inside. She tied off the mouth of the bag and rushed to Gromoth and hugged him.

"Thank you so much!" She wailed in his arms. "Thank you so much!"

Gromoth released Dawn; but allowed her to lean on him as they strode toward the dock. "You should thank Dura," he laughed. "She snuffed out that evil before I even thought something was amiss."

Dawn gazed toward Dura, who had been pacing alongside with her hand on the hilt of her blade. She stared toward the ground, watching her own feet as she walked.

"Dura?" Dawn called out. She continued to walk as if she had not heard a word.

"Although today we have victory," Gromoth started, "not all our battles have been won."

Dawn glanced between Dura and Gromoth. "What happened?"

Gromoth's tone softened. "After Dina ran off, Dura followed her sister across the plains until they were both out of sight of the rest of the tribe. What she discovered there was... disturbing."

"Dina is one of them," Dura said. "She helped orchestrate this mess."

"Dura watched as the illusion faded on the battlefield," Gromoth stated. "It must have been a spell these sorcerers were casting. A way to keep us orcs away, making us believe that a great battle took place with Grumuk's tribe. Simply a facade. I have always hated magic."

"Hear, hear!" Krom encroached on the conversation from behind. "From illusions to that stupid teleporting spell the witch used, the living world is better without interference from the gods."

Dura gazed back toward the ground, as if she were counting each brick that lined the road as she walked by them. Dawn wandered over to her and tugged on her shoulder. "Thank you, Dura."

Dura jolted up before calmly responding. "For what?"

"You came back."

As they approached the peacekeeper's boat, Dawn couldn't help but look out over the water adjacent to the port city. It sparkled in the setting sunlight, the gleams seeming brighter from the earlier stormy weather. As if in sync with Dawn's own lungs, the ocean breathed alongside her, the surface rising and falling with rhythmic ease. The waves crashing against the dock matched Dawn's pulse, and for the first time in a long time, she felt peace. She reached behind her head to feel for the wound that had been left from the skirmish before, but to her surprise, the wound had closed.

"Crazy, isn't it?" Dawn turned to find Krom standing with her, staring out over the ocean as well.

"What's that?" She asked nervously.

"Such beauty in this world," Krom stated. "When behind us there is so much carnage. How can something so beautiful exist alongside so much evil?"

"Dawn! Krom!" Ephras shouted from the boat. "Let's go! Your reaver still needs a healer!"

Dawn sighed, turning away from the beauty of the ocean.

"Don't worry," Krom reassured her. "He's going to be okay."

They both smiled and raced to the boat, where Gromoth and Ephras had already been making the final arrangements before setting sail. "What will you do?" Ephras asked, untying the rope anchoring the ship to the dock.

"We will stay here," Gromoth answered. "Clean the city up and give our tribe a place to call home."

Krom stopped in his tracks. "That is suicide! You know the Guild won't allow you to stay!"

"It isn't like the city has been very hospitable to humans recently either," Gromoth responded. "From the looks of things, the sorcerers have been holding their illusion over us for a long time. We will not bring trouble to the Guild, but we will defend ourselves if we need to. We hope this can be the beginning of the end of this war between orcs and humans."

Krom sighed. "Can't say I carry your optimism."

"But we trust to hope," Ephras interrupted. "If we can send help from the Citadel, we will do what we can."

Gromoth nodded, and smiled toward Dawn, "Goodbye, girl."

Dawn rushed to her orc friend and embraced him one last time before boarding the ship and setting sail across the sea.

As the ship embarked, Dawn examined its structure. The creaky wooden planks that made up the deck forced a queasy feeling into her stomach. Kaela pulled on some lines and red sails unfurled from the tall mast above. A winged horse brandished the sails, decorated in magnificent purples and golds.

The ship had been underway for a while when Krom approached Kaela with a smile plastered on his face. "Hey!" He flirted. "This is a great ship. Have you sailed much?"

Kaela turned away without saying a word, rushing toward the starboard side to maneuver some more lines, tying more knots. Krom couldn't be stopped though, as he followed her like a shadow. "Would you like any help?"

She glared at him with a piercing gaze, cold as a glacier, before turning her shoulder again. Krom's smile quickly dissolved, but before he could say anything, Ephras emerged from the depths of the ship and interrupted. "Don't worry about her," he said. "She will warm up as you get to know her."

"We just fought together!" Krom shouted back, making space between him and the standoffish woman. "You would think that we would be warmed up by now."

"And you would be surprised," Ephras laughed. "Kaela is special. Give her time, and you may see the same thing I see in her."

"How did you two meet?" Dawn asked, taking a seat on the wooden stairs leading up to the steering wheel.

"I have known Kaela my whole life," Ephras laughed. "She is my younger sister. Second youngest of the family, next to Alyina."

"And both of you are peacekeepers?" Krom asked with a gasp.

"It's kind of a family business," Ephras said. "Our sister Thea was a peacekeeper too. You could say that she inspired Kaela to join the ranks."

"Was?" Dawn inquired. "What happened?" Ephras was silent, gazing toward Kaela who hadn't stopped working around the ship. Before the silence had become unbearable, Dawn asked a different question. "What is a peacekeeper?"

Krom laughed, spotting the shock on Ephras' face. "She is a little sheltered from the world," Krom assured him. "Hadn't seen anything east of Oasis before a month ago."

"What a shame," Ephras smiled. His looming figure was

intimidating, yet comforting at the same time. Like a big stuffed bear, he was more reassuring than dangerous. "We will have to show you everything you need to see once we make land. Peacekeepers are the law of the Citadel. We investigate and arrest criminals, defend the streets, and do what we can to keep the Council safe."

"Why were you in Port Aurora?" Dawn asked.

"Well, we were investigating," Ephras answered. "Ulumbra, the cult that helped Moldolor come into power, has been making some waves recently."

That name again. Moldolor. Dawn had heard the stories, but had never thought that the danger he brought into the world was so real. Every time she heard his name mentioned, she couldn't help but to shiver.

"And we had reports that the witch Ariyah, who had been a right hand to Dark sorcerer, had resurfaced and was amassing followers in Quarrine. They had even infiltrated the Guild. Utilizing a higher position to support their own goals," Ephras continued. "Which I am glad we investigated, because we found all of that to be true. As well as meeting you." He smiled down at Dawn.

Dawn smiled back for a second before her face couldn't hide her questions anymore. "Ariyah..." She mumbled under her breath.

"She was the witch that vanished there at the end of our engagement," Ephras' voice sharpened. "There were always stories about how she had fled to the mountains of Quarrine after the war, but no one could ever find her. Kaela and I have encountered Ulumbra many times, but they always slither their way into tomorrow. Dealing with dark magic can be a tricky thing."

"Yeah. Tricky and dangerous." Krom agreed. "You're telling me that the Guild is partnered with those lunatics?"

"The Guild doesn't know they are being used," Ephras stated. "Wear a Guild insignia and suddenly you can search houses, or conduct raids. Even collect taxes. Imagine what you could do with a little bit of trust from the director himself."

The sun passed over the deep blue sky until it set in the horizon. Midnight came as Krom lay asleep on the wooden stairs leading up to the steering wheel where Ephras guided the boat. He waved his hands left and right, controlling aspects of the current with his magical hand. The sails cracked under the heavy ocean wind, pushing the ship across the deep sea.

"You don't have to stay up here, you know?" Ephras stated, gazing into the open ocean that lay before him.

Dawn peered up to the captain quizzically.

"I promise you won't be missing anything up here tonight if you go down and find an actual bed in the cabins below deck," Ephras continued. "There is even a spare bed in Cain's cabin, if you wanted to watch over him for the night."

"Are you sure you and Kaela don't need any help?"

Ephras grinned. "We have been doing this a long time," he stated. "Go get your rest. Embrace the new beginning this midnight delivers. Let the past pass, and recover your strength for the future."

Dawn descended below deck, checking each door for her mentor. Finally, she spotted him bundled up in canvas blankets, his chest slowly rising and falling as he rested beneath the deck of the peacekeeper's ship. She noticed another bed in the corner of the room, decorated with soft cloth blankets and pillows. Calmly, she approached Cain and grasped the small satchel he had dropped in the earlier skirmish and placed it on the nightstand nearby, resting her hand on his arm. Out of the corner of her eye, she saw a shadow shift near her bed, and she let out a sigh.

"Can you ever just leave me be?" Dawn asked.

The shadow emerged from the corner of the room, and materialized into her reflection. "I know you are stubborn," she responded. "But you aren't stupid. You have never been alone, Dawn. And you never will be."

Dawn silently gazed at her mentor, attempting to ignore the figure imposing on her time alone.

"Even when you experience the power we have together first hand, you still try to be rid of me," the reflection scoffed.

Dawn glanced up, but quickly returned her attention to Cain. "What do you mean?"

"You witnessed our power against that sorcerer!" The reflection responded. "You had never experienced anything like that before. That is what happens when you are in alignment with yourself. When you and I are in unity with each other." Dawn didn't avert her gaze from her friend, but her reflection now held her attention. "When we fight together, there aren't many who are more powerful than us. Not even Moldolor himself."

Dawn spiraled around to lock eyes with her reflection, glaring. "I don't want that kind of power! Especially if *THIS* is the price of that power!" She pointed to Cain. "I want a quiet, normal life. The life I had before. Before all of this. Before you." Tears formed in her eyes.

Her reflection laughed. "Your life has never been normal. From the minute you were born, we were destined for greatness. It's really too bad that village deprived you of our destiny for so long."

"That isn't true!" Dawn shouted.

Suddenly, the reflection disappeared. The air in the room lightened, and Dawn felt a weight release from her shoulders.

"Who are you talking to?"

Shocked, Dawn spun back around to witness Cain sitting up in his bed, rubbing his hand over his shoulder. Without a word, she jolted forward and embraced him, forgetting momentarily about his health. Wincing, he allowed the affectionate display. Dawn released after many seconds. "Sorry! I didn't mean to hurt you. But I am just so glad you are ok. How are you feeling? Do you need anything? I can get you something to drink, or something to eat. I think Ephras has kline on ice nearby, and I know how much you enjoy kline. Unless you aren't hungry? Whatever you need..."

"Woah!" Cain laughed at the sheer number of words unraveling from Dawn's lips. "Slow down there, hon. Thank you for the offer, but I am alright." He coughed a couple times before resuming. "I knew Ephras and Kaela would come through, just didn't know how. I imagine this is Ephras' ship?"

"Yeah!" Dawn answered. "Headed to the Citadel. We left Gromoth and the tribe back at the port to try their luck with the Guild. We didn't like the idea, but Gromoth and Dura insisted."

"How long was I out?"

"It has been a while," Dawn said, gazing toward the floor. "Close to 24 hours. Ephras confirmed that the tip of the arrow that struck you was poisoned."

"Ahh," Cain scratched his head. "I am starting to remember now."

"I'm..." Dawn's words choked in her mouth. "I'm so sorry Cain. I just left you, and I shouldn't have. You wouldn't be here if it weren't for me..."

"Dawn," Cain interrupted. "Do you remember when we left Oasis? We knew that the Guild would be looking for us. And yet, we chose to stay the course. I knew the danger. We all did. Maybe that fight on the roof could have gone differently, but what if something worse would have happened? The way the pieces fell, things are okay. Don't torture yourself with the 'what ifs'." Cain chuckled under his breath, releasing a cough into his elbow as well.

"You should get some more rest," Dawn said, holding back the tears from her eyes. "It seems to be doing you some good, seeing that you are able to wake up now."

Cain sighed, nodding in agreement. "Yeah, you are right. I won't be any use to anyone in the state I am in now."

Dawn slowly trotted to her bed, slipping under the soft blankets. When she looked over to check on her friend, he had already passed out of consciousness. She wiped her heavy eyes as she closed them for the night.

Nighttime faded into morning, and the sun's rays peeked in through the curtains covering the windows below the deck. Calls of the birds flying overhead were muffled by the waves crashing against the hull of the ship. The gleam of the sun shone on Dawn's face, warming her thoughts as she awoke from her dreamless sleep.

It had been months since she had a dreamless sleep. Terrors had haunted her nightly to remind her of her failures in her village. Dawn wasn't sure if this was her subconscious fearing the past, or if her reflection was humiliating her for her mistakes. But this night was different. A new day. Maybe Ephras was right, and the past could finally pass.

Dawn peered around the room, and saw that Cain was awake and already dressed in fresh, unstained clothes. "I thought you were going to try and sleep?" She asked with a look of disapproval.

Cain laughed. "I have been sleeping for many hours, Dawn. Just because I woke up before you, doesn't mean that I am putting off my healing." He opened the curtains and sat on his bed, gazing out across the sea. "So, yesterday..." He started.

"Yes?"

"Who is it you were talking to?" Cain asked with a more serious tone. "It seemed you were upset until I spoke up."

Dawn paused with her mouth wide open. Her face flushed tones of red and pink as the blood rushed to her head. "I..." She started, but she couldn't find the words.

"Sorry," Cain apologized. "If you don't want to tell me, you don't have to. You just seemed upset, and I wanted to help if there was anything I could do."

"Look at you," Dawn laughed. "On the brink of death, and the moment you awake, you are already putting others before yourself." Silence engulfed the room for what felt like forever. "I... don't know exactly who I was talking to,"

Dawn sighed. "I have been having these dreams and visions that seem so real. Like a reflection of who I am, but much darker. It seems so lifelike, but no one else has ever seen it. Even yesterday, the reflection was here in this room, but you obviously couldn't see it."

Cain responded. "Even though some things can't be seen, that doesn't mean they aren't real. You can't see the wind, but we all feel the effects of a hurricane."

Dawn peered down at the floorboards beneath her. "I am learning more and more about myself in these last few months. More than ever before." She glanced back up to Cain. "Normally that would sound like a good thing. People spend their whole lives discovering themselves. Though I don't know if I really appreciate who I am becoming. There is a part of me that I am getting more and more familiar with that I'm not sure I like. The part of me that attacked Greenwood at Ragnar's house, and left your side for the sake of revenge."

Cain took in this information and thought long and hard before giving a calm response. "Just because you are on a path to one destination, doesn't mean that you must arrive at that destination. Your destiny is yours to do with what you will. If you don't like the direction, you can change course."

"I wish it were that easy," Dawn responded. "It may just be surfacing now, but I think I have been on this path my entire life. How can you just uproot and do something different after all this time?"

"You have done it before," Cain said. "Maybe not to the extent we are talking about, but you have. You were forced to. And you may be forced to again."

"I hope not."

As Dawn spoke, a shout resounded from the deck above them. Puzzled, Cain stood to his feet, but crumbled under the weight of his own body. Dawn bolted to his side, placing his healthy arm around her shoulder to support him as they made their way toward the deck.

Dawn swung the door from the depths of the ship out to the wide-open airspace of the world beyond. Standing on the deck, Krom watched the skies unblinking, not noticing that Cain had woken from his sleep. Dawn peered upward, noticing beasts flying in the skies above, littering the sky like stars in the night. "What are they?" Dawn asked, never shifting her gaze.

"Those are the pegasus fliers of the Citadel," Ephras answered as he continued steering the ship. "Good to see you awake Cain! How are you feeling? I don't have all the skills of a Council healer, but I can make due when the need arises."

Cain glanced back at the peacekeeper, "I have been better, but at least I am awake. Thank you for that."

As the old friends caught up with each other, Dawn watched the skies above. Aside from the fliers, it was completely clear, as if the clouds had forgotten to roll in for the day. Suddenly, one of the winged horses descended toward the ship. The pegasus and its rider moved faster than anything she had ever seen. She hardly had time to think before the flier was upon them, landing on the deck of the ship.

The pegasus clad in armor decorated with jewels and colorful cloth. The sun shone brightly upon its bright white coat. Dawn had witnessed horses back on Quarrine, but this was no wild beast. It stood at attention like a soldier forming ranks. It didn't whinny or twitch. Even as its rider dismounted.

"Ephras! When you left, it was just you and your sister!" The man shouted toward the ship's captain. "Who are these you bring to the shores of Cirrane?"

"Silas?" Cain inquired before Ephras could speak. "Are you saying you don't recognize me?"

The man peered at the weak man, studying him from head to toe. "Cain?" He asked. "Cain! I can't believe it. You had been gone for so long, we thought you had died! Or worse, that you were staying in Oasis with your katze friend. Unpleasant character he always was." He paused as he looked toward Dawn and Krom. "What of these two? I don't recognize them. There is no way this boy isn't a Quarrine native." Silas sneered at the dark man standing on the other side of the ship.

Krom's hand wandered to the hilt of his sword, the grin disappearing from his face. Noticing the gesture of the Quarrinian, Silas followed suit before Cain could quickly interrupt. "No need for any of that!" He shouted, coughing into his shoulder. "These two are great people. Dawn has an aunt living in the Citadel, and Krom helped us in some reaver business. Helped kill an anguis in the canyon."

"He also assisted in the tracking of a fugitive of the Citadel," Ephras said, strutting down the stairs to the deck. "An Ulumbra witch that plotted to assassinate Council priests."

"I probably wouldn't be alive if it weren't for him," Cain continued.

Silas glared toward Krom, examining his demeanor. Slowly, he straightened back to the posture of the soldier he was. "They must check in with the Council once you land," Silas stated. "Taran must allow them to stay, otherwise we send them back."

"You don't need to worry about us, Silas!" Ephras laughed. "We are peacekeepers; we know the regulations of the Citadel. We could use your pegasus' speed though, if you don't mind. Cain needs a Council healer as soon as possible. Could you fly him to the Citadel for healing?"

Silas nodded and the crew helped Cain onto the back of the pegasus. Silas jumped up with him, and with a kick of his heels, the horse leaped over the ledge of the ship, and flew up toward the flock circling overhead.

15

The White Council

That night, the moon stood out as a giant in the sky, gleaming against the surface of the water. Dawn gazed out over the quiet sea, lost in thought. The still water reflected back up to her and she saw, for the first time, the scar on her cheek. She ran her hand up to feel the raised skin, but all tenderness had faded. The scar had fully welded the wound shut. Tears filled her eyes, shimmering there briefly until finally they dropped from her lashes to her new blemish.

She had been standing there on the deck alone for some time before the sound of footsteps clunking on the wooden floors startled her. She turned to find Krom and Kaela emerging together from below, laughing as Kaela took over for Ephras as the ship's pilot for the night.

Krom turned toward Dawn, who had since wiped the evidence of her pain away from her eyes. "You know," he started. "She really is a pretty cool person once she opens up."

"I am glad to see you two doing better," Dawn smiled. "How did you crack her shell?"

"I was rolling some dice downstairs, and she insisted on playing," Krom responded. "After that, it only took a couple minutes and she was actually telling me jokes. And funny ones too!"

Dawn nodded, turning back out to the sea, gazing beyond what she could actually see. Krom stood by her side. "It's moments like this that I am glad to share it with someone else." Dawn continued staring forward silently, unable to acknowledge her friend. Krom allowed the silence for a few moments before breaking it one more time. "Dawn, could you promise me something?"

Dawn turned to the Quarrinian, blinking away fresh tears that were threatening her eyes. "Anything, Krom. What is it?"

"We are finally going to be arriving in Cirrane tomorrow," he started. "And you are going to go see your Aunt Eva..." He searched for his words before continuing. "Don't forget about us. You know... When you get there?"

"Oh Krom..." Dawn smiled. "I will never forget you."

A warm breeze stirred the air around them. Krom sighed, a quiver shaking his voice. "Good. Because, while I do have blood family, those who are left. With the amount of time we have spent together... All of us... You, me, Cain, heck, even the peacekeepers. You guys are like my family now. I haven't been able to trust anyone like I trust you all since my sister..." His throat tightened.

Hearing this, Dawn nudged closer to Krom, resting her head on his shoulder. Krom's sleeves were rolled up on his arms, revealing several uniform scars climbing toward his torso. Silently, Dawn averted her eyes, and they gazed out over the ocean together, neither speaking another word until the sun came up the next morning.

As the light reinvigorated the world, the coast of Cirrane revealed itself. The pegasus riders soared through the skies, keeping watch over the borders of the country. Cliffs towered over the coast, making landing seem impossible, but straight ahead there was a small island allowing ships in and out. Ephras emerged from the depths of the ship and called out as he saw the land ahead. "There it is! Woke up just in time!"

He climbed the stairs to the ship wheel and took over command from Kaela, who sank downstairs to rest until they landed. Dawn followed her down to find Cain's room, where she noticed the bag she left for him was still on the nightstand. She pocketed it and rushed back upstairs to behold the cliffs towering higher and higher as they drew nearer to the shore. The walls of the port city overlooked the sea: guards patrolled the walls armed with longbows. "Barlo is the most well defended city in the world," Ephras stuttered to Dawn. "Aside from the Citadel itself, of course. Personally, I think Barlo is the greatest city in all the White Islands. Better than any elf city in Napora or Ardglas."

"I guess..." Krom mumbled. Dawn glanced over to him, but he quickly turned his head away, staring up at the walls of the fabulous fortress.

As the ship closed in on the wall, a gate opened to them revealing a passage into the city. They passed through the gate, eyes of the guards peering over the boat. Ephras continued to steer the ship through the passage until he found a dock where attendants waited to tie them to the dock.

Dawn stared in wonder as they made their way off the ship. Kaela stumbled out of the hold, having just woken up from her short nap. The stone streets of Barlo made an easy walking path for the weary travellers. Each stone was laid level with the adjacent one, no blemishes or scars.

Luscious green trees lined the streets accenting the grey rock that fortified the city. Heavily armored soldiers stood guard on each corner, clad in steel plate and wielding shields with a pegasus engraved on the face.

"The Sacred Order," Krom whispered to Dawn. "Watch this..." Krom broke away from the pack and tip-toed next to one of the soldiers. Suddenly he jumped out in front of him, screaming and waving his hands wildly, but the soldier didn't budge. He continued to scan the streets through the slots in his helmet.

When Krom returned, Dawn couldn't help but ask with a laugh, "What was that?"

"They won't budge for anything that isn't a real threat!" Krom responded. "No matter what. You couldn't even get one to laugh, let alone scare them. I have tried a few times, but to no avail."

"Maybe you just aren't very intimidating," Dawn laughed, pondering Krom's statement. "You have been to the Citadel before?"

"Yeah..." Krom mumbled. "Long time ago. Don't really want to talk about it." His demeanor shifted from his normal goofy self to a very solemn stare. Dawn sighed and continued the trek through the magnificent city.

Ephras and Kaela led them to a grand set of stairs set along a giant stone wall. As they ascended, Dawn noticed a bridge atop the wall that led across a deep ravine to another city. "Is that the Citadel?" Dawn asked in wonder.

Ephras laughed. "Of course not. That is just Barlo's upper level. You really didn't get out much, did you?"

Dawn sighed. "Farthest from home I ever got was Oasis. Definitely never left Quarrine."

At the top of the stairs, Dawn looked back over the city she had travelled through, amazed at its size. The sun shone high in the sky, gleaming off the city rooftops below. Near the center sat a large dome, dressed in grey stone and sparkling rock. "What is that building there?" She asked.

"That is the Other Observatory," Ephras responded. "They grow and cultivate wildlife that is not native to the White Islands. Many things from the Other, itself."

Krom scoffed, but without another word, the four crossed the bridge leading to the upper level of Barlo. The paving stones never lost their perfection as the trek continued. Dawn looked over the edge of the bridge to the waters below.

Soon they had arrived at the upper level. The architecture towered over them as they passed between buildings and under stone pathways looming overhead. People scurried through the streets, paying no attention to their surroundings. Dawn followed close behind Ephras, who led them forward with confidence, weaving his way through the crowds.

The sounds of hurried labor echoed through the streets; hammers clanging in the air, wheels creaking under the weight of cargo. Shouts from streets far away carried over to Dawn's ears. Her back tensed up and her neck shrunk back, but they continued onward.

"Not used to the city?" Krom mumbled to Dawn, noticing how tense she was.

"I guess not," she responded. "I like my wide-open spaces. It's how I grew up."

"Well," Krom started, "while the Citadel itself is just as busy, it is also much larger and open. Hopefully that will work better for you."

Dawn nodded as they continued onward through the upper level. Dawn noticed shops selling food and supplies the likes of which she had never seen before. As they passed one, 'The Citadel Loans Federation,' a man dressed in high class clothes rushed out, screaming at Kaela. "How dare you show your face on this street! Scum!"

"*HEY!*" Ephras drew his sword and stepped up to the crooked man. "She owes you nothing. Now go back inside, before someone gets hurt."

The man glared up at the Peacekeeper towering over him, grunted, and turned around. "You'd better hope you always have your big bad brother to protect you, girl."

Kaela rushed toward the shopkeeper, but Ephras stepped in the way, "Leave it, Kae... We are just passing through." Kaela sighed and turned her back to the storefront. Fury blazed in her eyes, and her fists clenched as she walked on, submitting to her brother. Dawn and Krom exchanged silent glances, as they moved forward.

Finally, the party reached the outer wall, exiting through a large gate that led to a thick wooded trail. Dawn tried to look past the trees, but couldn't see anything. "How far is the Citadel from here?" She asked.

"Someone is eager," Ephras laughed. "Don't worry; it is right on the other side of the woods."

They proceeded through the woods quickly. What was realistically hours felt to Dawn like minutes. When they finally reached an opening and looked upon the greatness of the Citadel itself. She stared in wonder as she looked up at the towering city, different levels and tiers, like a wedding cake, extending up to the sky. Just the first level's walls climbed four stories high!

As Dawn gazed in wonder, the walls shifted from a deep grey to white, blushing as the sun climbed over the central towers and shone on the face of the city. Dawn cried aloud as she peered even higher to the topmost walls and witnessed two great towers reaching into the clouds.

Ephras did not give time to gawk at the fantastic city, but instead pushed forward. Dawn scurried behind, never removing her eyes from the amazing sight. Krom walked softly behind her, chuckling under his breath as he watched Dawn's reaction to the metropolis.

As the party approached the walls of the great city, Dawn noticed more archers perched on the battlements overhead. Suddenly, the stone doors leading inward inched open and a soldier of the Sacred Order with a horn on his belt marched out to meet them.

"What is your business in the city?" The soldier demanded.

"Peacekeepers returning from an investigation," Ephras responded sternly. "Giving two Quarrinians residence with the approval of the Council."

The soldier revealed a scroll and unrolled it to read its contents. "Ephras?"

"Yes."

"You travelled back from Quarrine with a reaver?"

"Yes." Ephras wasn't caught aback by the questions, but answered them with confidence.

The soldier continued reading, until finally he placed the scroll back into a pouch, grasped the horn from his hip, and blew a long, loud blast into the air. Just then, the door to the city opened and the party gained access to the Citadel.

"Stay close, Dawn," Ephras hollered back to the awestruck girl. "Easy to get lost in the Citadel if you don't know where you are going." Dawn scampered forward to Ephras, her eyes wandering from structure to structure. "This is the Gate District," Ephras continued. "The lowest level of the Citadel. Stables, vendors, barracks, the works. Your aunt probably lives on the next level, in the Midtown District. Although we have to go up to the temples before we see your aunt or Cain. The Council would have you check in with them before running around in their city."

"How many levels are there in the city?" Dawn asked.

"Five total," Ephras said. "Like I said before, this is the Gate District. Midtown is the next level, followed by the Market District. Then it's Northtown, where Kaela and I live. Oh! And Cain has a home there too! And the final layer is the Temple District, home of the White Council. That is where we have to go first, and then we can make our way down to find Cain and your aunt."

Each district had stairs extending out of the walls barricading the next layer, elevating the travellers to the next level. At the top of each set of stairs was another gate, along with another gatekeeper asking the same questions that Ephras answered as they entered the city. Each time the party approached a gate, Dawn noticed a low growl escaping Krom's throat.

Each district was a tremendous size on its own. In her mind Dawn compared a single district to Oasis, wondering if each district by itself was larger than the Quarrinian capital city. She had no way to compare, but the thought itself was exhilarating.

Finally, once they entered the highest level of the Citadel, Dawn could see two magnificent towers. One climbed beautifully into the sky, decorated with brilliant crystals and elven architecture. The light blues and silvers radiated majesty throughout the court where she stood. It glimmered in the sky like a spike of pearl and silver. The other tower seemed to hardly stand at all. Grey stone shattered along the sides as small rocks tumbled down its broken face.

"The temples of the gods," Ephras stated. "Fos and Seor, the great gods of our time."

"Phh. That is one word for them..." Krom mumbled under his breath. Dawn cast a glare toward him, but he seemed not to notice.

As Ephras led the travellers to the light tower, Dawn dropped back to Krom and elbowed him in the arm. "Hey!" He shouted back at her.

"Why are you being like this?" Dawn asked in a hushed tone. "Ephras is doing so much to help, and you are choosing to be awful."

"You know my feelings about all of this," Krom responded. "Fos and magic. Even the Council themselves. Just wait till you meet them..."

"Krom!" Dawn interrupted. "If you want to be in everyone's lives now that we are here, you are going to have to get over all that. What is more important? Your hatred toward the Council and their magic, or your relationship with us?"

Krom sighed. "You're right. Sorry."

His words hardly had a chance to reach Dawn's ears by the time they had reached the temple entrance. Inside, gems and precious stones illuminated the corridor, shining just as brightly within the walls as without. Dawn stared in wonder at the gleaming golden walls trimmed with marble. Chandeliers made entirely of crystal hung from the vaulted ceilings.

As Dawn walked, captivated by her surroundings, a man came from around the corner, dressed in white and gold robes. "Something to behold, the temple of Fos," he laughed, placing his arm around Dawn and looking up at the chandeliers. Dawn jumped back, unnerved by the unexpected embrace. "Woah, there!" The man laughed. "I don't mean any harm, hon! Sorry to startle you."

Ephras rushed forward to greet the man. "Annias, my friend!"

"Ephras," Annias responded. "Welcome home! I hope you and your sister found what you were searching for in Quarrine."

"It seems they found even more..." Another man rounded the corner clad in similar robes as Annias, although this man's robes bore many insignias on the sleeves. "If I recall correctly, you left... *JUST* you and your sister, Ephras." His words, while matter of fact, were condescending. "Why have you brought home two Quarrinians?"

"Taran," Ephras stood at attention. "I apologize, I didn't see you there. These two had been travelling with Cain, the reaver. The girl has family in the city, while Krom here is escaping the conflict of the country."

Taran examined Krom, eyeing him up and down. There were so many things Krom wanted to say, but he managed to hold his tongue. "There are many Quarrinians who would like to take refuge in the Citadel," Taran said after many excruciating seconds. "Families. Hard workers. Children. But we can't take everyone who wishes to escape their mundane lives and enter our great city. Why should we make an exception for you?"

Krom grit his teeth, but before he could say a word, Dawn blurted out from nearby Ephras. "He is an amazing man!" She shouted. "He has fought against the Guild in many instances, is a hard worker, and brings life and energy to the most disheartening situations..."

"I had asked the boy, my dear," Taran interrupted, turning to Dawn to shush her. Though, when he saw her, his demeanor shifted. He scanned her person, before turning back toward Krom. "I guess, if what your friend says is true, I can allow you to stay. You must have a home though! The moment I find you sleeping on the street, you will go back to Quarrine. No questions asked."

"Don't worry about that!" Ephras interjected. "He can stay with us until he finds his footing."

Taran nodded, turning toward Dawn. "Now for the girl," he started. "Who is her family she will be staying with?"

"My aunt's name is Eva," Dawn said. "She is a tent maker in the city."

"Hmmm..." Taran thought for a second. "Her name doesn't ring a bell to me. Annias?" Annias shook his head. "I have much to do this afternoon, but Annias could look through the records and find her for you." Taran inched close and took Dawn's hand. "It's been a pleasure, my dear. You have my best wishes." Without another word, Taran strode out of the chamber.

"Don't worry about him," Annias sighed. "He has good intentions, just a little blunt on his follow through."

"I don't know about that..." Krom mumbled.

"Anyways," Annias continued, "I will go find that documentation for you. Wait just a moment, and I will be back."

As Annias walked away, Krom turned quickly to Ephras. "What is his problem?" He shouted. "Is it with just me, or all Quarrinians?

"Taran is the head of the White Council, and the ruler of the Citadel," Ephras responded. "He has a lot on his shoulders. His main priority is keeping his people safe, and with all the trouble happening on Quarrine, you can't blame him for being cautious."

"I guess," Krom sighed. "If that is the case, why is he so okay with Dawn being here?" He turned to Dawn. "He trusted you like you had known each other for years."

Dawn's head slumped. "At least he listened," she said. "I feel like this whole process could have been much more difficult."

"That is what I don't like," Krom said. "Why wasn't it?"

As Krom finished his thought, Annias returned with a map in his hands, followed by a hobbling Cain. "Good news!" He exclaimed. "We found your aunt!"

16

The Citadel

"I see you've met Annias," Cain said to Dawn, holding onto Krom's shoulder as the friends exited the temple. "He is a really good guy. Hopefully you will have more time with him while you're here."

Dawn smiled and nodded, but before she could get any words out, Ephras interjected into the conversation. "Did they get all the poison out already?"

"They did!" Cain exclaimed. "I just need to stay with someone for the next few days to make sure my recovery goes as expected. Would you mind if I stayed with you and Kaela?"

Krom laughed. "I guess your house is going to be a party for a few, huh?" Krom squeezed Cain from the side, "We are going to be roomies!"

"Ugh," Cain teased. "Maybe I will take my chances on my own."

They moved through the city slowly to stay in pace with

Cain, but Dawn couldn't help but to lead the pack. She moved swiftly ahead to scout out the street they were on, and which direction they should go next. She could have waited for Ephras to show her, but the anticipation pushed out the need for sound thinking. She felt like a rabbit, leading a pack of snails.

Finally, once they had passed through Northtown and the Market District, they had come to Midtown where Eva's home was on the map. Shivers ran up and down Dawn's spine, like lightning was coursing through her veins. Thoughts exploded in her mind, ready for her next season.

They stopped in front of a large building; stone stairs leading up to many doors. Dawn paused, staring up at the possibility of her new home. As if a fire was lit inside her soul, her eyes glowed in anticipation, but she couldn't move. Her legs froze beneath her. Her heart pounded in her chest.

"Dawn?" Krom had left Cain to place a hand on his companion's shoulder, causing her to jump out of her skin. "Your aunt is waiting."

"Yeah..." Dawn sighed, gazing up at the building standing in front of her.

"Are you ok?"

"I guess," she pondered the question silently for a moment. "I mean, she is all I have left. What if..."

"Don't do this to yourself," Krom grabbed her by her shoulders. "Stop putting yourself through a potential hell in your mind, and just go up there and experience the life that you are meant to." Dawn's friends all nodded in agreement. "We will wait down here for you. We won't leave until you tell us to."

Dawn exhaled a forceful breath, and strode up the steps toward her aunt's home. Two flights of stairs for her mind to play games. She felt like the voice of her reflection was speaking to her, but in reality, it was just her own thoughts. When she finally got to the door, she stood out front, staring at the slab of sturdy oak, as if she was waiting for it to open on its own.

"Okay," Dawn whispered to herself. "Here goes nothing."

Dawn raised her fist and tapped on the door, but quickly she retracted her hands as if the door was made of hot coals. Then she waited. No noise came from the other side of the door. Moments passed, and Dawn's heart continued to pound like a drummer, but nothing. No creaks in the floors, or voices echoing across the threshold. Only silence.

Dawn slowly reached her hand up again for her second attempt, but this time with much more confidence. Nothing. Still no noise from behind the door except the echo of Dawn's own knock. Tears welled up in her eyes, and panic set in. Her breathing quickened and her lungs felt heavy. She wasn't sure how long she had been waiting on the doorstep, but it felt like a lifetime.

Suddenly, her legs failed her and she stumbled backwards to the landing where she stood. When she looked up, she could see her reflection standing over her silently through her tears. "I don't want to hear it!" Dawn shouted, unashamedly.

"Dawn?" Krom's voice echoed up the stairwell.

Dawn stayed silent, crumbled in front of the door of her aunt's supposed home. Krom raced up the stone stairway, two or three steps at a time, to find her sitting in a puddle of her own tears, noticing the closed door in front of her. He dropped to his knees and embraced her.

"Hey, we can come back later," he started. "She may just be out for the day."

"Yeah," Dawn wiped tears from her eyes. "I guess."

"You can stay at the party house while we wait." Dawn smirked for a moment at Krom's comment, but quickly reverted back to her distress. "Hey," he continued. "Do you remember the promise you made to me?"

Dawn nodded.

"I make the same promise to you. You have us, you know. You have family, even if we aren't blood."

Dawn rested her head on Krom's shoulder until the tears dried up in her eyes, and then they made their way back down to the others. Ephras didn't need an explanation before offering his home to the young girl. The friends made their way back up to the Northtown District to Ephras and Kaela's home.

It wasn't anything too luxurious. It actually wasn't very luxurious at all. As Dawn walked through the doors, she was taken aback by the cheap furniture and lack of space. She had been expecting a place similar to Ragnar's home in Oasis, but this was half the size.

"I know, I know," Ephras said. "It's pretty big for a city home. The Council helps us with payment so we can afford to live here."

Cain eyed Dawn, chuckling under his breath. "Things are a little different in the city, aren't they? Not what you were expecting?"

"Not quite," Dawn laughed.

Ephras showed the friends around their home, escorting them to the places each person would call their quarters for the next few days. Kaela showed Dawn to the back of the house, where she would be sharing her room with the Quarrinian girl. If the foyer and the living area had been small, Dawn couldn't believe the size of Kaela's room. Hardly enough space for a bed, let alone another guest.

As the night progressed, the friends lingered in the living area, laughing together about the ins and outs of city life compared to life in the wasteland of Quarrine. "I guess space is a little harder to come by in the city," Ephras laughed.

"At least you have a home!" Krom shouted with a smile. "Even though there is space, there are so many people in Quarrine that have nowhere to go."

"You say that like it isn't the same in the Citadel," Kaela mocked. "Between the Gate District and Midtown, there are many who have to sleep on the streets. We are the lucky ones."

As they bickered, Dawn wandered the house, examining her new lodging. She found Cain's quarters, recognizable by the smell of spices from his pack. Quietly, she snuck in and placed his stash of souvenirs on his bed. In the corner of the room, set on a pedestal, sat a solid oak lute. The candlelight glimmered off the glossy finish, seizing Dawn's attention. She inched toward the instrument, but as she reached out to grab it, Ephras appeared and moved his hand between her and the lute. "You don't want to touch that."

Dawn snapped her hand back. "Sorry!" She apologized. "If you don't mind my asking... Why not?"

Ephras sighed, placing his arm around Dawn and leading

her back toward their friends. "That lute belonged to Thea, Kaela and my sister." Ephras' voice quieted, hushed and raspy. "She was killed nearly a year ago defending Kaela from those gangsters in Barlo. The Citadel Loan Federation. Long history there, but if Kaela were to see you with it, I'm not sure I could protect you."

"I am so sorry," Dawn murmured. "I had no idea."

They came back into the living area where Krom and Kaela were still arguing. "I'm not saying you aren't lucky!" Krom laughed. "All I am saying is sometimes, people would rather stay in prison than go back to their life on the streets."

"That is true," Ephras interrupted. "As peacekeepers, we have witnessed that many times. People who just need a meal, so they commit a crime, knowing we will catch them and have to feed them in the Citadel prisons. Our world is a dangerous place."

Dawn glanced over to Krom, whose demeanor had shifted from playful to downcast. "You ok, Krom?

"Yeah," he grunted. "Just not a great subject for me."

"Why is that?" Kaela asked obliviously.

"Kaela, respect his privacy!" Ephras snapped. "If he doesn't want to talk about it, he doesn't need to."

"No," Krom responded. "It's ok. I think it is finally time." He closed his eyes and inhaled a deep breath before continuing. "I have been to the Citadel one time before this visit, but it wasn't a vacation. I know that people sometimes prefer prison... because that was me."

"You were held in a Council prison?" Kaela asked.

"I was trying to get protection from the Guild, and had exhausted all my options. Back when the Council still had soldiers stationed on Quarrine, I attacked them. Never aiming for a kill, but enough for them to take me seriously."

"You are lucky they didn't kill you on the spot!" Cain shouted from his seat across the room. "That is more likely for Citadel soldiers nowadays."

"I was ready for whatever consequences awaited me," Krom replied, rubbing his arms nervously. "No matter what they were. Lucky me, they took me to the Old City Prison. I stayed there for six months until there were too many people getting arrested, and they didn't have room for me."

"Interesting," Ephras said. "That must have been some time ago, because that prison has been abandoned for years now. It is a piece of history. Hardly anyone ever goes there." Ephras paused for a moment, processing his thoughts. "I wonder if a visit there could help you with this discomfort you feel in the city?"

"What do you mean?" Krom scoffed, agitated at the remark. "What discomfort?"

"Oh, come on," Kaela interjected. "You have been squeamish since we disembarked in Barlo."

"That isn't true!" Krom shouted. He turned to Dawn, who nodded in agreement with the peacekeeper. "Well, maybe I have. But why would I want to revisit the place that causes my spite?"

"Because, this place has no power over you anymore," Ephras stated calmly. "It has no power over anyone."

Krom sighed, nodding in agreement.

"Great!" Ephras whooped. "Let's go then!"

"Wait a second!" Krom halted the housemates as they all

stood preparing for the excursion. "Is this a 'today' thing? It's getting a little late, isn't it?"

"You're funny," Kaela laughed. "Such a country boy. Just because the sun goes down, you can't go outside anymore?"

"That's not what I meant..." Krom mumbled.

"Don't worry, Krom," Ephras laid his hand on his shoulder. "It will be just fine."

Without another word, Krom stood with his friends and they left to find the Old City Prison. Under the cover of moonlight, Ephras led them through the darkened city streets. The way the lamps lit the streets surprised Dawn, almost as if the sun hadn't gone down at all. To the city dwellers, this was a shift from the burning sun throughout the day.

As Dawn, Kaela, and Krom chatted, Cain hobbled up to Ephras. "Kaela seems to be doing much better than last time I saw you two."

"Yeah," Ephras peeked over his shoulder toward his sister. "I don't know what it is about those two, but they have really pulled her out of her shell. I swear she was nothing like this before Quarrine."

"No matter what the reason for it," Cain said, "it's nice to see her joking around again. Not hearing her tease others had been hard."

"I just wish those gangsters would stay out of her life," Ephras grunted. "She has been trying so hard, and it seems like she just can't escape her past."

"Most of us spend our whole lives trying to escape our past," Cain sighed.

"Sorry, Cain," Ephras apologized. "I didn't mean..."

"Don't worry about me," Cain responded. "I've been healing for a long time."

"Is that why you have taken so much interest in this girl?" Ephras asked. "Is it a part of your healing?"

"I don't know," Cain peered at Dawn. "She reminds me so much of Roy. So much passion. So much raw ability."

"You can't replace your son, Cain," Ephras said. "Roy is gone."

"I know, Ephras," Cain grumbled. "But... maybe I can help her where I failed him."

The friends travelled through the city until they reached a gate separating the road from a stairway leading underneath the streets. Ephras summoned a fire to light the torches hanging on the walls, lighting the pathway ahead of them. He unlocked the gate and led the group downward.

"Welcome to the Old City," Ephras said. "Before the rule of the Council, this was the Citadel. Once the White Council took over power, they built the new city right over the top of what was already there, leaving the Old City completely functional, but in ruins."

Dawn gazed around at the ancient looking architecture, completely juxtaposed from the buildings on the surface level. The homes crumbling onto roads had been overgrown with weeds and greenery. Not even the paving stones could stop the advance of nature from the outside world.

Not far into the city they came across a building that stood out as newer; at least compared to the rest of the underground metropolis. The sign out front, covered in vines and moss, said 'Old City Prison.'

"This is the place," Krom shivered. "Definitely brings back dark times in my life."

A pair of pegasus statues stood watch over the front door, each standing more than ten feet high, and their wings spanning the same distance. Their eyes were a ruby red, as if they were laced with gemstones. As the travellers strode into the abandoned building, Dawn gazed up at the magnificent statues. Not even the onset of nature could disguise the majesty of the beasts.

Once inside the doors, Krom glanced around the facility. "Are my eyes twitching?" He laughed, looking back toward Dawn. "I swear, I don't even know what we're doing here."

"Come on," Kaela reassured him. "It's a piece of history now. Let the healing happen."

"I don't feel anything healing in me..." Krom mumbled.

Dawn examined a structure set upon the wall of the entryway. It had crumbled away so that its initial form was unrecognizable. She reached out to touch it, and as she wiped her hand against the stone she removed a thick, dark residue. Sticky to the touch.

"What is this?" She asked.

Ephras waved his hands, emitting a white light that engulfed Dawn's hands, removing the residue. "Something that probably shouldn't be here," he said. "Cain?"

Cain examined the structure, but remained silent. Him and Ephras gave each other knowing looks, but never spoke a word aloud about the severity of the residue. Dawn continued to search the ruin, walking with Krom farther into the prison. Cain and Ephras followed close behind.

They delved deeper into the compounds until they came

to the prison cells. Krom approached a set of bars and grasped them with white knuckles, resting his head on the cold steel. Dawn came up behind him and placed her hand on his back. "Can you believe that this place was actually a better option to me than being back home?"

"Healing can't happen until the wound is addressed," Dawn said to him. "If we were to leave a wound open, then time would only make it infected. But if you address the wound, then healing can truly take place."

"You guys all forget that I chose to come here," Krom laughed. "I wanted to be in prison."

"To get away from home?" Cain asked, approaching from behind. "Or because you wanted to punish yourself."

Krom's grin disappeared, hanging his head in defeat. Suddenly, he jerked away from Dawn and darted out of the compound.

"Maybe that's enough for now," Ephras acknowledged, leading the rest of the friends out of the prison to follow Krom.

Krom walked yard ahead of his friends as they exited the building. Dawn gazed up at the twin pegasus statues again with wonder. "Maybe being here was a difficult experience," she broke the silence. "But these pegasus are so cool. I would love to see some of those again."

"Had you seen any before you met Silas on the boat?" Ephras asked.

"No!" Dawn answered. "That was the first! And I really hope it's not the last."

"It won't be!" Kaela shouted in excitement. "Because we are going to take you to a Hilios match!"

17

Hilios

The sun had just begun to set as the companions traversed the city streets in the Market District. Dawn had now been in the Citadel for a little under a week, and had realized the Market District was exponentially larger than all the other districts. It was its own kingdom! Different social classes distributed throughout the streets, never crossing paths. Except for today, that is.

Excitedly, they approached the towering stadium. The roar of the crowds pressing toward the same destination was almost deafening. Ephras and Kaela led them swiftly toward the front of the mob.

Dawn glanced around as she followed her hosts, watching as people from all different backgrounds found their way to mobile food stands and souvenir stands, shouting out drinking songs as a preamble to the event to come. She had never experienced anything like it! People wore bright colors, all matching each other, waving flags, and cheering. Many wore wings as if they were eagles, while others had dressed in obviously fake body armor with matching helmets. Some had even colored their faces the same color as their vivid clothes!

The atmosphere of feverish excitement was highly infectious. Dawn couldn't keep herself from grinning. They walked for minutes, joking loudly amongst the chatter through the streets.

Krom shouted as they approached a man carrying trays of fried bread, smothered in a special sort of sauce. "Oh my gosh... It has been forever since I've had Sunny Bites!" He cried out, pulling some coins from his satchel. "I'll take four!"

"Dawn," Ephras pulled her close so she could hear him over the noisy crowd. "This is your first Hilios match. Go ahead and pick a souvenir. It's on me."

Dawn grinned from ear to ear as she scanned the crowd for something that stood out to her. Across the sea of faces, she spotted a bow, glimmering under the rising moonlight. Pointing toward it, she turned to Ephras and asked, "What is that?"

"Ah!" Ephras laughed. "You have a good eye." He led her over to the stand selling the bow. Dawn glanced at it and now noticed that the bow had no bowstring! But it was still tight, as if there were tension from a string. "This is a blessed bow, the main instrument of the Hilios players. Its magic allows it to shoot the light ball when it is charged."

"You don't need a string?"

"Not on these," Ephras smirked, handing the salesman some coin and grasping the bow, along with a pair of blue leather gloves. "Put these on, and you will see."

Dawn slipped the gloves over her fingers and onto her hands. They were a perfect fit, almost like her old hunting gloves. Ephras handed her the bow, pointing up in the air at a target that had been painted on a building nearby. "Go ahead," he smiled. "Take a shot."

Dawn's brow furrowed as she reached for where the bow's string would normally be. To her shock, once the gloves touched the space between the upper and lower limb, a brilliant light appeared, connecting the two pieces of the bow together. A radiant arrow materialized between her fingers on the newly discovered bowstring. She aimed the magical instrument toward the target, exhaled, and released the string, launching the blazing arrow into the target's center. After a few seconds, the arrow dematerialized, leaving an indentation in the wall where it had landed.

"This is amazing!" Dawn shouted, embracing Ephras with a reckless hug. "How? How does it work?"

"The Council's magic is pretty cool sometimes," Ephras laughed. "They have blessed these bows to never need a string, or arrows through conjuration magic. Of course, the ones the Hilios players use won't do any real damage, many of the Sacred Order use bows just like this that are just as good, if not better, than any Quarrinian longbow."

With wonder in her eyes, Dawn and Ephras regrouped with Cain and Kaela who had found their own souvenirs while Krom was still devouring his fried foods. Finally, with their money bags considerably lighter, they came up on the stadium. Ephras and Kaela led them through the front doors, past the guards and security stations that held up the crowd.

"Perks of being with the peacekeepers," Krom whispered

to Dawn, wiping sauce from the corners of his lips. She could hardly hear him over the chanting fans just behind them, but she smiled toward him nonetheless.

They followed the expansive brightly lit hallways until they reached stairs leading upward to a platform. Once all were on the platform, it jerked and started to rise into the air above them, climbing higher and higher. Dawn's heart jumped into her throat, but as she glanced at Kaela and Ephras, who had been watching her and smirking at her reaction, she realized there was nothing to worry about. "Magic, right?" She laughed, still uneasy from the sudden shift in elevation.

The platform finally reached a stop, where they disembarked and walked around more gigantic halls. They approached an archway that led into the stadium seating, where thousands of seats overlooked a massive playing field deep in the ground like a crater. Dawn stopped in her tracks under the archway, unbelieving of the spectacle in front of her.

"Welcome to the Hilios arena!" Ephras shouted as the others moved along toward their seats. "We wanted to arrive a little bit early so you could see it all before people were here. And in case you have any questions."

"I guess I have a few," Dawn mumbled as she continued staring out over the crater. "Firstly, what is Hilios?"

Ephras laughed, "You're funny. Seriously though, is there something you want to know?" Dawn turned back toward him silently with an honest look in her eyes. "Wait, you actually have never even heard of it?" Ephras' jaw dropped in amazement. "You must have grown up on the far side of Quarrine, because even Quarrinians have teams for Hilios."

Dawn blushed, "I didn't even realize that I *was* sheltered until a few months ago. I don't plan to be anymore though!"

Ephras smiled, leading Dawn to the others who had already found their seats. "First thing," he started. "All players play atop a pegasus, and are equipped with one of your blessed bows and those gloves. Each team has five players on the field at once." He pointed onto the oval field at both ends where three different sized hoops hovered in the air.

"The goal is to shoot through one of those hoops as many times as possible before the time runs out. The largest hoop is one point, the next is two, and the smallest is three."

"That seems pretty simple," Dawn stated.

"Simple to understand," Kaela retorted, listening in on the explanation. "Not simple to play."

"A ball of light that is sent into the air at the beginning of the game, and that ball transfigures into the only arrow that can score. All other arrows that are shot are generally to incapacitate another player."

"That is where the gloves come into play!" Kaela interrupted again. "The gloves are blessed to catch the ball of light, as well as deflect any opposing shots."

"I can't believe you have never seen a match," Krom commented. "They even have an arena in southern Quarrine. A city called Silt, where they have pegasus you can rent to practice or play recreationally."

"Silt actually has a team playing tonight!" Ephras stated, people now beginning to flow in from the outside. "The Silt Guardians. They are doing really well this season, from what I have seen of them. Could even win it all."

"Oh, I hope so!" Krom shouted. Dawn eyed Krom, whose demeanor had completely shifted from that of a week earlier. Now he couldn't contain his energy. He was chatting their ears off, excited for something she couldn't have expected him to be excited for. Maybe going to this game really *was* a good idea, not just for her, but for him as well.

Dawn gazed out over the stadium, where now at least ten thousand people were piling in to find their places in their seats, which rose in levels around the long, oval field. The ceiling of the stadium emitted a golden light that suffused the entire playing field.

She peered upward to the only section that was higher than the section they were sitting in, to see Councilman Taran taking a seat secluded from the rest of the crowd. Suddenly, a flash of heat permeated throughout her body. She sunk deep into her chair as her vision darkened, and all she could see was that same familiar face. As if staring into a mirror, her reflection stared back at her. Silently. Her eyes blazed with anger... And fear.

"Dawn?" Krom had grabbed her and shaken her back to her senses. "You alright?"

"Yeah," Dawn responded hesitantly, glancing back up toward the councilman. "I guess I'm just a little overwhelmed by the enormity of all this."

"I promise, it will be fun," he assured. "You will forget all about being overwhelmed."

Soon, everyone had found their places, and ten pegasus riders flew out over the field. Five were clad in a burgundy and yellow uniform with the word, *'Guardians'* written on their backs. The rest were dressed in a luminous white with *'Angels'* across their backs. They practiced with the players of their own teams by shooting their bows at each other, and catching each glowing arrow with their magical gloves.

Just then, the blast of a horn resounded throughout the stadium. Another rider, clad in solid black, flew out to position the teams on their respective sides of the field, speaking to them under the roar of the crowds. "What is that one doing?" Dawn turned to Krom to ask.

"That is the official," Krom said. "He is explaining the rules and getting them prepared for the start of the match."

The black rider hovered in the center of the crater and the other players circled him with brilliant speed. They were alternating between teams, so that no player flew next to a teammate.

Once again, the horn blasted, and a dazzling ball of light exploded upwards from the black rider, and the players dispersed to their positions on the field. Two opposing players rushed toward the ball, racing each other to grab it first, but the Guardians flyer was hit by an arrow shot by one of the Angels, allowing her teammate to grab the ball of light.

"That is Phoenicia Rodes," Kaela shouted to Dawn, pointing out the flyer who had caught the ball. "She is one of the greatest players to play the game!"

Swiftly, Rodes drew back on her bow and shot toward another Angel. Catching the arrow in their enchanted gloves, the Angel repeated Rodes' play, shooting toward another teammate. Again and again, they caught and released, not allowing the opposing team a chance to come close, until finally, Rodes caught the arrow one last time, and shot it past the Guardian's goaltender into the smallest hoop.

"That's three," Krom sighed. "I was hoping Quarrine players would put up more of a fight against these guys, but it doesn't look like they stand a chance."

Again, the light emerged in the middle of the field from the black rider, and again Rodes caught it. Like clockwork, they accomplished the same play. Back and forth to each other without any disruption from their so-called opponents. Another three points.

Dawn watched the flyers race through the air as the Guardians tried their hardest to keep up with the professional level of the Angels. The game was extremely fast paced, never stopping for a second to rest or to recalibrate. Even just watching could be exhausting, trying to keep track of the lightning-fast ball being shot between the players.

"These guys give Quarrine a bad name!" Krom shouted. The score was now eleven to two. "Dawn, we could do better than this! And you have never even flown!"

"Have you?" Cain turned to Krom with a smirk on his face.

Krom scratched his head nervously. "I mean... legally? No..."

"Woah! I don't want to hear that!" Ephras shouted.

After an hour of play, a final horn blasted to signal the end of the game. The black rider raised his hand and drew in the light to his hand, releasing it into a small vial in his breast pocket. The score to end the game was twenty-seven to five.

"Just embarrassing," Krom said as they exited their seats. "I've never seen such a huge blowout."

"The Angels this season are something we have never

seen before," Kaela said. "Rodes lit a fire under the rest of the team and brought them to another level. It is her first year playing too!"

As they scuttled through the crowds toward the front doors, a familiar man approached with haste. Dawn examined his face, processing where she had seen him before, but couldn't pinpoint a time.

"Silas!" Ephras shouted. "Did you get to watch the game?"

"I did!" Silas responded. "I was keeping watch over Councilman Taran in the executive booths." He glanced over to Dawn. "Well, hey there! We met on the boat, right?"

"Yes!" Dawn remembered. "Nice to see you again."

"Was this your first match?" Silas asked. "What did you think? Even though it wasn't the best game, you got the experience."

"And I loved it," Dawn smiled. "Everything about a pegasus is just mesmerizing, isn't it?"

"That is why I do what I do!" Silas clamored. "Though playing Hilios is much more fun than watching over the coast. That is why I am putting together a team to compete next season."

"You don't need to be great to beat those Guardians," Krom whimpered.

Cain laughed. "Krom here seems to think he can do better than those professionals out there." Krom's face flushed with a kiddish smirk at the lighthearted teasing.

"Well," Silas started, "If you want your chance, you can try it out for our team." Silas watched Krom's face turn from embarrassment to excitement. "We still need two players to compete."

Krom glanced back and forth between all of his friends with giddy excitement. "You know what this means?" He shouted, patting Dawn on the arm. "Dawn and I can prove that Quarrine can actually play Hilios!"

Silas turned to Dawn, "Wait, do you want to play too?"

"Yes!" Dawn answered without even processing the repercussions. Like it was just an instinct, a reaction she couldn't control.

"That decides it then!" Silas confirmed. "We are allowed to start practicing together next month, so if you need flying practice, you should find the time before then. I will send all the information you need to Ephras' house." Silas then turned to Ephras, his demeanor shifting completely. "Though, I wish this could be the end of our meeting, I need to speak with you."

"Did you find her?" Ephras asked, turning to Dawn. "I had asked Silas if he could take a look around for your Aunt Eva, since we haven't been able to find her yet."

It was as if the excitement from the day had been extracted from the room. They had gone to her aunt's home every day to see if she had returned, and every day there had been no answer.

"We did find her," Silas uttered. "You're not going to like it."

18

Ulumbra

The streets calmed from the earlier clamor. What, just hours before, had been a jamboree of singing and eating and laughing was now silence. Torches had been extinguished and people had found their way back to their homes. Littered along their pathway were sour relics of discarded snacks and meals.

Walls of the buildings around them climbed high. Dawn didn't even bother to seek the already blackened sky through the jungle of rock and glass. Torches lining the streets cast a shadow like black over the deepest charcoal. She still gripped her new magical bow tight in her warm gloved hands.

A blanket of fog descended upon the city. As they passed alleyways, Dawn noticed glimmers of light in the corner of her eye. The fog had been condensing into an apparition, her reflection staring back at her. Watching her.

Silent.

Unmoving.

Silas led them to Eva's home. "We thought it was weird that she hadn't been home this week," he explained. "So, we finally broke down the door."

Dawn inspected to find that Silas' story was true: At the top of the stairs, the door lay in splinters inside the front room of her aunt's home. A feeling like acid filled her stomach. Bile rose through her esophagus in search of an escape route. The color in her face evacuated and the world around her began to spin. Krom placed his arm around her shoulder, holding her up as she stumbled into the house.

Then, everything she feared had been realized. They turned the corner of the charming second story home into the living area, and there she lay. Aunt Eva. Devoid of any color. Lifeless, along with the rest of the room. Her face was dry and wrinkled like a prune, her eyes seceding back into the sockets where they rested. The sight of her body curdled the blood of even Ephras and Kaela. Cain sighed, turning to Krom with a knowing nod.

Dawn couldn't even form tears in her eyes. She wanted nothing more than to cry and to feel the gravity of the moment, but all emotion had left her. No sadness. No anger. Not even pain. She felt nothing.

"How long?" Cain asked.

"Can't say for sure," Silas responded. "But it wouldn't take long for a body to start producing a smell, and you have probably noticed that there isn't one…"

"There won't be," Cain interrupted. "Don't have too much experience with dark magic, do you Silas?"

Silas shook his head. "Ulumbra was defeated early in my life. Long before I took up flying."

Suddenly, Dawn rushed out of the room toward the door, dropping her bow and knocking over furniture on her way. "Dawn!" Krom shouted following close behind.

Dawn turned to him, pressing her hand into his chest and never looking him in the eyes. "Krom, I am fine. I just need some time. I will see you at home." She continued down the stairs.

"But Dawn..." Krom started, but Cain grabbed him by the shoulder, shaking his head.

"Give her some time. She needs it."

"You guys go ahead and go home," Ephras said to Cain and Krom. "Make sure she has company if she returns. Kaela and I will stay here for a while and process what happened here."

Cain nodded, grabbing Dawn's bow and leading Krom outside. At the bottom of the stairs, they watched Dawn strolling down the street away from their temporary home. They gave each other a look, and headed back to Ephras' house.

"Kaela," Ephras ordered. "Check the rooms for any signs of assault. Her attackers got in and out somehow without anyone noticing."

Kaela nodded, closing her eyes and focusing. The room around her flourished to life, every life force radiating in her mind. She scanned the room for abnormalities; footprints left behind, auras still lingering in the air. Silas' aura glowed green, with Ephras glowing his natural blue. But deeper in the home, a deep red burned. As Kaela drew nearer, the crimson glow flushed all around her. It darkened as she immersed herself deeper into the hellish illumination.

Finally, she entered the bedroom, which was enveloped in the crimson aura. The atmosphere of the room had shifted from the other parts of the house. Dread filled the room, thick in the air like a deep fog. The mirrors and shelving had been ravaged and broken, thrown around the room in a storm.

She opened her eyes and the light disappeared. In one corner of the room, where the damage seemed the heaviest, there was a dark sticky residue splattered across the floor. "Ephras!" Kaela called her brother into the room.

Ephras rushed into the bedroom, glancing around at the destruction in the room. With one look at the residue he grasped the hilt of his sword. "Let's go."

Step after step, Dawn wandered through the streets. No aim. No destination. One step at a time she strolled from block to block, hardly looking up from the road beneath her feet. There could have been a battlefield around her, and she wouldn't have realized. As if the world around her had faded from existence.

She reminisced about her days in Quarrine. Waking early to the sound of birds chirping outside her hut. Hunting with the overly competitive Maron. They had grown up together their whole lives, and now she would never see him again. Training Cammie to be the greatest man he could be. Learning from her dad, and from Merlyn. She hadn't even touched a lute in months. The world that used to kiss up against her skin and laugh with her and create melodies in her head - no more. The world had shrunk to a cold void.

Suddenly, Dawn's feet stumbled over each other and she was falling; tumbling down stairs made of concrete. With a *THUD* she hit the bottom, sore and bruised from the descent. She reached for her neck to ensure the safety of her amulet, and exhaled a sigh of relief. Struggling to lift her head, she peered around where the world seemed to be spinning. "The Old City?" She whispered to herself. "Why?"

Her limbs weighed a thousand pounds, but she still managed to pull herself up to her feet. Torches on the wall illuminated a path from the stairs deeper into the ruins. Following this path, her mind hazed. The fog of the upper level had descended into her thoughts, blurring her decisions, and pushing her forward.

Soon, she was gazing up at the pegasus statues in front of the Old City Prison. Their eyes glimmered in the flame light like precious stones. When she encountered them before, she felt safe, but now, they seemed menacing. Full of hate and malice. Without another thought, she rushed inside the prison and slammed the doors behind her.

The dead air was cool. Torches and lanterns had already been lit inside the walls of the prison. The hallways and corridors winded on and on without end. Dawn wandered in, one hand leaning against the wall to support the weight of her increasingly heavy body. Her other hand grasped her amulet, which seemed to be burning a hole in her chest where it rested.

Aside from the crackling torches the prison was silent. Slightly eerie. A shiver slithered down Dawn's back. Her eyes darted left and right. A strange feeling overcame her. Like she was being watched. She turned a corner into a hallway filled with prison cells. The lights of the fires dimmed to a dark orange, casting deep shadows throughout the corridor.

A figure stood at the end of the hallway, shrouded in black. She couldn't make out the silent shape of the person ahead of her. "Is it you again?" She called out, her voice echoing off the concrete walls.

No reply. Her voice reverberated until there was silence again. Her heart fell into a vice, squeezing with so much pressure to cause her constant pain. Was she breathing? She couldn't tell. She had forgotten how.

Behind her, the sound of rushing wind gushed into the hallway. Suddenly, the torches on the walls extinguished one at a time, until they both stood in the darkness. Her necklace glowed, illuminating the corridor and revealing the figure ahead.

"Who are you...?" Dawn asked meekly, peering through the darkness.

Slowly, she backed away, but as she took a step backwards the figure stepped toward her. She stopped. Frozen in place. But the figure took another step. Her heart dropped. Squinting tensely through the darkness, she watched as the figure drew nearer, walking steadily past the prison cells until they were mere feet from Dawn.

She reached for her sword, but to no avail. She had left her weapons at Ephras' home before the Hilios match. Helplessly, she backed away from the approaching menace.

Quickly, she turned to run back down the halls toward the front doors. Shadows of more enemies encroached on her vision as she traversed the halls, zipping through the corridors.

The light of her amulet illuminated her path. Finally, she reached the entryway of the prison. But as she entered, a squad of hooded figures closed in around her, closing her off from her exit.

"It has been too long, young one," a disfigured man spoke in a particularly rough voice. A familiar voice that summoned a deep hatred in her. He had one blade in each hand, ready to attack at any moment. "We have been waiting for you."

"You won't be needing those, Greenwood," a feminine figure approached from behind. "She won't be fighting her way out this time."

As the woman spoke, the torches on the walls relit, revealing their faces.

"You..." Dawn realized. "What do you want with me?"

"I believe it's time we had a proper introduction," the witch said, removing her black hood. "My name is Ariyah. You have met my captain, Grendel Greenwood."

"I don't care who you are!" Dawn shouted. "Let me go!"

Ariyah snickered. "You really think you are going to leave here alive? I thought you were smart."

"I am so sorry Dawn..." a soft voice whimpered from the crowd of cultists. One at a time, the hooded figures moved until a prisoner was thrown to the floor before Dawn. The young man gazed at Dawn's feet from his knees, unable to lift his head. Tears dripped from his eyes to the cold stone beneath him.

"Maron..."

Ariyah snapped her fingers and her servants seized Maron by his tunic and dragged him to Dawn's feet. He gazed into the floor, never looking up at his childhood friend.

"He led us right to you, girl," Ariyah snickered, grabbing Maron by his scraggy hair and pulling him up to Dawn's eyes. "He knew so much about you. He knew about your aunt living in the Citadel. He gave us everything."

A spark lit inside Dawn. The fire of rage burned hot, blazing into an inferno within her soul. Maron silently wept in front of her. The revenge Ariyah offered through her lifelong friend knocked at the door of her heart. The anger from her eyes revealed the scared child within, a girl who was taught to fight and craved the love of family and friends. She had been wearing a mask, this new persona to defend her against the horrors of an evil world. Only, Maron knew the real her. A tender, soft soul. But she was fading.

Her reflection appeared ahead of her. It reached out its hand, and grasped her own. As her body reunited with this piece of herself, she felt power surge within her. Slowly, the apparition molded into her body, pressing itself into her spirit and fueling her rage.

"Show me your true power," Ariyah whispered. "Prove yourself."

Dawn clenched her teeth, light glowing from her hands. She clenched her eyes shut, images of her family shooting through her mind. The faces of the ones she loved lying dead in the dirt of her village.

She opened her eyes to Maron being held up by the witch's grasp on his hair. Last time Dawn had seen him, he was the pretty boy of the village. Unable to get his hands dirty and ready to flirt with whoever. Now, he was different. He still wore the same hunting tunic as that dreaded day, but it was ripped and torn. He still had the same brown eyes, but now they were afraid. Solemn. Mourning.

"No," Dawn whispered. The light shining from her hands faded. "That's not me!" Just then, her reflection tore away from her body, flying back through the room. The rage within her diminished until her heart felt cool again. She looked up at the apparition, who snarled at her from across the room. "He is my friend." With a growl, the apparition disappeared.

Ariyah scoffed, throwing Maron to the floor and smacking Dawn with the back of her hand. The witch grasped Dawn by her face, pulling her close. "To think, we were going to give you a chance," she growled.

Suddenly, the doors to the prison burst open and Ephras and Kaela rushed in, weapons in hand. Without hesitation, the peacekeepers cut down the cultists surrounding Dawn. Ephras waved his sword while Kaela whipped around her short spear. Maron scurried away to a wall nearby. Dawn watched a blade hit the floor from a fallen enemy, but as she dove to grab it, Greenwood wrapped his giant burly arms around her, holding a blade against her throat.

"Drop your weapons, or she dies!" Ariyah shrieked at the incoming peacekeepers. Without a word, they looked at each other in defeat, and their weapons hit the floor with a clang.

"No!" Dawn squirmed. "Save yourselves!"

But it was too late. The flames flickered and color faded from the room as long black tendrils extended out of Ariyah's fingertips, wrapping Ephras, Kaela, and Dawn in her magical grip.

"Now," Ariyah sighed. "Where were we?" Dawn kicked

and squirmed, but nothing could release her from the grip of Ariyah's dark magic. The witch reached out a hand and grasped Dawn's amulet. With one thrust, she ripped the jewel from Dawn's neck and pulled it toward herself.

"No!" Dawn shrieked. She thrashed and jerked, screaming empty syllables at her captors.

"Finally!" Ariyah exhaled. "After all those years." She held the jewel up over her head with one hand, and the rest of the cult kneeled in front of her. "Perry!" She called out with a shrill.

Quickly, one man stood and removed his hood, revealing a bald, tattooed head. Suddenly, a long lash of light extended out from Ariyah, grasping hold of the man. Life drained from his eyes and his skin dried and wrinkled. Soon, his lifeless shell lay flat on the floor, gazing with empty, grey eyes at the ceiling of the prison. The lash of light returned to Ariyah's hand and formed into a ball, which she pressed into the amulet. Pain clawed at Dawn's chest as the jewel absorbed the life force of the cultist. Her vision blurred until she could hardly see a few feet in front of her own eyes.

Just then, Ariyah held out the amulet, and chanted in a foul language. Something Dawn had never heard. It wasn't orcish, but it sounded just as brutish and harsh. As she spoke, the jewel illuminated the room like a star. Brighter and brighter it glowed until the entire prison was coated in a blanket of thick white fog.

The fog dissipated. Standing in between Dawn and Ariyah was a pale man with long black hair. His glowing bright blue eyes were marked with a hideous scar that extended the length of the left side of his face. Every breath that he inhaled whistled in the air. Slowly, he turned to examine the room.

"I see," his voice was raspy, but steady. "Ariyah, is this your doing?"

"Yes, master!" She bowed low, her voice quivering.

"How long has it been?"

"Nineteen years, my lord."

"Hmph," the man grunted. "Such a long time. And where is Drake?"

Dawn gasped at the mention of her father's name.

"Dead, I believe," Ariyah muttered.

"Shame," the man whispered. "I rather liked him." He turned to the cultists who were still bowing around them. "Are these your new servants?"

"Yes, sir!" Greenwood stood to his feet and lowered his head. "My name is Grendel, and I willingly give my life for Ulumbra."

The man slowly hobbled over to the captain. His eyes didn't blink once. Silence filled the air as he shuffled his feet across the stone floor. "That's good," he whispered. Suddenly, he reached out his long arms and grabbed hold of Greenwood's neck with his spider-like fingers. "Because I need your life."

All of a sudden, the air shifted in the room. Like all the wind had rushed out, or had been sucked in by the mysterious man. The captain remained silent, but his eyes screamed in terror as life left them. He squirmed helplessly under the talons of the man until finally all movement stopped, and he hung lifelessly from the hand of the fiend.

Dawn choked down a scream as the man tossed Greenwood aside like a piece of meat. He looked to the other cultists, ready for another sacrifice. "Are all of you ready to give your lives?" His voice had strengthened, carrying much more dread.

"Stop!" Dawn cried out. The pain in her chest intensified a hundred times. Her head felt like a giant was stepping on her temple, slowly placing all of its weight.

The man turned to the young girl, his eyes deep blue and menacing. He eyed her from head to toe and smirked. "You aren't really in a position to give commands, little girl."

Dawn fidgeted beneath the dark tendrils holding her hostage, attempting to summon magic of her own to free her. But none came. Her power had left with her reflection. She closed her eyes, mumbling a prayer to Fos under her breath, but still nothing.

"Girl," the man spoke, running his fingers against the scar on Dawn's cheek. "Open your eyes and face your future."

But Dawn kept her eyes shut and continued to mumble words under her breath. "Please, Fos," she whispered. "I need your miracle. I need your power. Now more than ever."

But still nothing. As she prayed under her breath, the man extended his arm and grabbed her face. "I said, look at me!"

"Stop!" Ephras shrieked. "Please, not her."

The man released Dawn's face and turned to Ephras, still tied tight by Ariyah's dark magic. "You care for this girl?" The man asked, slithering toward his prisoner.

Ephras pressed his lips together in a tight line, silently stared at his enemy. Dawn opened her eyes and watched as the man walked towards her friend.

"Fear. It is so much more powerful than death," the man

hissed. "When we are finished, she will be begging for the sweet release into The Other."

Kaela and Dawn both squirmed and thrashed in their bonds. Ariyah had now made her way back to her feet and was watching from behind with the other cultists.

"It seems both of these ladies care for you quite a bit, my friend," the man hissed. "They seem... scared. Don't they?" He grabbed Ephras' face and twisted it toward his sister. "What are they afraid of? I think they are scared they might lose you. That you may die."

With a jerk, the man released Ephras face and turned his back to the prisoners. "How pointless," he continued. "To fear death. It awaits us all."

He flipped back toward Ephras, who hadn't made a noise since his interjection. Ephras' glare could pierce the soul of a hardened warrior, but this man was different. Unshakable.

"Let's show them there is nothing to fear," the man snarled, reaching his hand out toward the peacekeeper.

"No!" Kaela could no longer hold it in. "He is my brother! I will kill you if you touch him!"

The man kept his hand on Ephras' neck as he turned toward Kaela. "You have some fight in you," he hissed. "Let's see how long it lasts."

Suddenly, just as before, the air shifted in the room. Ephras turned towards Kaela and mouthed words to her, but no sounds came out. All the breath had evacuated his lungs until finally his head slumped, and the dark magic tendrils released him to fall to the floor.

For a second that seemed like an eternity, they stared at Ephras' lifeless body. A steady stream of tears flowed down

Kaela's face as she gazed into her brother's expressionless eyes. Open and grey, they were like the windows of an empty house. Vacant. Deserted.

Kaela's sobs filled the room like a child's screams. Her body convulsed violently. Her shrieking only paused long enough for her to draw breath. Dawn stared at the lifeless husk, then back to Kaela before squeezing her eyes shut again. To be so close to such pain changes a person. The faces of Dawn's passed loved ones rushed through her mind, and the image of Ephras met them in an open field.

But quickly, the moment had passed. The field in her mind caught fire, and all she could see was the face of the man. The inception of all her problems. This man in front of her. Dawn opened her eyes, a fire burning again in her soul. The man stood in front of them, watching carelessly as the pain of losing Ephras washed over them. His eyes then met with Dawn, and his carelessness passed.

"There is something different about you, girl," he stated coldly. "Even in the face of death, you seem to only grow stronger. I see a bit of myself in you." He gestured to Kaela, who continued to sob in her shackles. "This would be most people's response to what has just happened. Some even lose all emotion as if to protect themselves from feeling at all. But you! Death fuels you." He paused momentarily, examining Dawn's silent hateful gaze. "Let's see if we can stoke those flames?"

He then turned to Kaela, whose terrified eyes jetted upward to meet with his own. Panic suffocated Dawn like a pillow sitting over her mouth and nose. Suddenly she couldn't breathe. As if the spell the man was casting had missed its target. Her heart pounded to the point of causing her body to ache. Her stomach lurched and her legs grew weak as she watched the man extend his arm out to Kaela.

But then, he stopped. His head twitched toward the front door of the prison, listening intently for... something. Dawn hadn't heard anything. From the look of terror still plastered on Kaela's face, neither had she. But the man continued to listen. It may have been seconds, or it may have been minutes, but Dawn watched as the man waited for more sounds to reveal themselves.

Then, Dawn smelled it. The smell of snow. Her nostrils tingled as the cool air traversed its way into the room. Frost crept under the door along the cold rock floor, biting at the feet of the cultists. Soon, flurries of flakes danced throughout the prison in a light, choreographed ballet, conducted by a gentle wind.

Suddenly, the doors flew off their hinges in a blast of cold air and wind, crashing into two of the cultists. The incoming blizzard nearly knocked everyone off their feet. Dawn couldn't even see through the stinging wind filled with frost flourishing through the prison. The entire room quickly became an ice field, as if they had been teleported to the northern island of Ardglas.

Just then, the tendrils that held Dawn and Kaela as prisoners loosened, and they fell to the cold floor with a hard *THUMP*. There was a split second, maybe, that Dawn had considered running for it. Racing for the door and finding her way through the storm back to the surface. But as she stood to her feet, she noticed Kaela, embracing her lifeless brother's body in tears.

Fire filled her soul. She reached for the blade of a fallen cultist and grabbed its leather laced handle. The blade was frozen and frosted over from the blizzard, but it would serve its purpose anyways. Her head now on a swivel, silhouettes of characters stood out through the thick snowy haze, and she charged with ice and hate in her eyes.

As she cut down the hooded men, she heard shouts coming from throughout the room. "Get her out of here!" One man shouted, his voice confident and weathered.

Dawn listened, but soon she felt a tingle on the back of her neck. She swung her blade around to strike her pursuer, but her blade met with metal as the weapons resounded a loud clang in the air.

"Dawn!" Krom lowered his weapon and wrapped his arms around her. "We have to get you out of here!"

"We can't go without Kaela!" Dawn shouted.

As she spoke, the wind died down, and the snow fell to the floor. No longer was the room filled with cultists, but instead, Cain, Krom, and Silas stood in the room with weapons out, ready for battle. Ariyah had been knocked over and was finding her way back to her feet. The man stood near her, glaring at Cain with hate in his eyes.

"Yet another failure," the man grunted. "This could have been it."

Ariyah stood hunched right behind him. "I am sorry, my lord," she stuttered. "I thought we had the time."

The man glanced at Cain, who had taken a step closer

and formed more ice in his hands. "You are a powerful mage, reaver. Even I know the sting of defeat."

Then, something like a flash of lightning struck the man and his subordinate. Once the light had dispersed, they were both gone.

"Okay," Krom nervously glanced around the room. "What the heck was that?"

"Dark magic," Cain responded. "They are gone now."

The rescuers rushed over to Kaela, who still sat embracing Ephras body. She buried her face into his chest, crying out in muffled screams. "Please. No. Please, Ephras. No."

As Cain approached, he knelt next to her and placed his hand on her shoulder. She gazed up into his caring eyes and wiped away the flood of tears. "Can you bring him back?" She stuttered. "Y-you are the mage! You know h-h-how these things work." Cain continued to gaze silently in her eyes. "You overpowered that goon! You are the most powerful mage I have ever met! Could you bring him back? Please? Cain?"

Cain pulled Kaela in for an embrace, whispering in her ear,

"Kaela. I am so sorry."

Maron glanced up from his fetal posture in the corner of the room, shivering under a blanket of frost. Dawn trudged toward him with her sword still in her hand. As his eyes met hers, he quickly diverted his gaze back to the floor. She kneeled in front of him, lifting his face by his chin. "Maron," she whispered. "We are going to figure this out. Together."

19

A New Dawn

Deep, red flames climbed high toward the setting sun. Ephras' body lay burning on a pile of wood in front of the two spiritual temples. Councilman Taran had been speaking about the afterlife for a few minutes before the fire had been lit, but Dawn hadn't listened to his words. She just gazed, silently into the roaring flame.

Inside the fire, she could almost see the faces of all those she had lost. As each flame shifted and changed, the faces took on a deformed shape for a moment, and then left without a word. Her unblinking eyes dried up from the heat of the fire as she watched. Tears had all but left her. She couldn't even tell if she was in pain.

Soon, the fire died down, and the crowd that had gathered to pay respect had thinned and dispersed. All that remained were those who had been present when Ephras was killed, as well as the White Council. Annias, who had been talking with Kaela on the other side of the courtyard, approached Dawn with sorrow written across his face. "I am sorry for what you have gone through," he said, offering his hand.

Dawn glanced up at the councilman and reluctantly took his hand. "What happened to Maron?"

"He is being watched at the Northtown Prison," Annias responded. "Until he can give us something of interest regarding the events of the last few days."

Dawn released Annias' hand, clenching her teeth shut in her mouth. Before she could respond in any way that she would regret, Cain came up behind her and rested his arm around her shoulder.

"Councilman," he started. "Thank you for being available on such short notice."

"No need to thank me, Cain," Annias responded. "I know Ephras was an important person to everyone here in the Citadel. Not just to you." Annias glanced around the courtyard, seeing Taran speaking with the others. "Have you had an official statement with Taran yet?"

"Not yet," Cain responded. "I don't know when that will happen."

Annias continued to look around the courtyard. "I don't know what your thoughts are about him," he stated, reverting his eyes back to Dawn. "But if you want, I can take your statements. Councilman Taran can be off putting to some people."

Dawn couldn't help but smirk at that statement. She hadn't known them for very long, but she understood exactly what Annias meant.

"I don't know what you want from the statement," Cain

said. "But I do know one thing. The man who killed Ephras wasn't some random thug or cultist. I will never forget his face. The man in that prison was Moldolor."

Dawn shuttered at the name, shocked by its mere mention.

Annias' eyes furrowed. "Moldolor," he sighed. "You are sure?"

"Beyond any doubt," Cain responded. "He is back. Not yet as strong as he was nearly twenty years ago, but he was in that prison. I am sure of it."

Annias' grim face spoke for him as silence ate away at the conversation between them. "This is terrible," he said. "I must report this to the Council and see what our next steps will be. Cain, if you could come with me."

Cain nodded, giving Dawn a look and heading off with the councilman over to Taran, interrupting his conversation with the other people who were still mourning the death. It didn't take many words, and the councilmen were leading Cain into the Temple of Fos.

* * *

Nearby, Kaela and Krom had sat down on a stone bench, gazing at the still glowing embers of the pyre that had been lit just moments before. Tears had stopped flowing from Kaela's eyes, as if the source had been cut off. The pain still ate away at her heart, but her face told a different story.

"You know," Krom mumbled. "I lost my family too. My sister and my parents were all taken from me."

"Is that supposed to make me feel better?" Kaela sneered.

"No!" Krom insisted. "I mean... Yes! But that isn't what I meant! I was just trying to say..." He paused to catch his breath, flustered at the hole he had dug for himself. "I know what it is like. To lose someone you love. If you need to talk, or even a shoulder to cry on, I am here for you."

Kaela peeked up to lock eyes with her friend, silently affirming his gesture. They continued to watch the courtyard as more and more people left to find their way to their homes. "I can't believe my family isn't even here for this," she whispered. "They probably don't even know yet. What am I supposed to tell them? How am I supposed to tell them?"

"You don't have to tell them alone," Krom replied. They sat silently for a moment until Krom noticed Kaela watching Dawn on the other side of the pyre. "How long do you think you are going to be mad at her?"

"Mad?" Kaela's head jolted up in surprise. "Am I mad at Dawn?"

"Well, aren't you?" Krom asked.

"Dawn didn't cast the spell," Kaela stated. "Yes, it may have happened because we followed her. And it may have been her necklace. Heck, it was even her friend that led them here. But I do not blame her for my brother's death."

Krom glanced at his fellow Quarrinian. "Does she know that?"

Kaela sighed, pushing herself off the bench and shuffling over to Dawn, who had found herself a seat on the front steps of the Temple of Fos. "Can I sit?"

Dawn nodded with a forced smile.

Lowering herself onto the step next to her friend, Kaela took a deep breath. With a long exhale, she turned to Dawn, but words couldn't come out. She couldn't even will her lips to move. As if underwater, everything seemed to slow and warble. They both sat together, staring across the courtyard.

As they sat, Dawn began to hum aloud to herself, growing increasingly more confident in volume, until finally her melody grew into words:

> *I am fall leaves under the frost.*
> *The chill is in my blood.*
> *I'm unsure if what I feel is pain.*
> *I'm unsure if it is not.*
> *Can I endure this hopeless winter?*
> *Will I be sleeping through the night?*
> *Or will my heart stay cold and bitter?*
> *Even as darkness turns to light.*
> *For now, I wait for spring.*
> *Where the sun will return and glow ever bright.*

* * *

With the moon set high in the sky, the friends journeyed back through the streets to Kaela's home. They walked through the door to the dark, empty foyer. As Krom lit the candles throughout the home, they all sat in the living area. Quiet warmth filled the room.

Dawn glanced out the window of her host's home to find her reflection staring back at her from the street below. Silent and brooding, it watched her, but she quickly turned back to her friends inside.

The next morning, Dawn woke up to the smell of bacon and eggs cooking on the stove in the kitchen. She discovered Cain preparing them all breakfast. "I should have known it was you," Dawn laughed. "It's always you when I smell food."

"At least it isn't kline this time," Cain smiled back, sprinkling some spices over the meal. "How are you doing?"

Dawn glanced back to the living area where Krom and Kaela were sleeping. "She seems to be doing alright. She hasn't cried since the funeral, but I can tell she is definitely hurting."

"That is to be expected," Cain sighed. "But how are *YOU* doing?"

"I..." Dawn stumbled over her words. "I just don't get it. When we were in Quarrine, I defeated Greenwood with my own power. I fought him with my magic. I used my magic to fight. You taught it to me. So why couldn't I fight back this time?"

"*Your* magic?" Cain asked. "It isn't your magic, Dawn. It is a blessing, remember? A gift. You're not the one that held off Greenwood, it was Fos."

As Cain spoke, Dawn's reflection appeared behind him in the kitchen, silently watching the conversation. "I'm not sure that is entirely true," she mumbled.

Cain paused his cooking, watching Dawn's eyes as they darted back and forth. "What do you mean?"

"I don't know," Dawn pondered. "I don't know if Fos has ever been the source of my magic. I don't know how, but I think it was actually coming from me."

Cain approached Dawn, laying his hands on her shoulder.

"You have many talents, Dawn. You truly are an incredible person. But even the most incredible person has their limits. You can accomplish all sorts of marvels, but eventually we all come to the end of ourselves. We are mortal, and weak. Even the strongest of us. But when we tap into a source that is greater than ourselves, that is where true power lies. Not in our own ability to accomplish great things, but in the source where we pull our power from."

"I don't know how to do that," Dawn admitted. "I have always relied on myself. Everyone relied on me and my father in my village."

Cain smiled; his eyes glowing bright. "We can all learn," he said. "If we are willing to be taught."

He returned to the flame to tend to the breakfast he was making for his friends. He waved his hands and released a few small magical blasts to perfect his cooking process, and then placed the food on four separate plates. As he turned, plates in hand, he noticed Dawn's blank yet thoughtful stare.

"It isn't your fault, you know," Cain stated clearly.

"How is that?" Dawn snapped back. "Remove me from the equation, and none of this would have happened."

"If that is your only judgment," Cain responded, "then there are a lot of people to blame." Dawn's questioning eyes demanded an explanation. "If Ariyah wasn't there, then you may never have even been captured. If Greenwood wasn't there, then Moldolor may not have had the power he needed to do the damage he did. If Krom hadn't taken us to the prison a week ago, you wouldn't have even thought to go there. If Ephras and Kaela hadn't gone to look after you, knowing there was something amiss, then he may still be alive, and you would have died instead. But in all of these scenarios, there are an infinite number of other possibilities that could have happened as well.

"The reality is this: Ephras gave up his own life so that you can live. Don't cheapen his sacrifice by drowning in your own shame. The greatest honor you can do for him is live the life he has allowed you to."

Dawn gazed into the floor, the food on the plates beginning to feel the brisk chill of the air as the fire died down. "I guess there is still a lot I need to learn," she sighed.

"You know," Cain started while handing the plates to Dawn and picking up the other two and leading her into the living area. "Some time ago I promised you that I would teach you magic. I think there is more that I can teach you than just magic. And, while there is some learning that can happen through conversation and lessons, there is no better way to learn than through experience."

Dawn glanced up at her mentor, questions in her eyes. "What do you mean?"

"I mean," Cain continued. "I would love to take you as a disciple. For you to become a reaver. Fight off the evil forces that slither in the darkness of our world. Prepare ourselves for the next time we encounter those cultists. What do you say?"

Suddenly, there was something like an explosion in Dawn's mind. One that carried possibilities. More than she could be conscious of. Possibilities of challenges and tears, as well as great joy and peace.

Only one word came into her mind.

"Yes."

End of Part 1

About The Author

Brandon Hargraves is the Youth Pastor at Faith Family Church in Milton Washington. Him and his wife, India, spend much of their time finding ways to show love to the community, and helping those in need. Brandon started writing his first book amidst the pandemic, but that wasn't the beginning of his writing. He has had stories in his heart for as long as he could remember. He is excited to finally be able to share his stories with the world.

www.ingramcontent.com/pod-product-compliance
Lightning Source LLC
LaVergne TN
LVHW010311070526
838199LV00065B/5522